Emyr Humphreys was born in the Welsh seaside resort of Prestatyn, the son of a Flintshire schoolmaster. He was educated at the University of Aberystwyth, where he began to develop his lifelong interest in Welsh literature, language and politics. He has worked as a teacher in London, as a radio and TV drama producer for the BBC, and as a drama lecturer at Bangor University.

Winner of the Hawthornden Prize and the Somerset Maugham Award, his highly acclaimed novels include: *Flesh and Blood*, *The Best of Friends*, *A Toy Epic* and *Jones*. He has also published books of poetry and non-fiction in Welsh and English, and in 1983 he won the Welsh Arts Council Prize for *The Taliesin Tradition*, a book about the Welsh character. He lives with his wife in Anglesey.

Also by Emyr Humphreys
in Sphere Books:

Flesh and Blood
The Best of Friends

Salt of
the Earth

Emyr Humphreys

Sphere Books Limited

Sphere Books Limited
27 Wrights Lane, London W8 5TZ

First published in Great Britain by J.M. Dent & Sons Ltd 1985

Copyright © 1985 Emyr Humphreys
Published by Sphere Books Ltd 1987

The author wishes to thank the Welsh Arts Council
for an Award which helped him to complete this novel.

TRADE
MARK

Set in 10/11 pt Plantin

Printed and bound in Great Britain by
Cox & Wyman Ltd, Reading

I

Andrew

1

Miss Sali Prydderch was already smiling as she ascended the steps of the Ivanhoe Hotel. The sun was shining, the sea was blue and she had abandoned her motor car at an untidy angle against the curb of the promenade. As an inspector of schools in a land still reverently devoted to education, she could conduct herself with something of the confidence of an hereditary ruler on a visit to one of the several strongholds of her fief. On visits of inspection the staff of any school or hotel could recognise at once her wide brimmed hat and her cloak. As a sartorial theme they softened the authority of her office with a hint of deeper artistic inclinations. Near the reception desk, Amy Parry was waiting for her. She clasped the young woman's hand in both her own and held on to it as she spoke.

'Amy. How well you look. And how beautiful. I'm so glad you could come. I really am.'

Amy blushed. Sali Prydderch appeared serenely unaware that their encounter was under general observation. She continued to talk in a loud voice as they progressed along the thick carpet. They were shadowed down the corridor by a waiter in a white jacket. His manner became theatrically suave as soon as Sali Prydderch showed that she was aware of his presence. The lounge was empty and she paused to survey it like a chatelaine viewing a favoured apartment. She pointed briefly at the largest bay window overlooking the promenade and in an instant the waiter took up a position behind her chosen armchair, ready to adjust its angle to any direction she desired. There was also a chair to be drawn up closer for Amy's use. A dull flush in the waiter's cheeks added a temporary lustre to his performance. He saw Sali Prydderch settle comfortably in her chair and extract a cigarette from a lacquered case, while she watched the people strolling on the promenade that stretched its great width between the yellow sand and the road. He produced a lighter from the pocket of his white jacket and held one hand in the other to keep the flame steady at the end of her cigarette. When she had inhaled, he withdrew silently to see to their afternoon tea. Sali Prydderch looked around her as though she were seeing the hotel through Amy's eyes.

'I suppose you find this a pretty awful place,' she said.

'Oh no.' Amy blushed again.

'Enid makes fun of the names. Ivanhoe, Balmoral, Waverley. "Those places you hide in, auntie." She has always been very frank with me. I encouraged it. From when she was a little girl. She was always bright, you know. Always very bright.'

'I know.'

Amy could not prevent herself from sounding despondent. Sali Prydderch waved an arm about so that the coins on her bracelet made a jangling noise.

'Neo-colonial shelters for expatriates and commercial travellers. That's what she calls them. For such a gentle girl she can be quite sharp, you know.'

Amy felt obliged to speak up in defence of her best friend.

'On matters of principle,' she said.

'Oh quite. There never was a girl with so many principles.' The inspector of schools stared disconsolately at the view and the cloudless sky. People passing on the promenade were casting lengthy shadows in the afternoon light.

'I was totally opposed to the marriage.' She leaned forward in her chair to screw her cigarette into the black marble ashtray.

'I thought it was a terrible mistake. And I still do.'

She stared at Amy challenging her to respond.

'They say History is a sequence of mistakes,' she said. 'That may be so. But that doesn't absolve us from the responsibility of trying to avoid them.'

She looked consoled by the proposition and even pleased to see the frown on Amy's smooth forehead. Pronouncements of this sort could help to restore her confidence in her own judgement.

'She was so pitifully young and innocent,' Miss Prydderch said. 'It was a terrible shock to me. You can't imagine. She and I were so close, you see. When she was growing up. I was always her chum and her champion. Her mother resented it quite honestly. Enid was so bright. She simply shot up out of

2

her reach. And then suddenly she shot up out of my reach as well. And I suppose I resented it. We can go on examining our motives for ever. But meanwhile life goes on. Separating us further and further, like victims of a flood. How is she? My little Enid?'

Sali Prydderch bent forward as though she were begging a favour rather than asking a question.

'She's very well,' Amy said. 'Apart from the minor discomforts that go with pregnancy. At least that's what she calls them.'

They both began to laugh. It warmed them both to contemplate Enid's personality and share their knowledge of its more endearing characteristics.

'I miss her so much,' Miss Prydderch said. 'It's ridiculous really. Cutting off my nose to spite my face. But I did everything I could to stop it. And she knows that. Her father and mother would sulk for ever but they would never do anything. Never take action. I took action. Ineffective of course. Totally useless. But at least I tried. And in the process, I lost her.'

Again she was looking to Amy for comfort. For any crumb of reassurance.

'I said extreme things about him,' she said. 'I said he was self-absorbed, weak, and self-pitying. I'm sure I'm right. He may be a good poet, a national winner and all that sort of thing. But does that make him the right husband for my Enid?'

'She thinks he's a genius,' Amy said.

Miss Prydderch threw up her arms in helpless exasperation.

'He may be a genius in Pendraw,' she said. 'But does that make him a satisfactory husband?'

Her question hung in the air. The waiter was approaching with afternoon tea. With professional skill he gauged an intensity in the atmosphere. He refrained from the jolly remarks he would have been inclined normally to make and laid out their tea with reverential care. Miss Prydderch rewarded him by addressing him by his first name as she thanked him. The meal brought her some comfort. She

3

indulged in a bout of rapid eating. From her handbag she produced a handkerchief with a lace edge which she used to dab the corners of her made-up mouth.

'This business of the Great War,' Miss Prydderch said. 'He treats it as if it were a personal affront. All right, he volunteered under age and saw terrible things. Saw his friends killed. Lost his best friends and so on. What he doesn't seem to realise is it happened to millions of people.'

Miss Prydderch stared soulfully at a chocolate eclair. Her mind seemed partially engaged with the problem of how to eat it with the minimum of mess.

'A catastrophe is the sum of a million personal tragedies. I can testify to that. And it must never be allowed to happen again. But that is no excuse for a person to allow himself to sink into a rut of self-pitying despair. It seemed terrible to me that a man like that should snatch up my darling little Enid and lock up the poor child in his great Castle of Despond for the rest of her life. You can imagine how appalled I was by the mere idea. Why are you smiling?'

Miss Prydderch watched Amy intently. The younger woman was about to eat with fastidious care.

'I would have said it was she who locked him up.'

Miss Prydderch looked puzzled. She gazed at Amy with a new respect as the girl contended with a mouthful of cake.

'Will she ever forgive me?'

Amy's mouth was still full. The inspector of schools could not bear to wait for a novice teacher's verdict.

'She was such a glorious child,' Miss Prydderch said. 'I remember once, we were staying at my cousin's farm in the Vale of Clwyd. Pant Gwyn Mawr. Such a glorious place. Like the Garden of Eden. She couldn't have been more than nine years old. We went out in the early morning and little Enid became absolutely absorbed in the drops of dew on the grass. Such a little thing. She said "Each drop is a world with a sky inside it." Imagine her saying a thing like that, at that age!'

Amy grinned cheerfully. 'She's still doing it,' she said. 'She's much more of a poet than he is really. I think so anyhow.'

Miss Prydderch clasped her hands together as though she

4

were longing to applaud Amy's perspicacity. She bent over the arm of her chair to extract her cigarette case from her handbag.

'Ah, my dear, it's wonderful you understand them so well.' She pressed her palm along the smooth surface of her cigarette case.

'Do you think she will ever forgive me?'

'Of course she will.' Amy was robustly certain. 'It's her speciality.'

Miss Prydderch gave Amy one of her most brilliant smiles. They could move closer together. The twenty years difference in their ages would be no obstacle to their becoming friends. Amy would be her advocate on her niece's hearth. Amy would open the door of that tall forbidding terrace house and let her in. She would even mediate on her behalf with the difficult gloomy poet and make it possible for a dialogue to be resumed and for old wounds to be neatly healed. She opened her case and offered Amy a cigarette. To smoke together would set a seal on their new alliance. There was so much to discuss between equal partners with equal powers: a new range of enticing possibilities would open before them like a new view of a landscape when the mist rolls away before the rays of the morning sun. Amy was about to lean forward and take a cigarette when a man's hands descended on her shoulders and held her back by force.

'What's this? Corrupting the young?'

The man's glossy head was bent above Amy's fair curls and his pliant features spread out in a confident grin that demonstrated that he had no doubt but that his presence would be welcomed. Standing behind her, he could not see the young woman's face was rigid with distaste. The waiter hovered in the background pleased to have been the agent of such a sociable reunion.

'Professor Gwilym.' The waiter made the announcement in a quiet parody of ceremonial presentation. The deeper flush on his cheeks suggested he had been drinking. He seemed particularly to enjoy enunciating the title.

'May an old sinner like me beg to be allowed to join the ladies,' Professor Gwilym said.

The waiter sniffed as he savoured the privilege of

overhearing the whimsicality of the request. With a discreet flourish he lifted a comfortable low chair without arms and placed it neatly next to Amy's. The professor sat down with the contented sigh of a man taking a well-earned rest from exacting labours.

'Committees are the bane of my existence,' he said. 'And yet what is one to do?'

Somehow he contrived to bring his chair closer to Amy's so that he could lean over and rest one arm on the arm of her chair. His hands had gripped her shoulders, gaining a physical closeness that he was loath to lose. He straightened his waistcoat and gazed sincerely at Sali Prydderch: this was a delectable encounter much to be preferred to even the most crucial committee.

'I stood over there watching,' he said. 'Your *tête-à-tête* made the most delightful picture. If I had been born with the gift of a Renoir instead of the gift of the gab, I would have rushed for my brush and palette. As it is I shall have to make do with a paean of praise to the ineffable charms of Celtic womanhood. "The Flower Daughter meets the Princess from the Sea." Alas my poor muse is so inadequate. How could I ever do justice to the subject.'

As he chuckled, his body shook up and down in a way that allowed him to lean over closer to Amy. She held on to her cigarette waiting for Miss Prydderch to light it.

'My dear ladies, don't mind me!'

Professor Gwilym gave a generous flourish with his left arm and let it sink again to rest on the arm of Amy's chair. He was studying her legs appreciatively. When she became aware of this she tucked them as far as she could under her chair.

'I am entirely broad-minded in these matters. If ladies feel inclined to smoke, in public or in private, then by all means let them do so.'

Amy held out her unlit cigarette so that Miss Prydderch could replace it in her case.

'I am great partisan of feminine emancipation as Miss Sali Prydderch will tell you. In every conceivable direction. Miss Parry isn't it? Miss Amy Parry. Recently appointed to the staff of Pendraw County School. My old school let me add.'

6

He paused to allow them to savour with him this piquant fact. 'I have my spies you see in every corner of the Cymric world. Not that I have any power. Unless knowledge is power, which I very much doubt.'

Miss Prydderch was smiling nervously to show that she appreciated the nuances of his discourse.

'Only this morning you know I picked up a tabloid and reading between the lines I glimpsed something of the frightful power those Hollywood moguls exercise over impressionable young ladies who yearn to become film stars. Something between old fashioned prostitution and serfdom. You know sometimes one despairs utterly of the human race.'

The professor's elastic features quivered with generalised concern before he turned his attention to Amy.

'But you like it there, Miss Parry? In Pendraw of the Western World. At the end of the line.'

He smiled broadly to show that he was joking.

'Not that I take that view. Pendraw is a seaside gem attached to one of the strongholds of our native culture. Like a jewel on a beautiful woman's throat. That's the way I look at it. And now that you are there, Miss Parry, that seaside gem sparkles even more brightly. Wouldn't you say so, Miss Prydderch?'

'Yes indeed I would, Professor Gwilym. Should I order you fresh tea?'

The Professor raised a restraining hand like a policeman on point duty holding up the traffic. A look of deepening concern darkened his face.

'Mr Val Gwyn,' he said. 'A man I admire very much. Is he still in that new sanatorium?'

Amy was able to nod with a legitimate excuse not to speak. The professor leaned closer as though overcome with the desire to bring solace to a young woman deprived of the presence of the man she loved.

'Poor fellow. Poor fellow.'

He established an interval of respectful silence.

'We are all on the same side,' he said.

He seemed to feel he had established a clear right to a more intimate level of conversation.

7

'There goes a young man who has sacrificed his health for the good of his country. And very little thanks he has had for it. He tries to speak out and as soon as he opens his mouth he gets attacked from the left and from the right in our weekly press. Do you know I can say this from personal experience, in this Wales of ours, nothing is more difficult than steering a moderate steady middle course. That may surprise you. The way I'm putting it. But I'm sure it's true. Words fly in all directions. Everyone is led to believe that the millennium is around the corner. And meanwhile, nothing gets done. I tell you in all seriousness for the next ten years this little country of ours must prepare itself for the worst. England holds on to her ramshackle empire, the city of London rules the roost and all we have to look forward to is the spectre of want and suffering hovering over our heads. What industrial base we have is crumbling to decay and our young people, our hope for the future, leaving their homeland in droves for the back streets of Birmingham, Coventry and Slough. Val Gwyn is quite right you know. But what are we to do about it?'

The professor raised both his arms in a gesture of cosmic despair.

'Red Revolution? I fear that remedy is worse than the disease. Apathy and acquiescence? The habits of inertia? There again, you see, our friend is right. A people who have lost their sense of independence have also lost the capacity to stand on their own feet. They will let anything happen. They have abrogated the right of decision to a Higher Authority. The serf mentality fears freedom more than death itself. And what are we to do?'

The professor did not expect an answer to his rhetorical question. He sprawled back comfortably in his chair and began to fill his pipe. He raised his eyebrows at Miss Prydderch and she watched him filling his pipe as though mesmerised by the virility of the ritual.

'There isn't much time left,' Amy said.

The professor sat up, startled by the music emerging from such delightfully youthful lips. Not content with this exaggerated reaction he lifted both arms in the air again, this time to make manifest his limitless admiration for her intelligence, her impetuous sincerity and the general

8

radiance of her appearance. Amy jumped to her feet. He continued to look up at her admiringly.

'Such purity of spirit,' he said. 'If I may use such a phrase. That's what Val Gwyn possesses. Such integrity. When you see him next, Miss Parry, do tell him that he can count on my sympathy and support.'

He reached out to squeeze her forearm in order to press home his message of goodwill. By moving closer to Miss Prydderch Amy placed herself out of his reach.

'I must go,' she said. 'My aunt will be expecting me.'

'Must you?' Miss Prydderch gazed pleadingly at Amy. 'But must you, Amy?'

Now it was Miss Prydderch who reached for her arm. The professor paid close attention to the bowl of his pipe. He cleared his throat.

'You mustn't let me spoil your *tête-à-tête*,' he said. 'If you'd like me to leave I could come back later. All I would like to say is that it is up to us to give the young people every support. I think you would agree with that, Miss Prydderch?'

'Indeed I would. Of course.' Sali Prydderch was eager to please them both.

'Thank you very much for my tea, Miss Prydderch,' Amy said. 'Good afternoon, Professor Gwilym.'

She withdrew with determined correctness. Miss Prydderch made a brief signal in the professor's direction and followed Amy to the lobby. Amy was moving so quickly she was obliged to seize her arm with one hand and balance her wide-brimmed hat with the other. The waiter in the white jacket lurked in the corridor watching their encounter with unrestrained curiosity. There was little time for confidences yet Miss Prydderch was impelled to make them.

'Amy,' she said. 'Amy.'

Amy stood waiting patiently for her to speak.

'You won't tell Enid, will you?'

Holding on to her arm, Sali Prydderch escorted Amy to the hotel entrance. Her voice was lowered now to an agitated whisper.

'She dislikes him,' she said. 'Quite unreasonably in my view. In some ways she can be very intolerant. I just don't

9

know why. But his very name is like a red rag to a bull. The poor man. We meet here you see, to play bridge. He's my partner. I don't enjoy it very much to be honest with you. I get so terrified of making the wrong bid. But he loves it. He says he finds it very relaxing.'

The polite but detached manner in which Amy listened to this spate of confidences seemed to agitate Miss Prydderch even further.

'I know it's an illusion,' she said, 'For a spinster of my age. The illusion of comfort and a bit of attention. The kind of thing one doesn't get living with relatives. You've seen enough of Ivydene. You must admit it is a bit lacking in interest and sophistication. But what am I saying? It's Enid that really matters to me. You understand that, don't you?'

When Amy nodded she seized on the small measure of reassurance.

'I wasn't sure he would turn up today,' she said. 'I was rather hoping he wouldn't. But I can't very well tell him not to come. We are allies after all. In all sorts of ways. He has some influence. Not much but we do achieve our little successes for the language in the field of education. Nothing spectacular, but Gwilym is good on committees. There are people who listen to him. He's very good with county councillors. It's uphill work of course. But it helps us to survive.'

She squeezed Amy's arm.

'Don't judge him too harshly,' she said. 'That's all I ask. I long for you and I to be frank with each other. Is that possible?'

Amy was beginning to blush again.

'Will you call me Sali? I would like that.'

When Amy smiled at her, she let her arm go.

'We could co-operate, Amy, couldn't we? I know Enid is closer to you than anyone else. But we could conspire together to protect her, couldn't we? She's vulnerable. She does need protecting.'

'Oh,' Amy said, 'Enid is a lot tougher than you think.'

'Is she?' Sali Prydderch said. 'Is she really?'

Anything Amy said she was prepared to accept gratefully.

'She'll manage him,' Amy said. 'I'm quite sure of that. In time. She is the stronger character, I would say.'

'Is she? Is she really?'

Sali Prydderch began to adjust her hat and her dress in front of Amy as though she were standing in front of a mirror.

'Could you bring her home?' Sali said. 'Or should we meet on neutral ground. Or should I wait for the snow and walk barefoot to her front door?'

Amy took a little time to think.

'If you came to the school,' she said. 'In the normal course of your duties. Or for some special reason. We could go down then and see her. In the most natural way in the world.'

'Wonderful. Oh wonderful.'

For a moment it seemed as if Sali Prydderch was about to kiss her.

'We are friends,' Sali said. She took Amy's hand and seemed about to raise it to her lips. 'Sweeter than a prize,' she said.

She squeezed Amy's hand and let it go reluctantly. 'I must get back to him,' she said. 'Don't think too badly of us.'

Amy watched Miss Prydderch's progress past the reception desk. The waiter was following in her footsteps almost mimicking her imperious step. His tray was tucked tightly under his arm ready to receive the professor's order.

2

The Austin Tourer jerked cautiously down the narrow lane. John Cilydd More gripped the large steering wheel tightly. Deep furrows appeared on his forehead under his grey Homburg hat. His grandmother, Mrs Lloyd of Glanrafon Stores, sat alongside him. His wife Enid was in the back, steadying herself by pressing her right hand against Amy Parry's shoulder.

'"Strait is the gate and narrow is the way..."'

The car jumped forward as he changed gear awkwardly and interrupted Enid. Amy was ready to complete her cheerful quotation.

'"And few there be that find it!"'

Mrs Lloyd frowned disapprovingly and stared ahead through the windscreen. John Cilydd raised his voice above the noise of the engine.

'Are you all right in the back there?'

'Of course I am.'

Enid was happy to make light of the minor discomforts of her pregnant condition.

'I'm not made of crystal,' she said. 'At least I don't think so.'

'This stupid gear-box.'

He muttered angrily to himself. His grandmother was nursing her gloved hands in her lap and scrutinising his performance with an uncompromising gaze that did nothing to improve it. Mrs Lloyd peered grimly at the overgrown hedges and the rough surface of the lane.

'It's pitiful to see the place,' she said. 'I've never seen it look so untidy. In the old days this lane was beautifully kept.'

Cilydd raised his voice so that Enid and Amy could hear.

'This vehicle is no longer a car, ladies,' he said. 'It's a Time Machine taking you back fifty years.'

'Only fifty! Are you sure you don't mean a hundred?'

Enid was ready to respond light-heartedly. Mrs Lloyd ignored her attempts at playful banter.

'It's that woman I blame.' She addressed them in a determined tone. 'That Dossie Evans. That so-called housekeeper. All she does is pamper cats all day. Instead of looking after your great-uncle properly. It's an absolute disgrace.'

Cilydd glanced in the reversing mirror and caught Enid and Amy smiling. The lane widened and he was able to relax at the wheel. He attempted to make his grandmother smile.

'Dossie is nursing a secret ambition as well as a cat,' he said.

He spoke loudly enough for the girls in the back to hear.

'Don't talk in riddles,' his grandmother said. It was a fond enough rebuke.

'Dossie hopes to marry him. She's got her eye on great-uncle Ezra!'

'Don't talk such rubbish,' Mrs Lloyd said angrily. 'A grown man and a qualified solicitor. You should be ashamed of yourself. I'm quite serious now. Your great-uncle is a sick man. He is old and sick. You'll be old and sick yourself one day. It grieves me to see him not properly looked after. If I had my way he would be living with us at Glanrafon. In warmth and comfort. And since he's made a will already in your favour, you and Enid could be living here. In Cae Golau. Instead of in a terrace boarding house down that Marine Terrace with visitors parading to and fro outside your front window.'

'Nain Lloyd!'

Enid was able to allow herself an affectionate protest.

'I'm not interfering,' Mrs Lloyd said. 'It's just that I like to see things properly arranged.'

The high hedgerows were abruptly replaced by a length of suburban-looking laurel on either side of the lane. A few yards ahead they were confronted by a wide iron gate. The front elevation of Cae Golau had been broken by an ill-proportioned portico made entirely of blue slate. Two monkey-puzzle trees had been planted in the circular lawn in front of the house. They made the clumps of daffodils dotted around them look pale and fragile.

'So this is Cae Golau,' Amy said.

Enid looked at her eagerly to see if her friend approved of the place.

'The Field of Light or the Fair Field?' she said. 'Which is it?'

Amy did not answer. She got out of the car to deal with the gate. It had sagged on its hinges and she was obliged to exert her strength in order to drag it through the moss and gravel. Cilydd tapped the steering wheel with his fingers.

'Temperance Towers,' he said.

His grandmother's hearing was sharp enough to hear him mutter.

'Don't mock,' she said. 'You have a most unfortunate tendency in that direction, John Cilydd. Your great-uncle Ezra was the President of the North Wales Temperance League for twenty-three years and very widely respected.'

'Well, of course. Of course.'

He let out the clutch and the car lurched through the gateway.

'Appearing on public platforms,' said Cilydd. 'With such notable abstainers as Lloyd George and Llewelyn Williams.'

The tourer came to a halt between the lawn and the portico. Mrs Lloyd hissed out her protest so as not to be overheard should anyone open the front door.

'A life of service,' she said. 'No one has the right to mock that. It seems to me the young people of today are bent on mocking everything. No matter how sacred. Your great-uncle has a good opinion of you. Always has had. Though there have been times when I have inclined to wonder why.'

She turned around in her seat to communicate with Enid. She made an effort to adopt a gentler tone.

'What will you do?' she said.

Amy was walking towards the car, smiling and smartly dressed. Enid raised her voice.

'Amy? Shall we two take a walk down to the river?'

She came out of the car and took Amy's arm. They walked under the sycamore trees that thrust out of the hedge at irregular intervals between the outhouses and the walled garden. Cilydd and his grandmother watched them as they waited for the front door to open. The young women were already deeply engaged in conversation, their heads bent close together.

'Miss Parry is doing very well at the County School,' Mrs Lloyd said.

She spoke with generous impartiality.

'Why don't you call her Amy?' Cilydd said.

'I don't know her well enough for that, do I?'

The front door was open and Dossie Evans the morose housekeeper stood in the doorway. Her plump arms were folded and she stood with her feet apart as if she were resolved to prevent their entry. Her sagging cheeks were flushed. She made no attempt to smile or offer any formal greeting.

'I had no word you were coming,' she said.

Mrs Lloyd said nothing. She stared at Dossie's swollen feet in their carpet slippers as though willing them to move.

'Mr Ezra More is not at all well,' the housekeeper said. 'I have been in two minds whether or not to call the doctor.'

At last she moved to one side. Once inside the house Mrs Lloyd Glanrafon sniffed audibly.

'The smell of cats,' she said. 'That can't be good for his throat. If I were you, Miss Evans, I would open some windows. The spring is here.'

Resentfully the housekeeper led the way to the study and tapped gently on the door before opening it. The Reverend Ezra More sat alongside the oval table in the centre of the room, his dark sleeve resting on the red plush cloth. Both his sideways position and the high white stock he wore were designed to conceal from the over-curious the hole in his throat. The books on the table within reach of his fingers were unopened. His white hair was arranged forward in a style favoured by distinguished pulpit orators of the previous century. A fire blazed in the black grate. A tassled fringe of red plush concealed the edge of the marble mantelpiece. The room was stuffy and smelt of old books and clothes impregnated with camphor.

'I've done very little today.'

As soon as he spoke he automatically raised his hand to protect his throat. He also intended to muffle the faint whistle that accompanied his speech. He husbanded his voice with prolonged silences. Cilydd's eye caught the gold lettering on six copies of *Temperance for Everyman by Ezra More MA* wedged side by side on the middle shelf of the glass-faced book cupboard.

'I am not idle,' Ezra More said. 'You must tell people that if they ask. Do they ask?'

His eyes moved imploringly from Cilydd to Mrs Lloyd before he raised his eyebrows to dismiss the housekeeper lingering in the doorway. When the door was closed Mrs Lloyd moved confidently towards the fireplace. Cilydd observed his grandmother closely. It was never her habit to flatter, but he could hear her at it now with the skill of a lifelong practitioner.

'A dedicated man,' she was saying, 'who gave his all to the Connexion and the great cause of Temperance. Out in all weathers. Addressing as many as four meetings a day. Neglecting his health. Sleeping in damp beds. Writing far into the night. All to make this land of ours a cleaner place to live in.'

She sat down on the edge of a button-back horsehair chair.

'When my voice is restored I shall have things to say. You can tell them that if they ask you.'

Mrs Lloyd nodded, curbing her tongue as she waited for the old minister to say more.

'There is no such thing as the pleasure of retirement,' the Reverend Ezra More said. 'It is nothing less than a Babylonish captivity. Enforced inactivity. Tell them that if they ask you. Tell them that he longs to resume his all-out attack on the cohorts of Satan.'

He raised a finger to point at Cilydd.

'Was it you who reported to me that our soldiers were plied with strong drink before going into battle?'

Cilydd cleared his throat.

'I don't know, uncle,' he said. 'It might have been. I was very young at the time.'

'I brought it up at the monthly meeting,' Ezra More said. 'But there were pusillanimous figures there. Wanting me to tone it down. But it's all over now. Let the Truth come out!'

He raised his hand to his throat clearly regretting the volume of his outburst. He leaned forward towards Mrs Lloyd to whisper.

'Is the world any nearer Reform?' he said. 'Give me leave to doubt it.'

'We are here to see if you need anything,' she said. 'And we are here to ask your advice.'

'Advice?' He mouthed the word, savouring its taste.

'There are people in the chapel who want to extend a Call to the Reverend Tasker Thomas.'

Ezra More pointed a finger at Cilydd.

'You never heard the Call,' he said. 'You took up the Law.'

'That's right, Uncle,' Cilydd said, 'I followed your advice.'

He smiled to show he was prepared to give a more light-hearted direction to their conversation.

'I remember you telling me, "How can you expect to hear the still small voice when you are mesmerised by a cuckoo?"'

Ezra More's shoulders rose and fell in a measured outburst of silent laughter.

'I told you that?'

'Yes indeed you did,' Cilydd said. 'I think I was fifteen or sixteen at the time.'

'I was quite right too,' Ezra More said.

'Indeed you were.'

Mrs Lloyd was getting impatient.

'What about this Tasker Thomas, Ezra More?'

The old man was not to be deterred from pleasurable recollection.

'I put it to them like this,' he said. 'On more than one occasion. "What do you have in mind, brethren, spoiling a good poet to make a poor teacher, or spoiling a good teacher to make a poor poet?"'

Cilydd laughed more loudly than usual as though he were making a noise also on his great-uncle's behalf. The old man enjoyed the sound, but Mrs Lloyd was frowning her disapproval.

'Tasker Thomas,' she said.

'Listening to the leaves in the trees and the mountain brooks and all that sort of animistic nonsense,' Ezra More said. 'What can a mountain brook tell you that you don't know yourself already?'

Cilydd held his head to one side, showing that he was ready to argue if the occasion allowed him to do so. His great-uncle turned his large head towards Mrs Lloyd.

'I know a little of what is going on in the world outside,' he said.

'I know you do, Ezra More,' Mrs Lloyd said.

'You can tell them that if they ask you.'

He smoothed the red plush with the palm of his hand.

'Tasker Thomas,' he said. 'Grandson of Thomas Edwards, Tywyn. One of the greatest preachers I ever heard.'

Mrs Lloyd contained herself.

'I never saw, never heard, a greater master of a congregation. He would start slowly enough. Groping for the words. Searching for them like a man in the dark. That could go on for some time until you felt sorry for him, until a light came into his eyes and then, the strangest thing, he would grab the Bible under his arm and the thoughts and the convictions would come pouring out of him like a mighty torrent.'

Ezra More's hand rose protectively towards his throat. His eyes were moist. He gathered strength for a further pronouncement. The fire crackled in the prolonged silence.

'If the grandson is quarter the man his grandfather was, he would be good enough for any church.'

Mrs Lloyd stirred impatiently in her chair. The oracle was hardly shaping up the kind of pronouncement she wanted to hear. Ezra More drummed his fingers thoughtfully on the plush table cloth.

'But we have to allow for the spirit of the age. Heresy and strong drink have this in common: they make the wisest men mad. You can tell them I said that. If they ask.'

Cilydd could not help speaking.

'He campaigns for Peace,' he said. 'Just as you used to campaign for Temperance, Uncle Ezra.'

His great-uncle stared at him resentfully.

'I shall have things to say,' he said, 'when my voice is restored. Dabbling in heresy is the spiritual equivalent of being drunk on sweet wine. Set a heretic at the helm and be prepared for discord and dissension. Be prepared for shipwreck.'

He raised a hand to show he did not wish to hear Cilydd's comment or argue the case. Mrs Lloyd rose eagerly to her feet.

'We must not tire you, Ezra More. We shall leave now. But I must add this. If you feel at any time the need for greater comfort and more careful attention, there is a place reserved for you at Glanrafon. Your own establishment with all your books around you and so on.'

Ezra More nodded graciously. The concentrated effort of giving advice had tired him. He was ready to be alone.

'It's time for your hot milk,' Mrs Lloyd said, 'I'll remind Miss Evans. And have her whip up an egg to strengthen it. Come along, John Cilydd. We mustn't tire your great-uncle.'

3

The terrace house faced east and the blinds of the bow window which had been half lowered against the morning sun, had still not been raised. The sparsely furnished room was filled with a haze of amber light. Amy stood by the window with an index finger hooked into the tightly drawn net curtain. Cilydd was slumped in the larger of the two armchairs, his chin on his hands, the heel of his right boot furrowing the hearth rug. He stirred briefly at the sound of footsteps on the floorboards of the bedroom overhead and then lapsed into another posture of melancholy inertia, fixing his gaze on a heap of oranges in the fruit bowl on the table. These seemed to offer some consolation as they shone with a light of their own.

'She expects too much from me,' he said.

His chin sank on his chest as though he had been further deflected by the effort of confession. Amy smiled, secure that he could not see her face. The silence of the room was embroidered by the delicate clip-clop of a pony-trap she watched returning empty from the promenade to wait in the station square for a fresh party of holiday makers. The driver wore a flat cap, a stiff collar and the ends of his moustache were proudly waxed.

'She thinks too highly of me,' Cilydd said. 'That's the trouble. How the hell can I live up to it? Do you know what I mean?'

He sat up with a sudden access of energy and turned to look at Amy standing in the window, demanding an immediate and honest response.

'She thinks too highly of us all.'

He was unable to understand why Amy was smiling.

'About the War,' he said. 'She's right. The whole thing lies deep down inside me. Thirteen years ago or whatever and I still haven't digested it. Still haven't digested the experience. So how can I possibly write about it? Perhaps I'm more keen on forgetting it. After all I was only a kid. Under age and terrified. How do I write about that? Do I parade my own cowardice? Do I celebrate the slaughter or what the hell do I do? You can understand, surely? I'm keenest of all on forgetting it. I still hope to wake up one morning and discover it never happened. And what will happen then? Do I close my eyes for ever to what is happening in the world around me? Or do I become a cynic?'

He waited for Amy to speak. She withdrew her finger from the net curtain and gave him her complete attention.

'We have to make certain it shall never happen again,' Amy said.

'Easier said than done.'

He turned away. In the light from the window, Amy's figure appeared too assertive and confident for him to contemplate for any length of time. She wore a dark blue dress with white circles around the neck and above the wrists.

'We have to do what we can,' Amy said.

'Of course we do. I've arranged a meeting. But doesn't that sound ridiculous? "I've arranged a meeting." Where? In a chapel vestry. And meanwhile the governments of this world are at it again. Piling up armaments as fast as they can. How can you expect a man not to become a cynic?'

A thought occurred to him that suddenly cheered him up.

'What is the punishment decreed by heaven for the cynic?'

He was ready to face Amy again. He stood up, straightened the hearth rug with the toe of his boot.

'To be married to a saint,' he said.

'Well there you are . . .?'

Amy spread out her hands as though to display the great prize he had won. For a while they were content to laugh together: but the intimacy that their laughter brought created an urge towards confession.

'I'm not good enough for her,' he said. 'And I know it. But it's worse than that. I'm jealous.'

'Jealous?' Amy reacted with emphatic disbelief.

'I know. It's shameful. Disgusting. Talk about "A Heap of Filth". If only some of those pontificating academic reviewers knew what was really going on in my mind.'

'She thinks you are a genius,' Amy said.

The light glittered on his spectacles as his head moved to give her a sharp glance.

'Evidently you don't,' he said.

He began to apologise for the remark as soon as he had made it.

'I'm sorry,' he said. 'I didn't mean that. What I meant was, it doesn't matter whether I am a genius or not. I'm simply not good enough for her. And then on top of that to be jealous.'

'Jealous of what?' Amy said.

He looked at her as though he expected her to provide him with the answer. He closed his eyes and muttered in a hurried voice.

'Oh God, practically everything.'

'That's silly,' Amy said resolutely. 'You have to be jealous of something, surely?'

'Of? All her causes to begin with. When I see the both of you on the march shoulder to shoulder for the Language, for Social Justice, for this and that and the other. For Peace even. I know I really don't count. Do I disgust you?'

'Of course not.' Her impatience was patently stronger than her denial. 'You have a wife who adores you,' Amy said accusingly.

'I know,' he said. 'Or at least I try to know. But this feeling. What the hell does it mean? How can one penetrate the murky depth of one's own unconscious? How?'

He seemed to be pleading with her. She considered the question as something which had never occurred to her before.

'Do you have to?' she said. 'Is that important for a poet?'

He was moved by the simplicity of her enquiry. He held out his hands towards her ready to talk at length.

'Amy.'

He heard the brisk tap of high heels on the stairs. The district nurse rapped a knuckle on the door panel and leaned into the room to beam amiably at them both. She was a plump and energetic woman. Constricted by a corset her body was permanently tilted forward on the high heels she wore.

'That must be it for now then, and there we are then, dear people. All is well and I'll be off now then.'

Without moving, she managed to imply she was already on her way in spirit. She peered with short-sighted but unconcealed curiosity at Amy. Her repetitious manner of speech gave her more time to take in every detail without detracting from her aura of brisk efficiency.

'I mustn't stop,' she said. 'Miss Parry isn't it? I've heard the Reverend Nathan Harris and his sister Mrs Rossett praise their lodger to the skies! It is right that you should know. You've brought them more than a little brightness into their lives at number seven, Eifion Street. Poor Nathan Harris. The worst case of arthritis on my beat. And in a damp place like Pendraw that's saying something. I attended your great-uncle Ezra More last week, Mr More. Cleaned out his windpipe, poor man. Disgusting job. Mucus, you see. Mucus. Worse than bedpans for me, I must confess, but when duty calls there must be more action and less talking, from an acting district nurse!'

'Mrs Nevin Jones. Are you sure you won't stay and take a cup of tea?'

Enid had appeared behind her, both her hands raised as though they were about to settle on the plump little nurse's shoulders. Cilydd moved forward anxiously to greet his wife.

'Are you all right?' he said.

Enid's cornflower blue eyes shone in the dim light of the passage as she smiled fondly at her husband. The district nurse stood between them in the doorway.

'I'm fine,' she said. 'There's nothing wrong with me, is there Mrs Nevin Jones?'

'Nothing at all,' the nurse said confidently. 'A little varicose vein, that's all. And which mother-to-be is without those, I'd like to know?'

22

Her small head went into a pecking motion to draw attention to an expectant father's traditionally anxious state.

'"Let patience have her perfect work",' she said. 'It's the only way we all slip into this troubled world, the one and only way and that is the case.'

She shifted nimbly to one side so that Enid could walk into the room. Enid took hold of her husband's arm and leaned against him.

'I haven't reached the point of carrying my femininity around with me like a great burden,' Enid said. 'But doubtless that stage will come.'

Cilydd was anxious to lead her to an armchair. Mrs Nevin Jones watched them closely.

'She is inclined to be saying clever things all the time,' the nurse said. 'Takes all my time to keep up with her. But we understand each other don't we, Mrs More?'

'I hope so,' Enid said laughing.

She resisted Cilydd's pressing invitation to sit.

'Now then.' She nodded towards the district nurse. 'The Peace Movement. Can I persuade you to join it, Mrs Nevin Jones?'

The nurse winked knowingly at Cilydd.

'There she is, you see,' she said. 'That's how she is all the time. Join this. Join that. Last time it was the Welsh Nats. This time it's the Peace Movement. Now then I say to you, the time is coming to concentrate on being a wife and a mother. Leave politics to the men, isn't it Mr More?'

Cilydd frowned.

'We all have the vote,' he said. 'Men and women alike.'

The district nurse's glances shot swiftly from Cilydd to Amy and from Amy to Enid and back to Cilydd to pick up the smallest signals that would give her an accurate reading of their relationship and their reactions.

'I can tell you this,' she said, 'and I tell you in the best and fairest spirit, this little town of Pendraw is split from top to bottom all because of politics. You can vouch for that, Mr More. You know something about the place and its history. These two young ladies are strangers to the district but it does no harm to know the way the land lies. Party squabbles hold everything back in this place. In my opinion. One political party, the mighty Liberals just like the town itself split down the middle because of an ungodly hatred between two men who ought to know better. Instead of working together they are at each other's throats from morning 'til night. And that if you'd like to know the truth, is why we do not have a Cottage Hospital. And not even a wing added on the Workhouse to give us an ideal Maternity Ward, hospital or home or whatever you like to call it. But are we likely to get it? Not on any account. And why? Because Alderman Llew wants it in one place and Doctor DSO wants it in another. It's as simple as that. You knew this I dare say Mr More, but the young ladies didn't know it.'

Both Enid and Amy were shaking their heads in pained disbelief.

'This Pendraw of ours could have a Cottage Hospital tomorrow if someone strong enough would come along to knock those two stubborn heads together. Now there's a job for your Peace Movement, Mr More.'

'Tasker Thomas!'

Enid pronounced the name as triumphantly as the instant solution to an intractable problem. Mrs Nevin Jones took in the name.

'The man from the South,' she said. 'I understood Giboah and Salem had not given him a Call.'

'Ah!' Enid clapped her hand over her mouth and enlarged her eyes. 'Am I on the verge of giving away secrets of church and state?'

The district nurse nodded eagerly to encourage her.

'Let us just say that Tasker Thomas *may*, I only say *may* be in our midst before very long. Is it all right to say that?'

She looked doubtfully to her husband for approval.

'There is a possibility he will take on the Harbour Mission,' Cilydd said. He made the pronouncement judiciously. Information given to the district nurse rapidly became public.

'A little place like that?' Mrs Nevin Jones could not suppress her incredulity.

'There is the Manse that goes with it,' Cilydd said. 'And a small church would leave Mr Thomas free to pursue his other interests, other causes.'

24

'Yes, yes,' the nurse said. 'Yes, yes. It is generally known that he moves about a lot.'

'Causes!' Enid said. She waved her arms in the air and the district nurse stared at her suspiciously. 'We need them all!'

Taken with Enid's unstinting enthusiasm, the nurse still appeared loath to agree with her.

'The Peace Movement,' Enid said. 'All these beautiful children you help to bring into the world, Mrs Nevin Jones. You want them to have a decent future, don't you?'

'I mustn't stop,' the district nurse said. 'No. I mustn't. Sweet as it would be to stop and talk and no doubt a special privilege.'

She spoke as if she were leaving, but in fact she advanced marginally into the room, bringing her voice down to a level of more intense confidentiality.

'Gobaith Terrace,' she said, 'where I'm off to now. The dirt. The filth. The absence of sanitation. Owned, I may say, by Alderman Llew's brother-in-law. But let that pass. The woman in number eleven is expecting. A woman incapable of learning. And the husband, you see, a chronic loafer. That house leaks, but the landlord does nothing about it. And the loafer refuses to do a thing for himself. On principle, if you please, and him on the dole with nothing to do all day except drink. And they are so dirty. Soap is cheap and water is free, is what I tell them every time, but will they ever listen? Good habits I tell them are like Bible verses, all there for the learning. And do you know what he had the face to tell me? "I never learnt a verse in my life." What do you do with people like that, Mrs More?'

Enid looked at her with intense sympathy. 'Just what you are doing now, nurse,' she said, 'only more of it.'

Mrs Nevin Jones smiled and shook her head addressing herself to Cilydd.

'Never without an answer,' she said. 'Never at a loss. Well I really must be off. My bicycle is in the back. I'll see myself down the little stairs.'

4

Enid More was out of breath. She paused in her climb along the narrow path that led to the higher ridge of dunes. She clutched the pair of binoculars above the curve of her belly and turned to grin at Amy who was following carefully behind her.

'I talk too much, don't I?' she said.

A wayward breeze from the sea stirred her loose-fitting dress and made it billow out. Amy pointed authoritatively to a hollow in the sand.

'Take a rest,' she said.

She trampled the marram grass to make the site more comfortable. Enid was concerned for Amy's polished shoes and the immaculate pleats of her white skirt.

'Oh bother the skirt,' Amy said.

She sat close to Enid ready to give her any support she needed. The sea was out of sight behind the dunes. They looked back at the town across the inner harbour. Everything was bright and attractive in the mid-morning sunlight. A railway engine, shunting towards the GWR terminal, let off puffs of steam like childish smoke signals. The sea water in the harbour looked as tame and as smooth as a lake of milk. The slate roofs of the chapels that were a conspicuous feature of the town's architecture glistened in the sun. A flag flew from the tower of the Town Hall. The sun shone most brightly of all on the windows of the County School building, which stood like a neutralised castle on the hill that overlooked the town. Amy held out her hand to borrow the binoculars. She turned westwards and trained them on the Beach Road that crossed the embankment at the end of the harbour.

'I see a car parking outside your house,' she said. 'Sali P, do you think?'

Enid sat forward in alarm.

'Relax,' Amy said. 'I was only joking. Bird-watching. Only human beings are more interesting than birds.'

Amy shifted the binoculars to observe the school on the hill.

'Not a bad old place,' she said. 'Apart from the headmaster's wife. And she's quite funny really. Or at least, if I think that, it helps me to put up with her. Interfering old dragon. It's not such a bad old place is it, Pendraw? On a day like this.'

She handed the binoculars to Enid and lay back against the slope with her hands behind her head, studying the white wisps of cloud high in the blue sky.

'We should never give way,' Enid said. 'That's what I think.'

'Give way to what, O pregnant sage?'

Enid smiled apologetically.

'Go on,' Amy said. 'Tell me. I'm always willing to learn. I mean, if I don't follow what you're on about there isn't much hope for anybody else, is there? Go on.'

They settled comfortably against each other. Enid closed her eyes with the effort of attempting to express herself precisely.

'We live in difficult times,' she said. 'In dark times. Any intelligent creature can see that. The easiest thing is to give up, lie back, and do nothing.'

'*Touché*,' Amy said.

'Seriously. Give up, give way, do nothing. In the case of the artist, the poet, the easiest way out is to submerge yourself and your talent in a trance of impotent melancholy.'

'Now I wonder who on earth she can be talking about,' Amy murmured humorously.

Enid nudged against her in ineffective protest. 'Now listen, Parry,' she said.

'Yes, Mrs More.' Amy nodded obediently.

'My theory is, what is true for the artist is true for the rest of us. It has to be. If there wasn't a potential for poetry in everybody there would be no need for poets, minor or major. What I tell him is this. We all get weighed down by the sheer sadness of things. The stupidity and the folly of the world. The misery and the despair.'

'Does he listen?'

Enid did not pause to measure the extent of her friend's curiosity. She was too intent on unravelling her own excited thoughts.

'Of course chapels can be awful,' Enid said. 'Especially small-town bourgeois chapels. Or rather the people that attend them. Or rather the people that dominate and control them. But they are there. You can't ignore them any more than you can ignore history. Just shouting "socialism" or "Karl Marx" or "Lenin" is no sort of answer. Either you tear them down or you repossess them. I think that's what Tasker Thomas is saying and it's still quite a daring thing to say in this day and age.'

She paused for breath. Her mind appeared to be racing forward at greater speed in defiance of her physical condition.

'It is time to lay the foundation for something new,' she said. 'That's what I tell him. In art and in life. The 1930s are a breathing space. Just time enough to breathe. To create rather than destroy. That's why Tasker is important. He is a sign of the times and a sign for the times. A special phenomenon. A spark of hope for Welsh non-conformity at the very moment when it seems to be dying on its feet.'

Amy turned to pat her friend's hand and calm her. 'Don't expect too much,' she said.

'Am I talking too much again?' Enid said. 'Am I getting on your nerves?'

'Yes,' Amy said. 'Of course you are. That's why I'm always listening to you. No, I was talking about Tasker Thomas. He used to turn up on his travels at Plas Iscoed. You know what a suspicious mind I've got. I thought he was sucking up to the Honourable Eirwen for the sake of her honourable money.'

'Amy!' Enid was deeply shocked. 'How can you say a thing like that?'

'Well, he had all the principles and she had all the money. Fair swap, that's the way I looked at it. You can imagine my staggered surprise when I discovered that in the dim and distant past they had been engaged to be married.'

Enid's eyebrows shot up. She was interested in spite of herself.

'For five terrible months in 1912,' Amy said. 'He bought her a ring. It cost him ten guineas.'

'How do you know all this?'

Amy grinned and tapped the side of her nose.

'They didn't even like each other. The thing was their respective mamas were related by marriage. That's history for you. Tasker's mum was worried about her unworldly son and wanted to see him make a wealthy catch. Eirwen's mum couldn't wait to match her ugly duckling. The one thing the two had in common, it seems, was being unbearably pious. Apart from that they could hardly stand being in the same room. The fact is, I don't think old Tasker likes women.'

'Amy!'

'I'm sorry, my dear. But you know me. I like to see the truth and see it whole. "With the greatest respect", as Mr Samwell says. I love watching him trying to get his own way with the Headmaster when Mrs Price isn't looking.'

'Honestly, Amy.'

'Sorry.'

A herring gull swooped low over their heads. Amy watched its shadow cross the sand. It soared to circle high over the dunes and broke the quiet of the place with a piercing isolated wail. Amy got to her feet and held out her hand to pull Enid up.

'Who is to say what is good or bad in this world?' she said. 'I don't know. On the other hand, I do know that you are good, from first-hand experience. So what else can I do except follow Mahatma Enid More.'

'It must mean something,' Enid said. 'That's all I'm trying to say.'

Amy turned back to drag her friend over an awkward patch of eroded ground.

'There has to be a living link between saving society and saving the individual soul,' Enid said. 'I think that is the real core of Tasker Thomas's message. Well now if it's true, as I think it is, then it has to affect the poet and the artist even more deeply. Do you see what I mean?'

She gave up speaking and began to laugh as Amy pulled her to the top of the dunes.

'There it is! There's Dic Bont's boat.'

In the whole expanse of the bay the green boat was the only conspicuous object. They took it in turns to study it through the binoculars. The engine had stopped and the boat had begun to veer about on an aimless course, drifting gradually closer to the shore.

'There he is.'

Enid trained the binoculars on the Reverend Tasker Thomas who sat high in the bow with his arms spread out along the gunwale. Even at a distance she could see that above the heavy-knitted collar of his white jersey his sunburnt face was wreathed in smiles. His bald pate, as bronze as his amiable face, was fringed with a coronet of reddish hair that fluttered in the sea breeze. Down the middle of the boat and around the bare mast, hobbled sheep from the island were contained by a cargo that seemed to consist chiefly of camping gear. Enid's eyes began to water. She handed Amy the binoculars.

'Oh my goodness,' Amy said. 'How Biblical. How many disciples are there? Not to mention the sheep.'

'Amy!'

'And I'll tell you something else. It's the engine. The engine has conked out and at this moment the whole thing is drifting. Let's hope not towards the rocks.'

'Oh my goodness. Do let me look.'

Enid held out her hand in vain for her binoculars. Amy was intent on detailed observation.

'Master Mariner Dic Bont has his head right in the works. Probably to muffle his curses. I can tell even from here he's in one of his mindless rages. In a minute he'll start kicking it. Something's got to be done. Let's get down to the jetty.'

They descended as rapidly as they could from the dunes to join a rough road that led to the outer harbour. It skirted boat-building sites in an advanced state of decay. At one point the road itself had subsided into a long barricade of brambles. Amy guided Enid's footsteps across the narrowest section. Below them an unfinished hull still stood on its blocks in the middle of a growing heap of marine scrap and rubbish. Sunbeams etched out the discoloured ribs.

They arrived at the jetty to find it deserted. They picked their way to the water's edge through stacks of unwanted roofing slate covered with layers of grey dust. By now the green clinker-built boat was close at hand. A more modern motor-boat was following it at a respectful distance. Dic Bont stood by the mast with a heavy spanner in his hand grinning in toothless triumph. When he saw Amy and Enid he waved the spanner.

'Look at him,' Amy said. 'Did you ever see a man so proud of his clumsy old bucket?'

She chatted cheerfully as they walked alongside the boat entering the mouth of the harbour.

'Just look at Eddie Meredith,' she said. 'Did you ever see a young man look so pleased with himself?'

A young man with black curls was standing up in the boat, waving at them. He had begun to sing and they could hear his pleasant voice wafting across the water.

'Always acting,' Amy said. 'Quite shameless. What do you suppose he imagines he is now? A Neapolitan or a Viennese tenor?'

They could see his companions listening with open admiration. And so was Tasker. None of them knew his song but Tasker was beating time contentedly. At the mooring point, Eddie was first off the boat. His companions seemed perfectly content to handle his gear. He confronted Amy and Enid on the quayside, stamping his feet delightedly. He held up a pack of cards in his hand.

'I thought they'd melt in the sun!' he said, 'You've no idea how hot it was out there. No protection from the sun. Becalmed. I felt just like the ancient mariner. And we had to sail through mist coming out of the island. Quite dangerous really. Anyway I fished these out and started to teach Martin and Otto how to play contract bridge.'

He was smiling at the girls in anticipation of their approval and praise.

'Where's the Bard?' he said. 'Where's our National Winner? You don't mean to say we are going to have to walk home?'

The other passengers were assembling behind Eddie waiting to be introduced to the young women. Two Danes, a Norwegian and a young Austrian with a round solemn face who seemed particularly anxious to kiss Amy's hand.

'This is Fritz the son,' Eddie said. 'Fritz the father is still on the island and I doubt if we'll ever get him off there again. He's absolutely entranced with the whole idea. Rebuilding an ancient Celtic abbey to create a new centre of International Brotherhood of Peace and Reconciliation.'

Having raised Amy's hand to his thick lips, Fritz the son was ready to recite phrases he had prepared on the prolonged trip from the island.

'If it is a sanctuary for birds' – he posed in front of Amy as he spoke – 'why cannot it become again a sanctuary for men, as it was in the Age of the Saints?'

'Isn't he marvellous!' Eddie slapped Fritz hard on the back. 'He does this all day long. Gathers up all his strength and then makes philosophical pronouncements.'

Behind the young men Tasker Thomas was in deep deliberations with Dic Bont. The seaman's face was wrinkled up with the effort of understanding, his open mouth exposing his toothless gums. The young men sorted out their camping gear and shared out the load between them. They explained to Amy and Enid how little food they had left and how hungry they were, sitting in the boat in sight of land.

'Near and yet so far,' one of the Danes said.

He was proud of the English idiom. Amy was moved to present him with an even more apposite Welsh phrase.

'*Boddi yn ymyl y lan*,' she said. 'Sinking in sight of the shore.'

He repeated the phrase, obviously glad of the excuse to walk alongside her. Tasker Thomas caught up with them and placed a fatherly hand firmly on Amy's shoulder.

'A brief word, Miss Parry. Between ourselves.'

They stood to one side and allowed the company to pass so that they brought up the rear.

'I thought you would like to know,' Tasker Thomas said. He beamed at her with deep benevolence.

'I called to see Val Gwyn last week,' he said. 'We had a long talk.'

Tasker touched her arm and lowered his head in a mute suggestion that they should pace out a complementary conversation on the road back to the town. Amy had begun to blush. Her mouth settled into a defensive firmness.

'In some ways we are very close,' Tasker said. 'And in others there is a great distance between us. But we are perfectly frank with each other. I have my reservations about his nationalistic stance. And I suspect he thinks my internationalism is woolly and idealistic. But for all practical purposes as far as the welfare of the common folk is concerned, and the language of course, and above all the well-being of religion, we are on the same side.'

He stood still on the road to study Amy's face and make certain she had absorbed the major point he was trying to make.

'He was a little sceptical about the Island venture,' Tasker said. 'As far as dear Val can be sceptical about anything. What he did say was perhaps an improved sewerage system for Pendraw was more important than a symbol on Saints Island. But when I riposted with "Why not both?..."'

Tasker spread out his hands dramatically. Amy stared at the ginger hair and healthy sunburnt skin of Tasker's large hands.

'He laughed you know. That charming quiet laugh of his. And he agreed.'

Tasker walked on deep in thought.

'He was so pleased to know I was coming to Pendraw. He was so anxious I should contact you. That we should be friends. And work together. I had a feeling you know I was coming to the very place in the world where he would most want to be. Tell me, Miss Parry, do you mind if I call you Amy?'

'Of course not,' Amy said.

'Tell me Amy, when did you last pay him a visit?'

Amy looked very unwilling to answer the question. Tasker Thomas smiled easily, unembarrassed by her silence.

'He seems to know everything that's going on in Pendraw,' Tasker said. 'I was quite amazed really. He gave me a political profile of the place. He knew all about the enmity between Alderman Llew and Doctor Davies DSO. And warned me of the pitfalls, moreover.'

Tasker shook with quiet laughter as if the complications of political life in Pendraw were a quaint epitome of the human comedy.

'Enid,' Amy said briefly. 'She writes him long letters. A mixture of local gossip and philosophical discussion. Something I couldn't do. They call them "Despatches from the Front".'

'Do they? Do they really?'

Tasker paused to marvel at the invention. Then he gave a deep sigh.

'I hope you will forgive me for saying this,' he said. 'A pastor should sympathise but should never pry. Believe me, I speak now out of loving sympathy. That man loves you more than anything in the world.'

Amy put her hand to her cheek. She could feel it burning.

'You think I'm treating him badly?'

He pushed his head forward to catch her whisper.

'You think I'm behaving selfishly?'

'Oh no, no, no.' Energetically he did all he could to disperse her suspicion.

'I only want to help,' he said. 'If there is any way I can. Two people for whom I have the highest regard, the deepest affection.'

'We are not engaged,' Amy said. 'Because of his condition. That's what he wants. I can't force myself on him.'

Tasker looked at her tenderly. Her eyes were almost closed and filling with tears.

'He tells me to look after myself and enjoy having my own job,' she said. 'And that's what I'm doing.'

Tasker stood still and nodded sympathetically.

'Yes, I see,' he said. 'I see. I hope ... I hope you don't think I was interfering. I felt so overwhelmed with sorrow when I left him there in that sanatorium bed.'

'I was willing to marry him,' Amy said. 'And look after him every hour of the day. He didn't want it. He wouldn't have it.'

She dried her eyes and stared defiantly at Tasker Thomas. He gazed ahead at the backs of the rest of the company. They were crossing the sandy waste ground between the inner harbour and the Beach Road.

'What do you expect me to do?' Amy said.

He sighed deeply and shook his head.

'Forgive me,' he said. 'I shouldn't have interfered.'

34

'It's his wish that I shouldn't go there too often,' Amy said. 'Apart from the distance or anything like that. It disturbs him. And it disturbs me.'

'I'm such an interfering fool,' Tasker said. 'Now you must forgive me. Promise?'

Amy smiled at last and nodded. They walked on emotionally relieved and in some degree of harmony.

'Is it such a bad thing to be content with one's lot?' Amy said. 'I work as hard as I can. The time passes more quickly that way. Not that I want the time to pass, and yet when I think of how long Val may have to be at the sanatorium I have to think in years, not in weeks and days.'

'Work,' Tasker Thomas said. 'My goodness yes. Work. A marvellous antidote for so many ills. That's why un-employment is such a spiritual scourge as well as a material blight. Ah!'

He raised a finger to show he had suddenly remembered something.

'I met a Bolshie friend of yours. A Red Revolutionary. At least he said he was a friend of yours. Been to Russia if you please. Very interesting to talk to. Working class but very acute mind. Very acute. First-class debater. Pen Lewis.'

'I hardly know him,' Amy said.

She sounded stern, resolute and self-possessed. Tasker was smiling broad-mindedly as he considered Pen Lewis.

'Very cheerful manner he has,' Tasker said. 'I rather admire that about him. "Give my regards to Miss Amy Parry", he said. "Tell her I might drop in one day for a cup of tea and a chat."'

'I don't want him here.'

Amy did not raise her voice, but Tasker Thomas was plainly taken aback by the force of her reaction.

'He's very fond of joking,' Tasker said. 'I rather like that about him. I don't think he meant any harm.'

Amy increased the speed of her walk. She seemed intent on catching up with the others. He heard her mutter angrily under her breath.

'Why can't people just leave me alone?'

5

When she reached the steps of the chalet, Amy saw Val
Gwyn sitting up in the bed which had been wheeled out on
the verandah and cranked up to allow him an uninterrupted
view of the landscape. His iron bedstead pointed like the
needle of a compass towards the majestic fir tree that stood
alone on a ridge to the left of the chalets on the hillside. A
massive root-system had taken over a half-excavated hollow
of what could once have been a hill fort. The two main
branches reached up like powerful supplicating arms
towards the ever-changing pattern of high cloud. Beyond the
tree the undulating hills were like the waves of a mysteriously
petrified green ocean. In the clear light Amy could see the
laundry folds on the jacket of his dark blue pyjamas. He lay
still in the bed contemplating the tree as if it were a living
presence with which he had established a form of
communication. Amy's approach was awkward and shy.

'You don't mind my coming?' she said.

He looked at her with the same quiet attention he had been
giving the tree. Then he smiled, delighted as she mounted
the steps and walked towards him.

'My goodness ... of course I don't.'

She arrived flushed after a rapid walk. Her raincoat was
unbuttoned. She wore a pale blue dress and a matching hat
that folded back and revealed more of her golden hair than it
covered. Her legs were bare and sunburnt and she moved
about with an athletic disregard for her appearance. She
extracted a letter from the pocket of her raincoat and handed
it to the tall man who lay so still in the sanatorium bed.

'From Enid,' Amy said. 'She managed to get it to me
before I left. Your despatch from the Front.'

Val accepted the letter gratefully but did not open it.

'I haven't brought you a thing,' Amy said. 'It was such a
rush. I thought I could stay the night down in the village and
do any shopping you wanted.'

A new silk dressing-gown hung within his reach. He
seemed to consider putting it on. The bedside table was

overloaded with books, magazines and papers. The extra weight he had gained in the weeks since she had last paid him a visit managed to make him look both well-fed and delicate. He was neatly shaved and his dark hair was more carefully groomed than it had ever been before he fell ill.

'I don't think there is anything I need,' he said.

'There must be.'

There were books on the floor. She bent to pick them up. Any form of action brought her some relief.

'Not now that you are here.'

He smiled but his welcome did not put her at her ease. He fingered the envelope of Enid's letter but made no move to open it. She grasped the wooden rail of the verandah and considered the view as if she could measure the degree of comfort it brought him. In the silence a red squirrel darted across the pine needles and roots among the rocks to scurry up the fissured bark of the fir tree on the ridge.

'Doctor Penryn says we should think of ourselves as passengers on the long voyage to recovery,' Val said. 'He's a strange chap really. A practical mystic. "Study the night sky", he said. "It's the best rehearsal for eternity."'

Val's shoulders shook with silent laughter. All his movements were constrained and limited by the experience of prolonged periods of bed-rest. Amy could hear him draw the envelope between his thumb and finger.

'Aren't you going to read Enid's letter?' she said. 'Report from the social laboratory. The great Tasker Thomas has now settled among us. Read all about it.'

'Up here the passage of time is different,' he said. 'I'm not pretending it doesn't hang heavy. If often does. But there are intervals of what I can only call lucidity. If I were a philosopher or a poet I could expand and explain as old Prof. Arnot used to say. But I'm neither. I'm only a would-be social worker on indefinite leave of absence.'

'Val!' She objected to his self-deprecating humour.

'Mind you, I can spend the whole morning cobbling up a single phrase about glimpsing traces of a universal consciousness through the cracks and interstices of individual perception and it seems a miraculous discovery until it evaporates in yet another bowl of cabbage soup.'

37

'Val!' She had so many things on her mind it seemed impossible she could find a way to unburden herself of half of them.

'Val,' she said at last. 'What about us?'

The question was so desperate he longed to bring her comfort.

'You exist,' he said.

This brought her no satisfaction.

'It is all I ask for,' he said.

Amy raised her fist.

'We must fight,' she said. 'We must fight together. That's the way to get you well. I'm sure of it.'

He was playing with the envelope again, drawing it listlessly between his fingers. She made a visible effort to prevent herself from stamping her foot and telling him not to do it.

'We've discusssed this,' he said. 'Objectively and subjectively. We decided on a free relationship. For you more than for me because I am effectively imprisoned.'

'I'm not free,' Amy said. 'Or if I am, I don't want to be.'

Her contradiction made him smile at her fondly. This brought her foot down on the bitumen-stained boards with unrestrained force.

'I've thought about this,' she said. 'I've thought about it for weeks. It doesn't matter twopence what I want or what I imagine I want. It's what I should do. That's what counts. I see that with absolute clarity.'

Her outburst did not disturb him unduly. His calm exasperated her further.

'Look at Enid,' she said. 'Just look at the way she writes every week. Without fail.'

'Freedom for each to fulfil him or herself in the way best suited to his or her condition,' Val said. 'We spelt it out. As far as Enid is concerned, writing is one of the ways in which she is best able to fulfil herself. You work. I would work if I could. As it is I am forced to lie here and I fulfil myself by learning to put up with it.'

Amy moved to the bottom of his bed.

'Val,' she said. 'It's so vital we should be absolutely frank with each other. I feel useless, utterly useless. Absorbed in myself and my own little job. As cosy as a pair of carpet slippers. That's not the way I want to live.'

He stared sadly at the glowing beauty of her figure at the bottom of the bed.

'I'm only half a man,' he said. 'Economically. Physically. Tuberculosis is an expensive disease. This place is too expensive really. We've been over it before.'

Shyly she thrust herself between the wooden partition and the side of his bed. He held on to Enid's letter. She took it and tossed it over to the side table. She took hold of his hand.

'It's not easy,' she said, 'for a girl to make the advances.' She leaned forward awkwardly across the high bed.

'Val. I want you to marry me.'

Her hand moved tentatively over his body eager to affirm how much she treasured it. With a shudder of pleasure he embraced her. Her hat fell off. He held her so tightly she had to struggle to breathe. It took him time to realise the extent to which he was overpowering her. He released her apologising profusely.

'Half a man, indeed,' she said.

He was eager to make light of his condition.

'I'm not supposed to be too much alive,' he said. 'It's not good for me.'

'I've settled it,' Amy said. 'I'll look after you. That's the simple answer.'

He reached out his arm for his dressing-gown. He swung his legs over the edge of the bed.

'It's degrading,' he said. 'Being afraid of the flesh of your own body. Thinking of your lungs all the time and wondering about their condition. I'd love to forget them. Leave them on some butcher's slab and fly off for a trip like an intellectual model aeroplane.'

Amy pushed her way out of the confined space between the partition and the bed. The table of books occupied the position where she could have stood or sat in comfort. She came closer to whisper her question.

'How much longer, Val? How much longer does Penryn say you'll have to stay here?'

He gave her a stoical grin. 'He tells me not to think about it,' he said.

'I want to know. Tell me everything. I want to know.' She spoke with the firmness of a woman resolved not to evade a single fact, however unpleasant, a moment longer.

'The AP's are not really working,' he said. 'Penryn says I have a choice. He calls it a choice anyway. There is a new operation, or a state of semi-permanent bed-rest that could last three or four years.'

'Three or four years?' Amy gasped as she repeated the phrase. The way she pronounced it, it could have been a life sentence. She struggled to control her dismay.

'But there are new cures, aren't there?' she said. 'One reads about them in the newspapers all the time.'

Val smiled at her sympathetically.

'Newspapers,' he said. 'The prime agents of myth and fantasy.'

Amy followed him to the open door of the chalet. He moved about with the unselfconscious ease of a man hospitalised over a long period.

'What's this new operation? What is it?'

She forced herself to ask the question.

'They call it a thoracoplasty.'

'What does that mean?'

'I think it just means chest surgery.' Val smiled and took a resolutely deep breath.

'What happens? What do they do?'

'They carve you up a bit. Down the back. Take out a couple of ribs or bend them. To get at the lung and press it down.'

The screen only partially concealed the tall naked figure that would be subjected to such drastic treatment. Amy stared at Val's well-proportioned shape and most intently of all at his long back as if it were being cut open in front of her eyes. Already there were dark marks between his ribs left there from earlier treatment like an earnest of more terrible intentions.

'It is in some ways the last resort,' Val was saying. 'But they seem very confident about it.'

'Oh Val...'

He turned around startled by her agonised cry. She was

40

stumbling towards him, her arms outstretched, half blinded by her tears.

'It's butchery,' she said. 'I won't let them touch you.' Her arms were around him and her cheek pressed against his naked back.

'I'll look after you, Val. I swear it. Every minute of the day, I'll nurse you. I'll look after you.'

She sank under the weight of her misery, kneeling at his feet. He sat down on a bench so that he could stroke her hair and comfort her. His trousers were still unbuttoned and his feet were bare. She held his hand and pressed her lips against his wrist.

'Old Tasker Thomas can marry us.'

She was ready to smile through her tears.

'Enid and John Cilydd can be witnesses. Nobody else need know. A secret wedding.'

She looked up at him, wide-eyed and longing for complete frankness, but his head was lowered and his eyes were closed. She knelt before him to concentrate her affection on his body as if to demonstrate that for her it had an infinite value. Shyly at first and with tender care her fingers touched his skin. Kneeling between his legs she laid her head comfortably against his chest. She listened to the pounding of his heart as her hand caressed the nape of his neck and stroked the length of his back. By her own unstinting efforts she would nurse him to health. Her hands and her lips would restore him. She whispered her spell as he bent over her as rigid and motionless as a marble statue.

'You're not ill. Not really. You're too beautiful to be ill. Too perfect. Too good.'

When she noticed the tense lack of response to her incantation she sank back on her heels weighed down once again with remorse.

'I'm not good enough for you. I know that. I never was.'

She turned away from him to stare at the half open door of the chalet. There was someone passing on the path outside. She waited until the footsteps had faded leaving a heavier silence between them in the hut which smelt of pine wood and soap and antiseptics. Pushing her fist into the corner of her mouth, she forced herself to confess.

'That Pen Lewis. I let him make love to me. I should never have let him.'

She crouched on the chalet floor abject with self-disgust. She waited for him to speak as if she were longing for him to pass sentence.

'I had to tell you,' she said. 'I couldn't breathe any longer without telling you. All I want in the world is to be as close as possible to you.'

She turned when she heard his teeth chattering. His arm was stretched out towards her offering her comfort. She scrambled to her feet and threw his dressing-gown over his shoulders. Then she wrapped her arms around him and pressed herself against his back.

'What else am I good for except to keep you warm,' she said.

'You mustn't torture yourself, Amy;' he said.

He kissed her hair and her face but carefully avoided kissing her on the lips.

'I told you when this thing started, in the other place, I told you, you were free. You were totally free. I told you.'

'I don't want to be free,' Amy said. 'I don't.'

In a state of near desperation, she embraced him recklessly, forcing him to kiss her on the lips even as he turned his head away to protect her from possible infection. She would have him understand that there was nothing she wanted more of life than to share his burden and bring him consolation and comfort. She would allow nothing to restrain her. She would trample on her pride and her lifelong habits of circumspection and offer her body as generously as she could in such an exposed and vulnerable situation. There were chalets with patients on either side of them and they were forced to whisper as they clung together and sank unsteady to lie together on the floor in the limited privacy offered by the changing-screen. Amy was slow to realise how much Val was struggling to restrain himself and hold himself back. She sat up and placed her hands on his face. It was covered with a cold sweat.

'Are you all right, Val?'

He nodded as though he were too short of breath to speak.

'Is it that you don't want me? You're thinking about Pen Lewis aren't you?'

He shook his head.

'He only wanted me because I belonged to you. He was trying to get at you, through me. That's all it was. He was envious of you.'

Val's understanding smile did nothing to comfort her. She shook his lifeless arms.

'What is it then? Val. Tell me. Please tell me.'

'I'm going to take that operation.'

Amy closed her eyes. Val moved away and began to get dressed for his afternoon walk. She lay on the floor behind the screen with a pillow held tightly in her arms.

'The chances of success are good. But not a hundred per cent of course. They never can be. But at least it will be some form of action.'

He wanted her to sit down so that he could explain his situation to her more fully.

'We have a poor record,' he said. 'A bad history, you might say. My father died of TB. So did my cousin Morlais. We were boys together. I don't know what my chances of survival are. But I want to fight it. We used to talk about my mission, didn't we? Well now it's shrunk down to this. But it's still the same fight for me. I feel it as a pattern of necessity. And it means I must leave this place. To take this operation I've got to go to a public sanatorium and that suits me well. Not a private chalet but just one more bed in a cubicle in a great big public ward, sharing the suffering. That's the only way.'

'You don't want me,' Amy said. 'I'm offering to marry you and you don't want me.'

She sounded almost childishly surprised and hurt. Val rubbed his forehead with his finger tips as he struggled to explain his position.

'I don't want privilege. I came here because I imagined I could do some thinking and some writing. Turn my condition to some kind of an advantage. But it doesn't really work that way. I suppose what it amounts to is that writing for me is a secondary pursuit. By nature and by desire I am a man of action. So this is no better than a pleasant prison.

Passivity doesn't really suit me. I'm talking a lot of nonsense, aren't I?'

Amy shook her head despondently.

'Oh no,' she said. 'Please tell me. Tell me everything. I want to understand.'

'Passivity encourages helplessness and lack of concern. It says we are all particles of the Great Nothing and the sooner we get used to the idea the better. That's what it says.'

Amy seemed tempted to agree with this: but she remained silent. She picked up a pair of thick woollen socks and pressed their prickly texture against her cheek before kneeling down to put them on his feet.

'Passivity,' Val said. 'It's very seductive. Socially and politically, it is absolute poison. It makes it easy for us to say that our fate is decided by things happening on the other side of the world that we can do absolutely nothing about. Like the restriction of credit. It wants you to accept that tuberculosis is like unemployment. A plague you can do nothing about. So you see the least I can do is submit to the best chance of a cure.'

'Who's that?'

A sniff outside had brought Amy's attention to an angular young woman in a long raincoat standing outside the chalet. Her sharp nose was running. She wiped it with difficulty since it was tilted upwards and she carried a small pile of books under her arm. Her approach had been silent because she wore tennis shoes on her feet. Under the raincoat the frilled hem of her nightdress was visible.

'Sorry to interrupt.'

She had a damp but amiable smile. Her eyes looked sore as though from too much reading. Her hair was tied back girlishly by a blue ribbon. Inside her drab raincoat she seemed to simmer with the desire to be jolly.

'Awfully sorry. Brought your books back. Great article on Lloyd George. Mind you, I don't agree with it. Do I have to?'

Val moved to the top of the verandah steps. Amy remained in the doorway, her hands held behind her back. The girl in the raincoat handed back the books she had borrowed.

'Well, if it doesn't convince you, it can't be much good,' Val said.

'No. It's not that.'

The girl screwed up her face and squinted at Val.

'I'm sure what you say is true. But it only dents the idol. It doesn't really knock him off his pedestal.'

She was waiting now to be introduced to Amy. Val considered her criticism in silence and then turned to make hurried introductions.

'Marian Mai,' he said. 'Our chess champion among her other accomplishments. Amy Parry. She teaches at Pendraw County School. Geography and Biology. Biology mostly, isn't it?'

Amy made no effort to corroborate the information. Marian Mai tried to lighten the atmosphere with a quick quotation.

'"Life isn't all biology",' she said.

She shook with pleasure at her own joke. This did little to commend her in Amy's eyes. Val tried to be amiable.

'Marian Mai has bardic connections,' he said. 'A vast knowledge. Very useful for crossword puzzles.'

Marian Mai pointed at the books Val was now holding.

'There is one very good line in that,' she said. 'Very telling I thought.'

She was addressing Amy to emphasise how much she appreciated Val's talent. As she spoke she gave her 'r's an elocutionary roll to embellish the quotation. The effort brought saliva to the corners of her mouth.

'"All Caesarism is based on the mass deception inherent in crowd psychology. Even the mealy-mouthed papier-mâché Welsh Liberal version." That won't go down at all well where I come from.'

She was eyeing Val with mild reproof and subdued admiration. Amy spoke out with such vehemence that Marian Mai stepped back in alarm.

'He ought to be shot,' Amy said. 'And all the people who are stupid enough to worship him.'

Marian Mai jerked about inside her long raincoat and one arm reached up after the other in precipitate farewell.

'Well, I must be off,' she said. 'I'll leave you in peace. Pleased to meet you . . .'

Val followed her a few paces along the path and then stopped to make cordial noises. He returned to find Amy sitting on the verandah steps playing with the brim of her blue hat.

'She was wearing a fancy night-dress under that mac,' Amy said sullenly.

'This is a very sheltered place,' Val said. 'Cut off. You could easily imagine some awful catastrophe happening in the world and the news just never reaching us.'

'She's keen on you. I could see that clearly enough.'

'On me?' Val found the suggestion incredible and absurd. 'Poor Marian Mai. She's a Blue Ovate by postal examination. Her father adjudicates recitation. He's a big Liberal.'

'Eisteddfodic twits!' Amy's exasperation was explosive. 'They get on my nerves. A couple of flower dances inside the Gorsedd Stones once a year and everything will be all right. And all that stupid get-up. Ostriches dressed as Arabs. I never could see the point of all that dressing up.'

Val sat beside her. He took both her hands in his to comfort her.

'Here, it's all temperatures and treatment,' he said quietly. 'We all try to make acceptable worlds. She's a bad case. I don't know how long she's got to live.'

Amy lifted his hands to her lips. 'I'm sorry Val,' she said. 'I was jealous. Really jealous. It's an awful feeling. Like being sick. I'm begging you to marry me. Isn't that funny? So that I can look after you. You can write. You could edit a weekly magazine like what's-his-name in Chester. It's not heavy work. And his condition must be far worse than yours. I'll feed you up. We'll manage together. I'll learn to help you in every little thing. And every big thing too. What's the point of living – What are we good for in this world if we can't learn to look after the ones we love and cherish the most? You've got a mission to get well. And then you've got a greater mission to go on to. I understand that. And that's what I want to share.'

Val was overcome with affection for her. He took her head

46

in both his hands and brushed her cheeks with his lips, savouring their softness.

'My dearest,' he said. 'My dearest.'

She waited patiently for him to say more. She swallowed her disappointment as she listened to him reverently murmuring her name.

'Your mind is made up then?' She stood up and offered him her hand to help him to his feet.

'Necessity,' he said.

'What does that mean?'

He thought about the answer and sighed.

'Well, take away all the philosophical stuff about constraint. All it means in my case is waiting,' he said. 'Just waiting.'

Amy gave a sad smile and shook her head.

'That's one thing I was never very good at,' she said.

'We'll walk a little,' Val said. 'That will help. I try to study nature. Not that I make a good job of it. I'll never be a nature-mystic, that's for certain.'

'Enid's letters,' Amy said.

She rested her arm lightly inside his. In the distance there were other patients taking gentle exercise.

'Does she say anything about me?'

Val began to shake with laughter.

'What's so funny?' she said.

'Nothing,' he said. 'I mustn't get over excited. But it's so marvellous to be with you.'

'So they wouldn't make me jealous?'

Amy threw her head back to breathe the mountain air more deeply.

'Go to your head more like,' he said.

'What does that mean?'

'She relies on you and admires you so much,' he said. 'That sort of thing.'

Amy rubbed his sleeve playfully, content to be at his side.

'Will you let me read them?' she said.

'We'll see,' he said. 'We'll see. If you are a very good girl. As a special treat.'

6

Amy sat in the women's staff-room correcting homework books. She had the room to herself. The hands of the clock on the iron mantelpiece stood at ten past five and the tick was as unobtrusive as a pulse; in this sanctuary at the top of the school it was a positive aid to concentration. It drew attention to the great silence in the school itself. Only a memory of the bustle of the school day lingered like a smell in the deserted corridors. There were two piles of books at Amy's feet. As one grew, the other diminished. The work seemed as pleasantly monotonous as a kitchen chore such as shelling peas. Each exercise book had an identical surface of white drawing paper on the left and a lined page with a glossy surface for written work on the right. Errors were quickly identified. Under cross-section drawings Amy inscribed brief comments in red ink. There was an earthenware bottle of the ink she used on the locker alongside her chintz-covered armchair.

A scratching sound made her lift her head. With great care she put down her pen and the exercise book to stand up and wait for the noise to occur again. The afternoon light came from ecclesiastically arched windows almost touching the high ceiling. A library steps had been left by the window that faced south, presumably to enable the shorter lady members of the staff to refresh themselves with an occasional glimpse of the sea. The overcrowded room was an odd shape. It was the last space under the roof where the two dominant concepts in the mind of a nineteenth-century architect had to be reconciled. Archivolts, eclectic curves and neo-gothic decorative motifs had to come to terms with squares and rectangles and the geometric accuracy of accommodating progressive work places and laboratories with sinks and bunsen burners.

With a mousetrap in her hand, Amy tip-toed towards the largest cupboard with an interior which penetrated in-definitely into the roof-space. The trap had already been charged with a tempting cube of red cheese. She pushed the door open with one finger. Inside, the cupboard was crammed untidily with assorted teaching aids, ancient and modern. Nothing seemed to have been thrown away since the day the school first opened in the 1890s, only thrust further out of reach to accumulate additional layers of dust and cobwebs in the perpetual night between the joists and purlings. Delicately Amy set the trap down inside the cupboard and closed the door.

While she stared at the cupboard, she placed her handbag on the mahogany table which took up so much space in the room. She lit a cigarette. There was no further sound and no reason for her not to return to her marking. She yawned comfortably as she resumed her work. As her head bent over the exercise book, the cigarette smoke was suspended in a canopy of soothing insubstantiality in the space above her. The pile of marked books grew steadily until a new noise in the corridor outside the door made her suddenly raise her head. As if some danger were approaching, she extinguished the cigarette on the blue tiles surrounding the fireplace and tossed the stump into the fan of newspaper that filled the grate instead of a fire. With her left hand she made a rapid attempt to dispel the smoke hanging above her. She continued with her marking, but her pen retraced the letters of the word 'drupe' as she listened for any further sound from beyond the door. She dropped an exercise book on the pile at the right of her chair and the noise was magnified to a thud in the silence. Again she held her breath. There was a modest tapping at the door. In the end it could be nothing more than a small child returned to school in search of something lost or forgotten. Amy elected to speak out with sharp authority.

'Yes! Come in.'

Eddie Meredith opened the door. With exaggerated caution he peered around the room as if to make certain Amy was alone before giving her an engagingly mischievous smile. He wore a trilby hat on the side of his head and a trench coat with the collar turned up.

'Miss Parry! Princess!'

'What do you want?'

Eddie was not discouraged. He tip-toed into the room intent on making her laugh.

'Do I look like a conspirator?' he said.

Amy picked up another exercise book and continued marking. She took her time to answer.

'You shouldn't worry so much about what you look like,' she said.

The engaging smile vanished from his cherub-like face. He flopped into the chair opposite Amy, tilting his hat to the back of his head. He gripped the wooden arms of the chair and gazed around the room determined to regain his composure and confidence.

'The Seraglio,' he said.

'You've no business to be sitting there,' Amy said.

'I'm overwhelmed by the nostalgia of an old boy,' he said. 'You've no idea how this little room used to intrigue us. Before your time, of course. This remote corner of the republic of learning reserved for ladies only. What I remember best is the blessed aroma of chalk and eau de cologne.'

Amy shut the exercise book and dropped it squarely on the pile of marked work. She had become the experienced school-mistress who could barely spare a steely smile as she gave her main energies to the task in hand.

'You are not exactly a model of reliability are you?' she said.

'Reliable?' Eddie said. 'What am I supposed to be? A motor bike or something?'

Briefly Amy pointed the top of her pen at him.

'An Oxford man,' she said. 'What else?'

Eddie raised both hands in mock self-defence.

'Amy,' he said. 'Miss Parry. Spare me.'

'The rising star of Pendraw,' Amy said. 'Tasker Thomas's white-headed boy. The Oxford man to end all Oxford men. How could such an important person be bothered with distributing our miserable little Peace pamphlets?'

Eddie surrendered without any further struggle. His hat dropped on the floor and he began to push his fingers ruefully through his thick black curls.

'My God, you're absolutely right,' he said. 'There are times I don't mind telling you when I absolutely disgust myself.'

'There's no need to go from one extreme to the other,' Amy said. 'All you had to do was distribute leaflets in three streets. And all you did in fact was dump them in Salem vestry.'

'Who told you?'

'Never mind who told me,' Amy said.

'Pendraw,' he said. 'The cesspool with eight thousand eyes. Please tell me. In the interests of Art and Science or whatever. I can't bear not to know.'

'My Mrs Rossett,' Amy said. 'My landlady. A woman of great resources and discretion.' She allowed herself to smile.

'Oh my God.' Eddie shifted about in apparent distress. 'You'll never forgive me. I can't bear it.'

He was about to sink to his knees and approach Amy as a penitent. Again Amy pointed the red ink-pen at him.

'Stay just where you are,' she said. 'If it comes to that you'd better clear out of here. The Head is still around. And that could mean his wife as well. She could march in here any minute.'

'I want to apologise,' Eddie said.

'What for? If I hadn't told you, you'd never have mentioned it. It's not my place to tell you, Eddie Meredith, but you have all the makings of a devious little monster.'

'Little?' Eddie raised his arms to exaggerate their length. He stood over Amy to demonstrate how much larger and more physically powerful he was. He struck a predatory vulturine pose in a last effort to amuse her.

'Spiritually little,' Amy said.

'Oh my God... You really mean it, don't you?'

'I usually mean the things I say,' she said.

He groaned in desperation and sank gracefully to the floor at her feet.

'Turn me into a spider or something,' he said. 'Or a dormouse. Put me to sleep. Strike me with eternal torpor. I'm making a mess of my own life in front of my own eyes and I'm so bloody sharp I know exactly the reason.'

'Get up, will you,' Amy said. 'And stop play-acting. You've got theatricals on the brain.'

He groped along the floor so that he could hold Amy's shoes in his hands. She drew her feet under her chair.

'Will you stop it?' she said. 'Someone could come in here any minute.'

He laid his fists upwards on the floor and pounded his forehead against them with a vigour which provided the gesture without the pain.

'If you despise me, there's nothing left to live for.'

'Get up, you fool.'

He lifted his face so that Amy could see there were tears on his cheeks.

'You are the goddess in my life,' he said. 'You have to let me go on worshipping you.'

To make up for her delay in discovering how much he was play-acting, Amy burst out into raucous laughter. It sounded so unseemly in the women's staff room that she clapped both her hands over her mouth to restrain it. Eddie leaned boldly against her knees.

'There's my girl,' he said. 'The most beautiful thing that's ever happened to this place. Will you come to tea next Thursday? At the Workhouse. My father says "The Union". But I say "The Workhouse" because that's what it is.'

'Why are you asking me?'

'For all sorts of devious reasons.' Eddie grinned at her. 'My father thinks you are marvellous. That must be the one solitary thing on earth I agree with him about. Say you'll come. Please. Please, say you'll come.'

'What are you up to?'

'Say you'll come and I'll tell you what I've got in my pocket.' He patted the left hand pocket of his raincoat to arouse her curiosity.

'What do I care what you've got in your pocket?'

'For the sake of the Cause,' he said.

'What Cause?' Amy said. 'The Society for the advancement of Eddie Meredith?'

'Oh you are a terrible goddess,' he said. 'The kind of beauty that brings strong men to their knees. So what chance is there for me?'

He drew out a folded sheet of notepaper and waved it in front of Amy.

'Proof positive that Alderman Llew is against the hospital wing at the Workhouse. Against the extended sewerage system. And determined to allocate the funds in question to the erection of the Llew Maurice Memorial Hall. Proof that the old monster has been lying himself blue in the face. He's got an Ozymandias complex. And proof that small town politics in a place like Pendraw is a microcosm of the machinations of great power politics. Only a million times murkier. I'm going to write a play about it. A glittering demonstration of the duplicity and baseness of human nature and human motives.'

As he worked himself up to a pitch of eloquence, Amy collected her exercise books and planted them neatly on the bench under the high window.

'You settle down here and do just that,' she said. 'For my part I'm on my way home.'

Eddie stood boldly in her way. 'Amy,' he said. 'Don't you understand? Don't you understand the significance of this scrap of paper? Don't you see what we could do with it?'

Amy looked at him sternly.

'I don't have to,' she said. 'Our Cause is right and just. In that case we don't need in any way to get involved with nasty little political machinations.'

'Give it to Enid More,' he said. 'And tell her to give it to Cilydd.'

'No, I won't,' Amy said. 'Give it him yourself if you think it's that important.'

'I came here specially . . .'

Momentarily Eddie was lost for words.

'Amy. Will you come to tea?'

A faint smile on her face was sufficient to encourage him. He leaned forward to peck a kiss on the tip of her nose. Amy pushed her fist angrily against his chest.

'Don't you dare.'

The unmistakable sound of the caretaker pushing desks around in the classroom below quenched the light of battle in Amy's eye.

'Get out!'

He was taken aback by her sudden fierceness. A new sound added to Amy's embarrassment. Female footsteps were approaching inexorably along the bare boards of the top corridor. Amy went pale.

'Mrs Pierce.'

She whispered the name of the headmaster's wife. She stepped away from Eddie so that the maximum space the overcrowded room allowed lay between them. The sharp knock on the door was accompanied by the rattle of coins on a metal bracelet. Amy sighed with relief before the door was pushed open and Miss Sali Prydderch appeared wearing one of her wide-brimmed hats and carrying a voluminous woven handbag on her arm. She beamed with delight at the sight of Amy in her graduate gown under the arched window.

'I knew I'd find you,' Sali Prydderch said. 'Don't ask me how. I haunt schools you see. That's my metier.'

She smiled approvingly at Eddie Meredith, waiting to be introduced.

'This is Eddie Meredith,' Amy said hastily.

To her own obvious annoyance she was blushing. She removed her gown and hung it up alongside four others on a row of pegs.

'I'm not sure that he shouldn't be at Oxford or somewhere like that,' she said. 'But at the moment he's here. This is Miss Prydderch, HMI, Mr Meredith.'

Sali clasped her hands together in wonder.

'Isn't that amazing?' she said. 'I have a letter right here in my bag all about you, Mr Meredith. You are going to Berlin to stay with the wonderful Pastor Otto Hartmann!'

Eddie stood deferentially poised in the centre of the room.

'I hope so,' he said. 'It's not quite settled yet.'

'Dear Tasker Thomas wrote me,' Sali Prydderch said. Her face was illuminated with the pleasure of offering the information. 'He knew of my connection with the Sternbergs. And he wondered if I would provide you with a letter of introduction. There never was a more thoughtful man. So resolved to go about the world doing good. Finding time for everything. And here we are – what a delightful coincidence!'

Eddie nodded to show his gratitude. He also continued to show that, happy as he was, he was still puzzled.

'I was engaged to Werner,' Miss Prydderch said. 'The second son.' She sounded both proud and happy. 'He was killed in the War. That War to end all wars as they used to call it. I still keep in touch. They have a house in Berlin but the estate is west of Gorlitz. I shall certainly write. If that's what you'd like.'

Eddie breathed deeply, held his breath and expelled the air in an explosion of delight.

'Oh my goodness,' he said. 'Indeed I would. That would be most wonderfully kind. I need all the support I can get.' He gazed appealingly at Amy and Sali Prydderch in turn. 'The trouble is, you, see my father's terribly against it.'

7

A beam of perpendicular light fell on the dusty counter of the front office of the Printing Works at the top of Glyn Street. Mr Evans, the manager, was a small asthmatic figure in a clean starched collar, determined to preserve some vestige of elegance in his appearance in spite of the nature of his work. He held one hand on the brass knob of the communicating door and the other pressed against his tweed waistcoat in order to help his breathing. Over his pince-nez he watched Enid fill a leather shopping bag with bundles of freshly printed leaflets.

'After all,' he said, 'we have a National Winner in our midst. That's not to be sniffed at.'

He smiled at Enid to show he was intent on paying her husband a friendly compliment.

'You know, when I was a young fellow the Roof Tree Circle was a worthwhile element in the cultural life of Pendraw. A nest of singing birds old Cromlech used to call it. I don't suppose you ever saw old Cromlech, Mrs More?'

Enid did her best to show a polite interest. She was wearing a loose overcoat over her dress and her hair fell untidily about her face.

'An old countryman of the old school. He used to march in

here you know and slap his manuscript down on this very counter and say to my father, "Now then Sol Evans, how much for printing this exalted rubbish?"'

Mr Evans's chest wheezed alarmingly as he tried to control his laughter. A commotion in the street made them both turn around and move towards the door. A herd of bullocks was being driven towards the station. In the narrow street, confronted with traffic and people on market day, the animals were at a standstill. From the doorway, Enid could see their black flanks throbbing with fear. Across the street, some visitors and day-trippers in holiday clothes gathered under the awning of a greengrocer, alarmed at the seething, lowing presence of the herd. Two men planted themselves on the pavement edge in front of Enid. One wore a flat cap and a stockman's brown overall. He carried a spare mackintosh folded neatly over his right arm which was parked ceremoniously on the small of his back. The form of his diminutive companion was made more bulky by the wearing of two overcoats. The general alarm gave them obvious pleasure. A young bullock thrust its tilted horns and clownish face in their direction in a vain attempt to avoid the pressure behind it. The open door of the printer's shop could have appeared to the animal as a possible avenue of escape. Enid could see its great eyes roll helplessly and the sticky nostrils wet and steaming with terror. The stockman raised his brown boot and kicked the bullock in the nose. He did this without disturbing the folds of his mackintosh hanging behind him from his right forearm. The bullock could not move because of the press of beasts behind him. The stockman kicked at him again. The animal could not shift. Blood trickled down its nostrils. Enid tugged at the mackintosh and the man was forced to turn to save it falling to the ground.

'Don't do that,' she said.

He glared at her angrily. His long face under the cloth cap wore an habitually sour expression.

'What the devil is this woman trying to do then?'

He addressed the diminutive companion alongside him as 'Mos bach'. Mos bach's most urgent function in life appeared to be registering the sour-faced stockman's

56

remarks and saving them up for repetition on convivial
occasions. His beady eyes glittered in the shadow of a cap
worn slightly askew. His elfin face had red cheeks that were
permanently inflated by the roguish smile stamped on his
face. It was he who recognised Enid. He whispered swiftly to
his companion.

'You see who it is,' he said. 'The Welsh Nash female. That
one we saw speaking on a cart outside the Town Hall.'

The sour-faced one restored the folds of his mackintosh
with care.

'In calf I see,' he said. 'I don't know what you'd get for her
either, Mos bach. Not in the peak of condition.'

Mos bach shrank inside his coats to giggle uncontrollably
to himself. Enid's face went white. She returned to the
counter and picked up a handful of pamphlets.

'They've no business driving their herds down Glyn
Street,' Mr Evans said. 'Especially during the season. I
brought the matter up myself at the town Council two
months ago. We must do something about it, I said. The
visitors won't like it.'

At last the bullocks had begun to move. Mr Evans turned
his attention to the leaflets. His thin cheeks creased as he
smiled at Enid.

'A printer can read upside down, you know,' he said.

He seemed to expect her admiration and approval.

'"Outlaw Bombing from the Air ... Support the League
of Nations Resolution ... Oppose the proposed Bombing
Range in Cadwal Bay ..."'

The meaning behind the letters was slow to penetrate Mr
Evan's consciousness.

'Ah well,' he said. 'Do you know what I think, Mrs More?'

Enid shook her head.

'You can't stop Progress,' Mr Evans said. 'That's what I
think.'

He sighed deeply and eased the spring of his pince-nez on
the bridge of his nose.

'Progress to what, Mr Evans?' Enid said. 'Progress to War
or Progress to Peace?'

'What can we do? What power have we got, little creatures
like you and me?'

Enid took out a bundle of leaflets and opened it, ready for distribution.

'If we do nothing, we shall all be driven to the slaughter. Just like those poor beasts in the street.'

She waited impatiently as he made out a receipt in English on an invoice with a letter head that displayed an exaggerated etching of Dawes and Evans Printing Works. Once in the street, she began to distribute the yellow leaflets to anyone who would accept them. She was making her way to Amy's lodgings in Eifion Street. At the cross-roads she encountered a tight group of farm workers in firm occupation of the corner site. It was a choice advantage point. Here they could watch the passing scene, ignore the visitors who wanted to pass, smoke cigarettes in cupped hands, cherish their second raincoats and polished boots and chaff each other at regular intervals. Breathing deeply to control her nervousness, Enid began to distribute her leaflets among them. They showed no great readiness to notice her or accept her offer. While she was attempting to interest them, Mos bach and the sour-faced stockman merged into the group, perceptibly strengthening it. Enid did not flinch from holding out a leaflet in their direction. The stockman shook his head staring at her suspiciously from the corner of his eye.

'Take one,' Enid said. 'It doesn't cost anything. It won't bite you.'

He resented her challenge. Mos bach held out a hand to ask for a leaflet eager to give the stockman time to formulate a biting remark. As he took the sheet he addressed an acquaintance on his other side through the corner of his mouth.

'Welsh Nash, this one,' he said. 'Seen her spouting in front of the Town Hall.'

He addressed Enid with sly amiability.

'What's it for this time?'

'Peace,' Enid said. 'It's for Peace. You read it.'

Mos bach averted his eyes. The stockman was speaking.

'A woman in your condition should be home,' he said. 'Not parading the streets.' Mos began to shake pleasurably inside his coats.

'It's about Peace,' Enid said.

The stockman looked at the leaflet.

'It's the right colour then,' he said. 'Conchie stuff I suppose.'

'You are lucky,' Enid said. 'You've never seen War. You don't know what war means.'

'Selling things on the street.' The stockman growled angrily. 'Stuffing things at people. Things they don't want. She'll be selling herself next.'

He was at a loss for any more biting phrases. Some of the farm workers had begun to read the leaflets with interest. Enid was standing before him as defiantly as any recalcitrant ewe guarding its offspring. Suddenly he flapped the panels of his overcoat and stamped his hobnailed boots.

'Huss!' He growled at her like a stockman urging on his cattle dog. 'Huss! Home! Go home!'

In a frightened state, Enid hurried down Eifion Street to number seven. She grasped the brass door-knocker and rapped it so hard against its metal base the noise reverberated in the street. She saw that the knocker was moulded in the shape of a sphinx head. It seemed disproportionately large for such a modest door. The men at the bottom of the street had turned their backs on her, already disclaiming any connection with her flight. Two children playing in the yard of the elementary school above the level of the road, ran to the protective fence to watch Enid with unrestrained curiosity. They wound their fingers through the plaited wire and looked down with innocent impartiality for anything to happen in the street below. Enid smiled at them and raised her arm to offer them a leaflet each. The younger boy reached his arm out through the wire but his sister plucked at the shoulder of his jacket to hold him back.

'Dear Mrs More!'

Amy's landlady had opened the door. Mrs Rossett was a tall woman. Her hands were clasped together beneath her stately bosom in an attitude of cultivated composure. She had prepared herself for the more leisurely activities of her afternoon with a light layer of pale pink face powder on her cheeks.

'Do come in!'

She became aware of Enid's mildly flustered state.

'Nothing amiss, I trust?'

'Nothing. Not really.'

Enid raised her leather shopping bag.

'I collected these at Dawes and Evans. Tried to distribute some.'

Mrs Rossett closed the door behind her. All her movements were deliberate and unhurried.

'I'm afraid Miss Parry isn't back yet,' Mrs Rossett said. 'She won't be long I hope. Her tea is ready.'

Behind Mrs Rossett's head Enid could see an oil painting of a ship in full sail and steam. Mrs Rossett was pleased to observe her interest.

'My father's ship,' she said. 'The Afon Alaw. Lost with all hands one week from Callao.'

'How terrible.'

Enid murmured respectfully. Mrs Rossett nodded and smiled sadly. With a delicate movement she reached past Enid and opened the door of the front parlour.

'There he is.'

Enid saw on the wall opposite an enlarged tinted photograph in a gilt frame of a sea-captain in uniform. The room was cold and smelt strongly of furniture polish. Beyond the mahogany sideboard hung another photograph in a heavy frame. The subject's dark hair was parted in the middle and his moustache was waxed.

'And that's my late husband,' Mrs Rossett said calmly. 'Also lost at sea. Time heals all wounds. Or so we say. And perhaps it is as well. And I still love the sea. I bear it no grudge.'

Mrs Rossett closed the door.

'Will you wait in Miss Parry's room? Or join us in the kitchen. My brother Nathan would be delighted to see you.'

The door of the room allotted to Amy was ajar. Enid could see a pair of felt slippers lying neatly inside a polished brass fender. Amy's own books were stacked along the surface of the brown cupboard on the left side of the ornate fireplace. A framed reproduction of a Chardin kitchen interior which Val had bought in Paris was propped against the books. Mrs Rossett smiled fondly at Enid.

'We do our best to make her comfortable,' she said in a low modest voice.

When she opened the kitchen door a black cat with a pink collar jumped from Nathan Harris's rigid lap and made for Enid's legs, eager to rub her fur against them.

'Well look at that!'

Nathan Harris could barely shift his large head with its crown of grey curls. Only his eyes moved and his pallid skin stretched in a skull-like grin that could equally represent pleasure or pain. He sat in a Windsor-back chair immobilised by arthritis. His clerical collar lay crooked around his neck and the black silk front had only been partially tucked in the wide neck of his grey pullover.

'She thought you were Miss Parry,' Nathan Harris said. 'Isn't that amazing?'

He had a penetrating tenor voice. He spoke loudly to compensate for the loss of physical mobility. Mrs Rossett muttered affectionately to the cat. She came up to her brother to tuck in his silk front.

'Mrs More has brought us some leaflets, Nathan,' Mrs Rossett said. 'For the Peace Campaign.'

Nathan Harris raised his arm as if he were about to give a cheer.

'I do apologise,' he said. 'These old cricks. I have to choose between sitting and standing. Some days are worse than others. I don't know why this should be so. Unless a rusty carcass is more responsive to the weather.'

He accepted a leaflet eagerly and read the print aloud in a ringing voice.

'Wonderful!' he said. 'Oh if I had the strength and skill and a splash of youth, I would be out in the world doing everything I could to put this little country back on its feet. Do you know Mrs More?' He raised a crooked finger. 'A conclusion I have come to? "What's good for Wales is good for the world!"'

He began to laugh at himself and his disability. 'Not much I know,' he said. 'The sum of Nathan Harris's wisdom. But I have to stand by it. We are glued together.'

His sister stood in the centre of the kitchen, her hands pressed together, listening to him appreciatively. He raised his arm again in an attempt at a lordly gesture.

'Bring Mrs More some tea, Annie,' he said. 'These young people. They restore one's faith in human nature. Not that I have ever lost mine. When you are a cripple, you know, you have a chance to see how good people can be. So good, they deserve better. And there you have what we have in common, dear Mrs More. The desire for a better world. They used to ask me you know, some of the older generation when I had this big church in the South, "Mr Harris", they would say, "Why should the church get involved in politics?" And then I'd say to them, good people that they were but nervous you see about unions and strikes and things like that, "My dear brethren, the church was born in politics."'

Enid listened to him intently. She sat by the window and looked at the elaborate tea Mrs Rossett had prepared for Amy. The brown bread and butter had been thinly cut. There was a fresh sponge cake and tinned peaches in a cut-glass bowl.

'It's a great comfort to have her in the house,' Nathan said. 'For Annie and me. She keeps us young, you know. I can venture to tell you this, Mrs More, as her best friend. Miss Amy Parry is one of those choice, one of those rare beings able to restore the poetry that belongs by right to living.'

They were smiling at each other in perfect accord when the rap of the front door knocker reverberated though the house. Nathan Harris chuckled delightedly. He raised his voice to address his sister in the back-kitchen.

'We are popular today, Annie,' he said. 'Number seven Eifion Street has become the hub of the universe.'

Mrs Rossett paused in the passage to examine herself in the mirror of the hallstand. She established an amiable smile on her face before opening the door. John Cilydd raised his hat politely when he saw her.

'Good afternoon, Mrs Rossett,' he said. 'I wonder if my wife Enid is with Miss Parry?'

'Do come in, Mr More,' Mrs Rossett said graciously.

Already she could hear her brother laughing merrily in the kitchen.

'I have captured her, John Cilydd!' His tenor voice echoed down the passage. 'You must ransom her with a poem.'

Cilydd shifted to one side so that Mrs Rossett could pass through to the back kitchen.

'An old cripple can say what he likes!'

Nathan Harris had developed a technique of chatting cheerfully to allow visitors to avoid the embarrassment of asking him how he was when it was so patently clear he could be no better.

'It's quite a privilege,' he said. 'Almost worth the discomfort should I dare say it. Why don't we all sit around the table and have tea together? To please an old cripple like me.'

'By all means,' Mrs Rossett said. She gestured calmly to demonstrate that her resources would be in no way over-stretched.

'You are very kind,' Cilydd said. 'But we should hurry home, alas.'

Enid raised her eyebrows in subdued surprise.

'I'm afraid we can't wait for Amy,' he said.

She moved obediently to his side.

'We are expecting my sister and my grandmother. And the district nurse calls at five.'

'All is well, I trust?'

Mrs Rossett muttered discreetly at Enid as they moved to the door.

'Perfectly well,' Enid said.

Nathan Harris raised his hand. He had something to say before they left.

'I'm stuck in my corner,' he said. 'And I can't do much. But I will say this. Tasker Thomas deserves all the support he can get. We both feel that don't we, Annie?'

Mrs Rossett nodded graciously and smiled. 'Yes, indeed we do,' she said. Her smooth murmur was intended to balance her brother's strident tenor.

'Even though he belongs to the tribe of Methodistia.' As a former Congregational minister Harris was determined to enjoy his little denominational joke. But his message was not finished.

'And you fortunate young people will allow an old man to tell you why,' he said. 'Because he is a man bent on the most difficult ministry of all: of practising what he preaches. Now that may sound a cliché of the most obvious kind. Most of the things I say seem to. But I see it as a comment charged with historical insight. And I'll tell you why as briefly as I can. I don't want to keep you. You see one of the side-effects of that terrible war was to turn poor old nonconformity out of its own home-made earthly paradise. Now you can argue that our worthy forefathers had no business to attempt making one in the first place. That's not the point. The point is, whether we like it or not, whether we admit it or not, we are turned out of the garden. We are in a new and frightening desert. A wilderness. And in the wilderness only the men who practise what they preach have any hope of leading the remnant of the faithful to the distant water-hole. And even then, so many will fall by the wayside.'

'Nathan my dear,' his sister said. 'Mr and Mrs More will have to call again to hear the rest of your sermon.'

His stiff frame was racked by a spasm of laughter. He still managed to speak.

'I hope there will be jokes in heaven,' he said. 'Or laughter at any rate. But not quite so painful.'

Mrs Rossett remained in the doorway as Cilydd helped Enid into the car. She looked pleased for them that they enjoyed such a convenient mode of transport. She raised her hand in a wave like a benediction before closing the door.

8

Enid oscillated gently in the swivel chair as she read with growing interest the second volume of William Lloyd's history of Calvinistic Methodism in Rhosyr and Dinodig. The book lay on the writing surface of the very roll-top desk on which it had been laboriously composed by John Cilydd's grandfather. The late William Lloyd had had the door removed and the doorway enlarged so that he could sit in the side parlour he called his office and attend to the drapery and haberdashery counter of Glanrafon General Stores even between the sentences. It was by now part of family tradition that the strain had turned William Lloyd's black hair prematurely white, ruined his eyesight and even shortened his life. The room still served as an occasional office but it was also something of a shrine. Nothing of any consequence had been changed since his death. His diaries and manuscripts were stored in two seaman's chests and the reference books he used, all printed in the previous two centuries, were locked in the glass-faced bookshelves. A small conservatory was attached to the side parlour. It was filled with palms and hanging plants that drooped for lack of water. The green paint was peeling and the pale sunlight showed the discoloured wood underneath. Beyond was a paved courtyard where grass sprouted between the stone slabs. A green door at the end led directly to the garden of the original eighteenth century farmhouse.

From where she was sitting, Enid could see her sister-in-law Nanw bent over an accounts ledger in the cramped Post Office section beyond the long drapery counter. Light from a small window revealed her lips moving as she recited figures to herself and picked at a red rubber thimble on her index finger to preserve her concentration. In the same light Enid could detect the resemblance between brother and sister; the flare of the nostrils, the vulnerable intensity, the pallor. When the shop bell tinkled Nanw did not raise her head. Enid could hear steel-rimmed clogs striking unsteadily at the bare floorboards of the shop. Robert Thomas the mole-catcher in his brown corduroy trousers and blue linen jacket confronted Nanw with only the grill of the Post Office section between them. He swayed slightly as he observed her concentrated state with respectful admiration. Enid for her part could see the sequence of emotions drift over the mole-catcher's weather-beaten face. He fumbled at an oval box of tobacco in his waistcoat pocket as he considered replenishing the quid of tobacco in his mouth. He gazed about the floor for somewhere to spit and thought the better of it. He was concerned also to learn if there were any other customers or members of the family present in the cavernous interior of the country store. The grocery display in the window was already covered with sheets of newspaper.

Robert Thomas paid particular attention to the door beyond the grocery counter with the word *dispensary* emblazoned in a semi-circle on the opaque glass panel. It was in that room that Mrs Lloyd, Cilydd's grandmother, practised her arcane skills in the disposal of wild warts. Robert Thomas had an equal awe of the practitioner and the disease. He took a step backwards to obtain a better view of the hardware section that was practically hidden by an imposing cupboard which occupied the centre of the floor space. This cupboard was reserved for animal medicines and dangerous chemicals. The glass doors were all locked and faded labels hung from each key. Robert Thomas's eyes narrowed as he peered into the shadowier regions of the hardware department. Someone could have been lurking where buckets, ropes, brushes, tools and cleaning utensils hung from the pitch-pine rafters like bats in a cave. When he had satisfied himself that he was the sole customer in the shop, he turned his attention to Nanw. He drew the edge of his tobacco box along the grill. Nanw's head shot up, startled by the sound. Robert Thomas grinned at her. The stain of tobacco juice on his teeth diminished the amiability of the grimace.

'Nanw fach,' he said in a sly ingratiating voice that could have been intended to hide the extent of his inebriation. 'Have you seen my new clogs?'

He stamped first one foot and then the other holding on to the edge of the counter to steady himself.

'Thought you might like to have a little dance with me,' he said. 'Nobody will see us. A little dance for two. A little jig.'

His calloused hand felt along the counter for the point at which he could lever it up on its hinge.

'Robert Thomas!' Nanw's voice was shrill with anxiety and accusation. 'You have been drinking.'

'Twt lol, woman. I know better than any man in this parish what every healthy woman needs, spinsters and all.'

'Robert Thomas!'

'I'm a man of course, as other men are. But better endowed than most. Due to my open-air life. And very gentle and understanding in spite of a rough appearance.'

Nanw pressed her weight on the counter to prevent him from lifting it.

'Don't you dare, Robert Thomas! I'll call my grand-mother. She's in the dispensary.'

Robert Thomas grinned gleefully.

'Ah no, she's not,' he said. 'No one about, my chick. No one here. So, nothing to be afraid of . . .'

'Good afternoon Robert Thomas.'

Enid greeted him from the far end of the drapery counter. The mole-catcher's mouth hung open. He stared at her as if she were a ghostly figure that had appeared from nowhere. He blinked as she came closer. A drivel of tobacco juice oozed out of the corner of his mouth and began to course down the crease in his chin. Nanw assumed control of the situation.

'Now then, Robert Thomas,' she said. 'Out of this shop! And don't you come back in until you are stone cold sober. Do you hear me?'

He shook his head to reassure her. His interest transferred to Enid's condition. He pointed at the bulge in Enid's belly.

'That's the way you want to be, Nanw fach,' he said. 'It has a wonderful sweetening effect on a woman's nature. And I speak as a man who lives close to nature in all its wondrous variety.'

'Get out of here!'

Nanw beat her fist on the counter. She could not bear the

increasingly self-satisfied look appearing on Robert Thomas's face as he gave ear to the flow of his own eloquence. Out of token respect for Nanw's insistence he took a step backwards and began to survey the shop.

'I never come in here,' he said, 'without calling to mind the immortal words of William Lloyd in recommendation of his business. Diawch, ladies, there was a man of talent gone too early to his grave. Of course it is easier to remember if you chant it you see.

The shop at Glarafon, a notable haven,
Is more than a warehouse we hope you'll agree
The prices are low but the quality fancy
Nothing is missing and the welcome is free!'

'Robert Thomas,' Nanw said. 'I've told you once and I won't tell you again. Will you get out of here!'

The mole-catcher had regained some of his confidence.

'Matches and sago, snuff and tobacco
Sapolio tablets and sauces gal-ore...'

He chanted on as he turned himself around and headed for the door. Half the panes of glass were obscured by venerable advertisements for Mazawattee tea, Cherry Blossom boot-polish and Colman's mustard. Above them the head of Tasker Thomas was gazing in, a seraphic smile on his face. Robert Thomas stepped back as though he had seen yet another apparition. He was beset by benevolent spirits sent to keep his unsteady feet on the narrow path of respectability. He pulled a face as if the tobacco juice in his mouth had turned into bitter medicine. Tasker could not resist making an entrance. He waited for the bell to stop tinkling before he spoke. His old raincoat reached within six inches of the bicycle clips that firmly gripped his ankles. In spite of his open necked-shirt and tousled sparse red hair he was still an imposing figure.

'The old Glanrafon family,' Tasker said. 'The salt of the earth!'

The mole-catcher smiled proudly. He pressed a hand against his chest including himself in the benediction. Shy as she was, Nanw could not bear it. With the smallest encouragement the mole-catcher would continue with her grandfather's metrical advertisement of his shop, and the praise poem had at least sixteen verses.

'He's no relation of ours,' Nanw said. 'That's Robert Thomas the mole-catcher. And he's come in here drunk, the shameless creature.'

Tasker took a moment to reappraise the situation. Robert Thomas began to blink under the large visitor's pitying gaze. He took off his cap as a mark of respect and tip-toed clumsily through the doorway. Outside a white hen with six chicks in train was strutting across the forecourt in search of grain and seeds spilt between the cobble-stones. The procession caused Robert Thomas to stumble. He regained his balance, aimed a kick at the white hen who was forced to flutter out of his way squawking. Remarkably, all the chicks were undisturbed and unhurt.

'I was passing the time of day with your Uncle Tryfan in his little cobbler's workshop across the way there,' Tasker said. 'Now there's a man for you.'

Enid leaned against the counter and nodded her whole-hearted agreement. Nanw stood erect, suppressing her impatience and plainly waiting for Tasker Thomas to state his business.

'Now there's a subject for a poem for you.'

Tasker addressed himself with some enthusiasm to Enid.

'A human gem. But how can you express it in words? The function of the poet is to find expression for the inexpressible. To sit there and watch him at work. Carving the leather. With a row of little nails in his mouth and those spectacles on the end of his nose. There are smart and would-be-sophisticated persons in this ever-so-modern day and age who would smile at him and call him a simple creature. But you know I could sit there for hours on end in his company and watch that golden aura of innocence shine like a halo around his head.'

A look of impatience on Nanw's face made Tasker rein in his eloquence.

'But that would be self-indulgence,' Tasker said. 'He doesn't need me nearly as much as I need him. And I suppose it is our business in life to be where we are most needed. My dear ladies, I am looking for that grand matriarchal figure of your grandmother, bless her. I must have a word with her.'

'She has gone to Ponciau with the trap,' Nanw said. 'She should have been back long before this.'

She was ready to return to her accounts ledger. Tasker showed he appreciated this. His russet eyebrows were raised and his sharp blue eyes were intent on being a source of comfort.

'You have so much work to do,' he said. 'So many duties to attend to and strangers march in here like the proverbial fool who rushes in where angels fear to tread. But let me explain what I meant by "salt of the earth". It's not the shop, you see, delightful as it is. It's what lies behind it. The economic base as our Marxian friends would say. There you have the earth and there you have the salt that gives the old Glanrafon family its savour. Two farms, Ponciau and Glanrafon. All maintained by family units and their dependents and all equal in the eyes of the Lord. Now there is the true soil of civilisation. Isn't that so, Mrs Enid More?'

'Well, I think so,' Enid said.

'And the seed-bed of poets. Or to change the figure, "the poet's cradle". Poetry needs roots in a community if it is to flower over a consistent period of time and not fizzle out like a firework or a nine days' wonder.'

'Excuse me,' Nanw said. 'I must finish these accounts before we close.'

Enid looked up at Tasker Thomas, pleased to see him. She spoke out loudly enough for Nanw to hear. What she had to say would be of equal interest to them both, a piece of research which established a link between the three of them and precedent for a fruitful relationship.

'I was just reading the second volume of William Lloyd's History,' Enid said. 'Such a curious coincidence. An account of your grandfather's visit to the district in 1852. There were so many people he had to preach in the open air. He preached from an open window. And his text was; "It is not for you to know the times of the seasons which the Father hath put in his own power."'

Tasker lifted both hands to share her wonder and delight.

70

Nanw's head was raised and held to one side as she contemplated a variety of comment.

'A young man,' Tasker said. 'And yet he had already accomplished so much.'

Family pride gave way to sense of personal inadequacy. His hands came down like broken wings to flap disconsolately against the folds of his loose raincoat. Nanw seemed to approve of his display of despondency.

'In times like these,' Tasker said, 'what can one do?'

His eyes shut tight as he searched his mind for an appropriate quotation. A sound outside caused Nanw to peer through the small window.

'Here she is,' she said.

Outside the hooves of the pony were striking the cobbles as Mrs Lloyd pulled out the reins to bring the trap to rest in the far corner of the forecourt. Tasker became intent on expressing his admiration for the vigorous old lady.

'Never says a word in the Presbytery,' he said. 'The only woman present they say and still the best man in the place.'

Tasker stepped towards the centre of the floor, rubbing his hands together like a man relishing the prospect of a sharp encounter. Mrs Lloyd came bustling in, drawing off her gloves.

'Mr Thomas,' she said. 'What's this I hear about you advising Huws the School to put away his cane?'

Tasker chuckled happily.

'It's a privilege to come here to Glanrafon Academy and learn a lesson or two, dear Mrs Lloyd. I can tell you that much.'

'The man was quite upset,' Mrs Lloyd said. 'I can tell you that much. A conscientious fellow, who always does his best. It doesn't seem wise to discourage him.'

'Nothing personal,' Tasker said. 'I told him that. In the friendliest possible spirit. A matter of principle.'

'Oh is that so? And what principle may I ask?'

'I don't need to tell you, dear Mrs Lloyd. Love, of course. "For God so loved the world". Well, now the time has come for the world to love God and the way to do that is clear, from the cradle to the grave. What do repression and harsh temper produce in reality? Cannon fodder. It's the recognised method of making soldiers, and perpetuating the thrust of aggression and the cult of militarism. But does the world we live in need that any more?'

Mrs Lloyd's feet were set wide apart. She kept a shrewd eye on her opponent, not prepared to give an inch.

'What about sin, Mr Thomas?' she said.

'Sin? Sin?' Tasker raised his arms and his raincoat flapped about like a surplice. 'Sin is the absence of love,' he said.

'Well I would say it was more than that,' Mrs Lloyd said. 'And so would your esteemed grandfather.'

Abruptly Mrs Lloyd concluded the floor of a shop near closing time was not an appropriate place or time for disputation. She turned her attention to Enid.

'Have you taken your rest?' she said.

Enid smiled and nodded dutifully.

'Is it to do with this Peace business?' Mrs Lloyd said. 'In that case you and I had better go through to the front parlour.'

Tasker was eager to explain himself so that Enid and Nanw could also hear.

'I'm a new boy,' he said. 'I realise that. My little church, God bless it, is one of the smallest in the Presbytery. But the message is urgent. "Alas to be born in such a sullen age, and God withdrawn beyond our reach".'

He was pleased to have recalled the quotation that had first eluded him and still find it apposite. He glanced keenly first at Enid and then at Nanw to make certain they had responded to the force of the words. Mrs Lloyd waved a hand impatiently.

'Come through, come through,' she said.

Enid could hear Tasker's voice in extenuated apology as he followed Mrs Lloyd down the dark passage that led from the shop to the family kitchen. She clutched her hands together and gazed hopefully at Nanw who was closing one ledger and opening another.

'Oh I hope Nain will support Tasker's motion,' she said. 'This campaign is really important. John Cilydd says it's the most important thing to happen in Pendraw since the Great War.'

She sounded eager for Nanw's approval. It was slow in forthcoming.

'Don't you think so, Nanw?'

Nanw's head jerked sideways as she ran her finger down the page of the ledger.

'It isn't of the slightest importance, what I think,' she said.

'Of course it is,' Enid said. 'Everybody knows how intelligent you are.'

'Adding up,' Nanw said. 'That's all I'm good for.'

'John Cilydd is always saying how bright you were at school. And how much he looked up to you.'

For a moment it appeared as if Nanw would start blushing. She took a firmer grip on her pencil.

'I can tell you one thing,' she said. She spoke in a coldly realistic tone. 'These antics won't do his practice any good. He's a lawyer. Starting a new practice. It's always a mistake to give people a chance to talk.'

'Antics?'

'Uncle Gwilym saw you and Amy Parry on a cart outside the Town Hall.'

'Oh, that.' Enid started laughing. 'That was the Home Rule Campaign. That was something else.'

'Whatever it was, it upset him.'

Nanw put down her pencil and concentrated on talking to Enid. They were at some distance from each other behind their respective counters.

'I'm not saying Uncle Gwilym isn't old fashioned. But so are the vast majority of people in this part of the world. Even I wouldn't dream of drifting about the streets of Pendraw on a Saturday afternoon.'

The note of condemnation in Nanw's voice grew stronger.

'And certainly not in your condition.'

'But Nanw, you are an intelligent woman. You know how desperately important these issues are.'

Nanw lifted the section of counter next to her position. It was time to lock up the shop. Enid followed her, ready to help. Her offers were ignored.

'What kind of a world am I bringing a child into?' Enid said. 'I have more right than anybody to share in the decision. I have the future of a child to think about. And John Cilydd absolutely agrees with me. He supports everything we are doing.'

'Where is it all going to get him?' Nanw said. 'He's a solicitor with a business to protect, not a politician.'

'He's a poet.' Enid sounded both proud and desperate.

'Oh yes,' Nanw said swiftly. 'And how much poetry does he write these days, I wonder? You need peace and quiet to write poetry.'

Enid began to blush. For the first time she was at a loss for a reply.

'The truth isn't always pleasant,' Nanw said. 'When you have to face it. Reality. Whatever that means. I don't know why I should always be the one to have to say it.'

9

Enid sat in a rocking-chair in the bay-window of the largest room on the second floor of their terrace house. Her knitting lay in her lap. She studied it ruefully.

'She thinks I'm hopeless,' she said. 'She's right too.'

John Cilydd was kneeling over books put down in uneven heaps against the wall. The room had been recently distempered in pale grey and smelt pleasantly antiseptic. The only furnishings were a white rug, two rocking-chairs, a green baize card table and a canvas chair. On the card table lay a white leather folder decorated with an intricate art nouveau design stamped in gold leaf. In the pouches Cilydd kept drafts of the poems on which he was working.

'She's jealous,' he said.

As he spoke of his sister he blew the dust off the covers of a book and opened it for cursory inspection.

'Of me?' Enid's mouth was open in a small circle of

surprise. It was plain that such an idea had not occurred to her before.

'Of everybody,' Cilydd said. 'But you chiefly now, I suppose. Poor old Nanw.'

Enid's smooth forehead was creased with the effort of incorporating a new concept into her understanding of their relationship.

'I thought she saw me as too young and inexperienced to get married,' Enid said. 'And in a way I agree with that. I'm no good at knitting and cooking and all that sort of thing. And she's so efficient. But I'm more than ready to learn. And they're not the most important things, really, are they? In a marriage.'

Cilydd was smiling at her.

'No they're not,' he said. 'Where shall we put the first bookshelf, Mrs More? There or there?' He pointed at two interior walls at right angles to each other.

'You've made me sorry for her,' Enid said. 'I can't bear to think of her being so unhappy. What should I do?'

'Forget about it,' Cilydd said.

'Darling!' She was shocked by his lack of feeling.

He stood over the card table fingering the leather folder, unable to decide whether or not to extract a particular sheet of paper.

'She's your only sister! She dotes on you.'

'She's like me,' Cilydd said. 'She enjoys being miserable. We wallow in it like a pair of water buffalo in the mud.'

He grinned at her cheerfully.

'Being possessive is her element,' he said. 'We have to accept that. The best we can hope for is that in time she will become possessive of you too. And in time you will develop a sixth sense, Mrs More. Or is it a seventh or eighth? An awareness of Nanw's emotional climate. The weather prevailing in her heart and mind. And then you'll know what to wear for the occasion. Whether to bring your umbrella or a bathing costume. On the other hand, you could be like me and ignore her moods completely.'

He sat in the canvas chair and with finger and thumb extracted a sheet from the folder. Enid stared at him as though she were contemplating a mystery.

'Do you think I'm hopelessly idealistic?' she said.

She was anxious not to disturb him but could not forebear to ask the question.

'No.' Cilydd was brief and business-like. 'And even if you were,' he said, 'it's what I like about you. The world is a murky place. Just a few days in a solicitor's office is enough to prove that. Hence the expression "Light of my life"!'

He smiled at her and she radiated happiness. She picked up her knitting and resolved to make a sustained effort to improve it.

'I'll be quiet,' she said. 'I won't utter a word.'

She raised the knitting to the light to decide how far she would need to unravel it. The room was to be reserved for John Cilydd's creative writing. It was to this eyrie with its uninterrupted view of the harbour, the dunes, the bay and the mountains on the eastern horizon he would repair, away from the mundane concerns of his practice and out of the reach of his demanding relatives to compose the new poetry that they both believed would extend the frontiers of their native literature.

Presently she could see that he was taken with the molten light on the evening tide as it crept into the inner harbour. Silently with a knitting needle she pointed at the pair of binoculars on the mantelpiece in case he should want to know where to put his hand on them. In the early morning when he thought she was still asleep she had seen him steal to the window to observe the waders on their feeding grounds undisturbed by the sleeping town. It gave him pleasure to identify them by colour and by flight. It was also possible that the permutations of light fascinated him even more than the behaviour of birds. For her part, she seemed content to observe him and wonder at the sensibility that would eventually bring forth a poem.

'Shonyn.' She whispered his pet name. 'Am I interrupting?'

He shook his head.

'Did you do anything about the idea of the warm viscous element in the womb giving birth to the human yearning for a lost paradise?'

Cilydd shook his head.

'I thought it was a lovely idea,' she said. 'Not surprising I suppose. Considering my condition.'

He turned to study her, resting his chin in the palm of his hand.

'A lifetime in the womb,' he said. 'In one way it's too big an idea, and in another just a whimsical notion. I'm not keen on whimsey.'

'I know this sounds obvious,' she said. 'Physical embrace creates every new human being. The foetus once it emerges from its perfect paradisical environment can only be sustained by unremitting love. And it is that love in one form or another that preserves the life-cycle of the human being. So that, in the very end, when our physical powers are worn thin, and beyond that when our bodies are burnt away by time, only this invisible power of love remains. And this is the trace element in the universe of the will of God. And that means the will of God is Love.'

'My goodness.' Cilydd sat back in exaggerated surprise. They both started laughing.

'To think I married a philosopher without knowing it,' he said. 'I can't manage the simplest things these days. Anything in the way of a long distance run appals me. It's a sprint or nothing.'

Enid picked up her knitting and set it down again.

'I have strange sensations,' she said. 'As if I had two brains. One asleep most of the time and the other one like a horse in blinkers going round and round like butter in a churn.'

'Of course you've got two brains.'

He stood up and began to pace about the room.

'I'm bursting with the desire to write all sorts of celebratory things about our marriage and your condition. But I'm inhibited somehow. It's all too close to me. I can't distance it or get anything into perspective. You can't go prancing around pouring out lyrics about your own breath now, can you? Can you?'

He stood silent with his hands in his pockets before stepping closer to take her more deeply into his confidence.

'I tell you what's on my mind,' he said. 'I don't know whether I can do it. But I'd like to have a try. Can you imagine a verse play about a community of birds?'

He stared at her hopefully.

'Does that sound daft to you?'

Enid shook her head quickly, anxious not to discourage him.

'Pendraw of course,' Cilydd said. 'Thinly disguised. Isn't there something in English called the *Parliament of Fowls*?'

'Morgan Llywd,' Enid said excitedly. '*The Book of the Three Birds*.'

Cilydd did not find the reference relevant.

'I'm thinking of a satire,' he said. 'Something that cuts really deep. Of course it's damn difficult to compete with reality. No one would believe in a figure like Alderman Llew if you stuck him on a stage in all his revolting reptilian reality. That's what Eddie wants to do. "Stick them up there", he said, "in all their gruesome reality. Including my old man."'

He expected Enid to laugh. Instead she became suddenly attentive to her knitting.

'He's a ruthless little blighter,' Cilydd said. There was a note of grudging admiration in his voice. He could have been speaking of a person who was treading down pleasant paths he himself would have liked to travel. Oxford was a gateway to a wider world through which he would never pass.

'You do it your way, Shonyn,' Enid said. She spoke in a quiet determined voice. 'Trust your own judgement. It's far better than his. He's only an imitator. He sees something smart and quickly imitates it. And exploits it. He's an exploiter really.'

'Hmm.' Cilydd sat down to consider the indictment.

'Perhaps he is,' he said. 'But does this society offer him much choice? What does an artist do under these conditions?'

'I don't see much evidence to support the idea that Eddie Meredith was ever an artist in the first place.'

'Look at my family,' Cilydd said. 'Our family. Our families. I mean if we didn't take whatever evasive action we do take, they would quite literally smother us!'

Enid smiled her relief as they embarked on an analysis where they could operate in comfortable agreement.

'You try and break loose,' Cilydd said. 'Regularly. In self-defence. From adolescence onwards. Oddly enough I'm sure that was the main reason why I joined up under age. But it's like a recurring decimal of one's existence.'

'Or a tide,' Enid said. 'Escape and return. Ebb and flow.'

'But there is no real escape,' Cilydd said. 'Not for us. Because of the way we're built. We're built loyal.'

'Well, that's a virtue,' Enid said. 'A negative virtue anyway.'

'Just look at my Uncle Gwilym. If you can bear to. Self-important, over-sensitive, interfering, a bundle of prejudice, a rag-bag of illusions, the fag-end of an exhausted culture pattern and worst of all... worst of all' – Cilydd wagged an admonitory index finger – 'a terrible portent of what I shall end up being myself!'

'Oh no, Shonyn, no!'

This was something Enid could never agree to.

'And what affection they have for us, these claims they never cease to impose on us, is not really for you and me as we really are. It is for some effigies they have invented in our likeness. And the end result is that you are tied up and hopelessly entangled in their illusions so that you can never escape even if you emigrated.'

'Shonyn.' Enid was disturbed by his frankness and even more by his increasing distress. 'It's not that bad.'

'Oh it is, you know. It is. If we face facts. "Reality", as Nanw likes to call it. It cramps, cribs, cabins, confines, inhibits, asphyxiates.'

Enid raised her arms, prepared to bring him comfort. He sank to his knees in front of her and close together they watched the outline of the mountains grow sharper against the eastern sky. The chair rocked gently to and fro.

'We are free here,' Enid whispered as she drew her hand tenderly across his head. 'Our own little territory.'

'Yes and even that they resent,' Cilydd said.

He sat up and wrapped his arms around his knees.

'I never saw such specialists in resentment,' he said. 'Every one of them has a talent for resenting in his or her own way.'

'Except Uncle Tryfan.'

'All right, except Uncle Tryfan. But you take Uncle

Simon. The master of Ponciau. Now if you please he resents us living in a terrace house in Embankment Road! "What do you want to live in a boarding house for?" he said to me. Only last week. "And keep it empty? You'd be better off to rent the place and come and live with us in Ponciau. Plenty of room in Ponciau."'

Enid smiled at Cilydd's crude imitation of his uncle's jerky manner of speaking.

'Well at least he wanted to help,' Enid said.

'Did he indeed! He wanted me under his eye and under his thumb. That's what he wanted. You've no idea how much he was opposed to me doing law. He wanted me as his pseudo-son and heir and unpaid farm servant, and but for my grandmother I dare say that's what would have happened.'

Enid was ready to smile again but she restrained herself when she felt a shudder pass through his body.

'Sometimes I think I dislike Simon more than Gwilym,' Cilydd said. 'And that's saying something. He's such a block. Such a swede. Such a turnip.'

He stopped speaking and crawled forward on his knees to lean on the low window sill and look down at the street. A blue car was drawing up outside their front door.

'Oh no,' he said.

He shrank back although there was no possibility of the driver seeing him.

'Your aunt,' he said. 'Sali Prydderch. HMI no less.'

From the centre of the room he looked at Enid, expecting her to show more signs of surprise and consternation.

'Are you expecting her?'

He had become nervously polite. He took off his spectacles, blinking rapidly as he polished them with a silk handkerchief from his breast pocket.

'Amy said she might call one day this week.'

'That was very thoughtful,' he said.

She raised an arm against the sarcasm. She also wanted help to get out of the rocking-chair. He was obliged to help her.

'Shonyn,' Enid said. 'Peace has to break out sooner or later.'

They moved to the bare landing, waiting for a knock on the door.

'She is contrite,' Enid said. 'Amy was saying she is in a state to walk down the cob in bare feet to beg our pardon.'

'Does she indeed?' Cilydd said. 'The trouble with our Miss Parry is that she has an inborn tendency to manage everything. And everybody.'

He turned to face his wife. 'I'm going out,' he said.

Enid grasped the banister as he took his first steps down the stairs, prepared to plead with him.

'I don't want to see her any more than she wants to see me,' he said.

Enid followed him down the stairs watching carefully where she placed her feet.

'But sometimes we shall have to meet,' Enid said. 'She's longing to see us.'

'To see you,' he said. 'Not me.'

'It can't go on,' Enid said. 'In any case it's gone on long enough. In any case it's against all our principles of reconciliation.'

Before he made for the basement stairs he turned to squeeze her hand and smile.

'Of course it is,' he said. 'But one likes a little warning. In any case it's better for her to make it up with you first. Let's take it in stages.'

The knock on the front door was tentative but it was enough to echo like a summons through the empty hall. It sent Cilydd hurrying out through the back without his hat. When Enid opened the front door, her aunt was on the pavement, facing the harbour, as if she had been in two minds to return to her car. She turned to look at Enid. Her lips had been trembling with the effort of holding back her tears. Her mouth opened with involuntary amazement when she saw Enid's pregnant condition.

'My little girl!'

She rushed forward to embrace her. The steps from the pavement made it an awkward encounter. But their mutual warmth towards each other overcame all the physical obstacles. With both hands Enid drew her aunt into the house. Sali Prydderch hung back. It was the only way she could express her sense of unworthiness for such an elevation. All the explanations and speeches she had prepared had fled from her mind: she was too overwhelmed with emotion to say anything except "my little girl, my Enid" over and over again.

They found it easier to talk about the state of the house. It had been decorated but there was still very little furniture. They stood close to each other in the front parlour where the most conspicuous feature to admire was the wallpaper. A muted pattern in two shades of grey excited Sali Prydderch's effusive admiration.

'We decided to furnish bit by bit,' Enid said. 'With things we really liked. As we could afford them.'

'My dear, my darling, how absolutely right.'

Sali Prydderch shifted her hands about outlining the shapes of choice non-existent pieces of furniture. She paused in the middle of her mime to press two fingers against her lips and make a confession.

'I tell you what I've done,' she said. 'I couldn't resist it. At a sale the week before last I bought an escritoire for John Cilydd. Do you think he'll accept it? A belated wedding present. A peace offering. If he doesn't like it I've also got an option on a very nice kneehole desk. One of the kidney shaped ones. But what am I talking about? You can have them both, for goodness sake. There's plenty of room for them in this place, goodness knows.'

She followed Enid carefully down the short flight of stairs to the basement. This part of the house was dark and damp and was still to be decorated.

'We can't make our minds up about the basement,' Enid said. 'Whether to have it done out or abandon it and make a new kitchen upstairs.'

Sali Prydderch wrinkled her nose and refrained from comment.

'You must make it easy for yourself, my darling,' she said. 'That's all I'd say. Housework can be a burden in a house this shape. All these stairs. Anyway housework can be a burden under any conditions.'

82

They both stood staring at the kettle on the kitchen range, waiting for it to boil.

'He's gone for a walk,' Enid said.

She blushed as she spoke.

'He thought it would be better for us to be alone to begin with.'

Sali Prydderch demonstrated her complete approval and admiration.

'Oh what tact,' she said. 'What sensitivity. But what else would one expect from a poet?'

They sat down at the breakfast table by the basement window. Shafts of sunlight burst through the clouds and penetrated the cobwebs hanging from the roof of the glass conservatory built against the rear wall of the house.

'I asked Amy to come with me,' Sali Prydderch said. 'She has such a wise head on her young shoulders. "No," she said, "it will be much better if you go alone." She's so devoted to you, Enid. You couldn't wish for a better friend.'

Enid gave a deep sigh.

'I'm worried about Amy,' she said.

Sali Prydderch looked surprised. In her eyes Amy appeared a self-reliant and competent young woman about whom it would never be necessary to worry.

'She hasn't been the same since she went to visit Val,' Enid said. 'Something happened, I'm sure of it. I can't get her to talk about it. It seems he has to face a terrible operation. She's so quiet. Sometimes I think she's breaking her heart.'

Sali Prydderch leaned across the table to cover Enid's hand with her own.

10

Alone in the third class compartment, Amy sat gnawing the top of her black fountain pen. She was trying, without much success, to concentrate on writing a letter. Through the window she saw a green island linked to the coast at low tide by an expanse of wet sand. Three men were bent low in the effort of dragging a boat up the beach. On the highest point the windows of a low white-washed building glittered in the morning sunlight. Only when it had all passed out of sight did she return her attention to the pad on her knee. Impatiently she tore out the sheet on which she had written a mere three lines. She crushed it in her fist, dropping it carelessly on the compartment floor as she bent over the pad again to make a more determined effort.

With a hiss of steam the train drew up at a Halt. Amy kept her head down refusing to read the name or even glance up and down the bare platform. She crouched above the pad as the nib of her pen drove purposefully across the page. A sudden cry of pain caused her to raise her head. It was as distinct as the squeal of a young pig being kicked into a pen. Almost immediately the cry was smothered in an outburst of boisterous singing. This sounded innocent enough. A school football team on its way to its last Saturday morning fixture of the season: youthful voices enjoying a release of energy, with some competing for the deepest notes and an edge of shrill hysteria to the bawling of voices still unbroken.

In its own inconsequential fashion the train resumed its coastal journey. Amy stared helplessly at her own writing which had come to a stop at exactly the same point where it had stopped before. Again she tore out the sheet, screwed it up in her hand and let it drop on the floor as she painstakingly rewrote the address and the date. The train rumbled across the long iron bridge at the neck of the estuary. The metallic thunder blotted out any other sound. Amy continued to write, her lips moving as she did so, as though some form of utterance would drive her pen beyond any obstacle. This time it was the flickering dazzle of the sunlight flashing through the girders that defeated her. Her head sank back into the dingy moquette. She pushed the pad aside and let the fountain-pen fall alongside it on the seat. She closed her eyes and allowed her whole body to become passive and inert until the train seemed to have shaken the frown from her forehead. Her light-blue beret was worn at a fashionably rakish angle, but it did not fall off. Once over the bridge the train began to pick up speed, the wheels groping their way back to the familiar four-four time. Amy opened her eyes and stared disconsolately at the writing pad. There was little point in picking up the pen if she could not find the words: nothing to do and nothing to say except listen to the numbing rhythm of the wheels.

The sliding door of a nearby compartment shot open. There was again the cry of pain, this time followed by hysterical adolescent laughter. She saw grinning schoolboys in flight down the corridor. She heard growls and shouts and a cry for mercy before the compartment door was slammed shut. Amy jumped to her feet. Her own compartment door was stiff to open. The train was gathering unusual speed as it took advantage of a track of geometric straightness down several miles of coastal plain. She swayed her way down the corridor, her face flushed with anger and frustration. She rapped her knuckles on the glass panel of the door of a compartment where five bulky senior boys sat side by side with arms folded and the space around their feet taken up with their football gear. The first-eleven blazers they wore did not belong to her school. She was not on duty. Somewhere near there would be a master-in-charge, accompanying the team. He should know what was going on. Amy was about to move off in search of him when she caught a glimpse of a figure under the seat almost completely hidden by the legs of the large footballers and their gear. Furiously she tugged at the compartment door. She saw the largest boy, whose dark eyes bulged aggressively in his small head, aim a surreptitious kick with his heel at the victim under the seat. As the door opened she heard him whisper hoarsely as if he didn't care much whether or not she heard him.

'Lie still, you turd! Don't you dare move.'

Amy now stood in the open doorway, a schoolmistress obliged to speak.

'What's going on here? Where's the master-in-charge?'

The large boy was sweating from his aggressive exertions. His eyes rolled and his gums glistened as he tried to smile innocently at Amy. With his arms folded, his lozenge form dominated the stuffy compartment. His first approach was a sly invitation to the schoolmistress to join in the joke. His bass voice was resonant with assumed innocence.

'Please miss, he missed the train. Slept late I expect, miss.'

The supportive laughter was half-hearted because the boys could detect no flicker of amusement in Amy's face. She pointed at the boy nearest her as though a teacher's instinct had led her unerringly to the weakest link in the chain.

'Get up! On your feet. Before I call the guard.'

Two in fact rose so that she caught her first clear view of the boy under the seat. He was older than she had expected. A lanky creature with both hands protecting his steel rimmed spectacles as he peered out. He blinked uncontrollably when Amy spoke to him.

'Come out of there, boy! At once.'

He wanted to obey but he had been deprived of his trousers. Once out of the space under the seat, he crouched on his bare knees like a penitent, his head lowered, overwhelmed, it appeared, with the shame and the humiliation.

'Give him his trousers! And be quick about it.'

Amy refused to smile. The tormented youth blinked and stuttered as he struggled to put on his grey flannels. His legs were too long and he was still unaccustomed to their length. Standing on one of them it gave way, too fragile to hold up even his negligible weight. He tumbled like a piece of luggage from the rack into the lap of his chief tormentor. He stuttered his apologies.

'S-s-s-s- Sid . .'

In a reflex of indignant revulsion Sid pushed the thin body of his victim away. He sprawled across the opposite seat, his bare pinched buttocks in the air. A dull red weal showed where his back had been pressed against the heating pipes of the compartment.

'I suppose you realise you have been torturing this boy?'

Amy concentrated her attack on the bulky figure of Sid. He pressed his lips together and sulkily refused to look up at her. Sitting down he was at an absurd disadvantage. Had he been standing he would have towered over her.

'That is a criminal act,' Amy said. 'It's not just horseplay. I suppose you know that, don't you?'

Amy controlled her indignation in order to be more relentless. Sid had to say something to maintain his position in the eyes of his companions, but he seemed to know it would have been better to remain silent.

'A little bit of fun, Miss. That's all.'

'Oh. Is that what you call it?'

Amy grasped the victim by his arm to twist him around so that his trousers once more fell around his ankles. With clinical precision she lifted his shirt so that they could see the weal.

'Just a few seconds more and that would have been a third degree burn. A hospital case.'

At last he was allowed to pull up his trousers. In his misery his body seemed to wilt.

'What's your name?'

Amy began with the victim. He lifted his head in a mute plea to be left alone in total anonymity.

'Dafydd, miss.'

'Dafydd what, for heaven's sake? The world is full of Dafydds.'

Her impulsive reply was a mistake. It gave some of the boys the release of a quick laugh. Annoyed with herself she gave Dafydd a push in the direction of the corridor.

'In my compartment, there's a writing pad. I shall want every name and address. Go and get it.'

Dafydd lurched into the corridor and then turned like a beaten dog that would prefer to return to his kennel and even another hiding rather than venture into the unknown.

'In my compartment.'

The very feebleness of Dafydd's reluctance to obey her began to undermine her position. She pushed him in front of her down the corridor. Even as she moved she could hear Sid's voice clearly enough as he confided in his friends nearest him.

'You know who she is, don't you? One of those Welsh Nashes on the staff at Pendraw.'

She paused in the corridor, uncertain whether or not to round on them again. Quite plainly she heard a deep voice say,

'It would have been much more fun to take her trousers down.'

This witticism was greeted with a roar of appreciative laughter. She could only pretend not to have heard the remark. In her own compartment she made Dafydd sit. He shifted as close as he could to the sliding door.

'Now then,' Amy said. 'In your own words. What was all that about?'

As she stared at him he began blinking uncontrollably. It was like the defence mechanism of an insect.

'I want to help you.'

She was trying a softer approach: but the boy seemed bent on retreating so far inside himself that eventually he would become invisible. The only sounds he heard came from the corridor. No other sound could mean anything to him. The football team and its supporters were in sole possession of the carriage. Nothing impeded their movements. They charged about opening and shutting doors, laughing and shouting. The larger boys had begun to line up outside the compartment pressing their noses and even their tongues against the glass. Amy tried to ignore them, concentrating her attention on Dafydd.

'Why on earth do you go with them? You don't have to, surely?'

Dafydd's jaw fell as he saw his chief tormentor push the boys aside and make a place for himself to open the door. Sid stood in the doorway excitedly conscious of his own size and strength.

'Excuse me, Miss,' he said. 'We'd like him back. Very valuable he is. Our deputy linesman.'

The title was such a familiar joke that even Dafydd ventured a shame-faced smile. Sid stood to one side and gave him a peremptory nod. Dafydd shot out of his seat and under Sid's arm to have his back slapped and thumped by his schoolmates as he burrowed through them. Amy lifted her pad and pointed the top of her pen up at Sid. Their positions had reversed, but she continued to exercise her authority.

'I want your name,' she said. 'And your address.'

Sid bent down suddenly to pick up a crushed sheet of paper Amy had left on the floor. Her cheeks became hot with anger and embarrassment.

'Give that back to me,' she said. 'You'll be reported to your headmaster. Every single one of you.'

'I don't know whose it is, do I? Just something I picked up. Keeping the place tidy.'

His team-mates had stopped laughing. They watched every move Sid dared to make. There were faces pressed eagerly against the glass on either side of the door. Sid was opening the paper in order to read it.

'"Dearest Val, what can I say"...'

Sid read the words out loud so that his supporters could hear.

'I don't know whether this is yours, Miss...'

He held out the paper like a trainer who expects his animal to leap up and grab it between its teeth. There were shouts of warning from the corridor. Blasts from the steam whistle announced they were approaching the next station. Sid realised his support was melting away. Hastily Amy collected the screwed up pieces of paper she had dropped on the floor.

'I'll have your name and address,' she said. 'Do you hear me?'

Sid had gone, leaving the paper behind him. She was more than ready to take the offensive. She saw him pushing and plunging against the tide repeating 'my togs, man, my togs' in response to their bellowing and shouting. They were all intent on making the quickest escape as though from a burning building. The carriage doors were flung open long before the train came to a halt. Amy was obliged to abandon her attack and concentrated on getting her things together. Like a flock of starlings the boys landed on the platform and dispersed. The guard was too late to stem the headlong scatter. The ticket collector waved his arms and shouted as the boys shot past him. Chaotic disorder had broken out on one of the quietest stations on the coastal line. Most travellers looked shocked. A young man on the platform wearing a tattered tweed overcoat that reached almost to his ankles tossed away his cigarette stump just in time to capture the last of the escaping schoolboys.

'Hello! What's this then? What's the hurry?'

He grinned down cheerfully at the wriggling form he held securely in his arms. He possessed reserves of strength and cheerfulness that no emergency could take by surprise. His dark hair was combed and parted with a precision that contrasted conspicuously with the ancient coat he was wearing. So did his pale skin which was carefully clean shaven. A bent nose and angled dimples in his cheeks gave his smile a fierce benevolence.

'What is it then?' he said. 'A riot or a revolution?'

His captive refused to listen. He found the undergrown schoolboy's panic effort to escape amusing, even when it included attempts to kick him in the shins with hob-nailed boots that looked too big for such spindly legs. When he saw Amy alight on the platform he let the boy go. He advanced to meet her giving her his undivided attention.

'You're here,' he said.

She ignored his greeting. Her eyes were still trying to keep track of the stampeding schoolboys as they galloped up the road the other side of the station fence.

'Monsters,' she said.

His presence did nothing to mitigate her condemnation of wanton and indiscriminate masculine aggression.

'Savages. No better than animals. The whole pack of them. That's exactly what they are. A pack. Worse than animals. Torturing the feeblest and most defenceless creature in the group. What kind of a school can it be? Absolutely no discipline.'

She seemed to expect some kind of an answer from him. All he could manage was a fixed smile he may have imagined to be a useful crush-barrier against any possible spate of frivolous comment. He was more than content to stand still, look at her and say nothing.

'Discipline,' Amy said. 'There has to be discipline. That's the mistake some people make. There has to be order.'

It was plain that his smile was becoming for her a growing

source of irritation. She squinted against the light in order to look up at the walls of a ruined castle commanding the rocky summit of the steep hill that overlooked the railway station.

'I would never have imagined such behaviour possible,' Amy said. 'Not in this part of the world at least. "The land of white gloves", as they call it.'

She breathed deeply and made a determined effort to sound more judicial and less personally involved.

'Of course the influence of the chapels is on the decline. Even here. Especially among the young, of course. What are you grinning at Penry Lewis?'

'I'm not grinning,' he said. 'I'm just looking at you adoringly that's all.'

Once he had spoken he could no longer resist the temptation of trying to be witty.

'Mustn't let it get under your skin,' he said. 'After all, it's not quite the end of civilisation as we know it. That's been postponed for another three weeks.'

He touched her arm to show that he was courteously prepared to escort her from the station. She shrugged his hand away.

'What is it exactly you want with me?'

Her voice and her stillness were so militant that he was reduced to rapid glances around the platform, calculating the extent to which their encounter could be under observation. The noise of the schoolboys had faded away and the passengers, settled in their places, had ample time to gaze through the windows. The round-shouldered porter was dragging his toe-caps as he sauntered along slamming the doors. As if to make up for his temporary lack of resolve, Pen came closer to mutter boldly,

'My God, you look beautiful when you're angry.'

Amy remained totally unmoved.

'I can give you exactly ten minutes,' she said. 'Then I have more important matters to attend to.'

The smile vanished from his face.

'Hey, Amy ... steady on.'

Ruthlessly she pressed home her advantage.

'Knowing you, there is probably only one thing that you

want. Since that is not available, there seems little reason why we should detain each other for more than a few minutes.'

Like an experienced orator unaccountably lost for words in the middle of a speech, Pen kept thrusting his arm out in a gesture of utter sincerity and a promise that he would complete the message and clinch the argument once the power of speech was restored to him.

'What a thing to say,' he said. 'Amy! What a thing to say to me.'

'It's the truth,' Amy said. 'That's what you like, isn't it? The truth.'

The train was moving out, but he was no longer concerned about how many eyes could be watching them, with how much curiosity. He would let her see the spirit of healthy self-criticism that would allow her to attack him as bitterly and as long as she liked, before he took up his inalienable right to defend himself.

'Now, where were you going to take me I wonder?' Amy said. 'That's an interesting question. What was the programme? You must have a plan, mustn't you? You of all people. Would you like to tell me the whole truth about that? Without your Marxian jargon. In simple language of course that a simple woman can understand.'

'Give me a hearing,' Pen said. 'A fair hearing. That's all.'

'Very well,' she said. 'Carry on. I'm listening.'

'We can't just stand here like this. It's going to rain any minute.'

They moved to the shelter of the wooden canopy that jutted out from the row of station buildings. Through an open door they could see a tempting fire burning brightly in the cast iron grate of the Waiting Room. Amy went in, but Pen hesitated on the threshold when he saw an elderly woman sitting in the back of the room with a large basket on her knees. She gave them both a welcoming smile, happy to share with them an amenity generously provided by the railway company. Pen stepped backwards so that when he was out of the woman's line of vision he could strike the side of his forehead with the side of his fist.

'Bloody hell. This is ridiculous.'

Amy watched him march up and down the platform feeding his own anger.

'Why the hell don't you listen to me?' he said. 'It's nobody's job but the worker's job to set the worker free. I'll sing the bloody thing for you if you like. I'll turn the world upside down. You've only got to say the word.'

He pointed at her, holding his head to one side. For the first time she seemed to concede the possibility that he could be sincere and disinterested. They walked purposefully out of the station to the bottom of the hill, but there they paused again. Amy was unwilling to take the steep road up to the centre of the old country town.

'You don't want to be seen with me in public,' Pen said. 'That's understandable.'

'It's not that.'

To explain her position would have meant taking him into her confidence and she was not ready to do that. While she hesitated, Pen looked around with his well-defined black eyebrows raised to demonstrate a new interest in what he saw. More than half a mile away across the fields and common land and the fairways of a golf course there was a conspicuous ridge of dunes, and beyond them glimpses of level sand and the dark blue waters of the bay. To the north, the stark outlines of the mountains were just visible through a curtain of approaching rain. As they hesitated, the gates of the level crossing swung open like an unspoken invitation. Pen's patience gave out.

'Let's walk, for Christ's sake,' he said. 'It doesn't matter about the bloody rain. I've got to talk to you.'

Amy frowned disapprovingly. The open gates had revealed an unfrequented country road that ran parallel with the railway line before bending westwards. It led to an ancient church surrounded by a circular walled graveyard. The consecrated ground stood in isolation among the fields, ineffectively protected by a straggling belt of trees. Without speaking, they began to walk in that direction. Amy carried an umbrella, but she refrained from opening it. It seemed that a few spots of rain were much to be preferred to the embarrassment of being obliged to offer Pen Lewis a form of shelter that would bring them closer together.

'A man goes away,' Pen said. 'When he comes back, everything looks the same. And yet everything has changed. His personal life doesn't count. It doesn't matter.'

He grew more emphatic and confident as they walked along. Her silence suggested that she was listening with some degree of sympathy.

'It's like being on what they used to call Active Service. I want you to understand that. But in some ways it's worse. No comforts and no public approval. No Sister Susie sewing shirts for soldiers and no concerts and no Christmas dinner. I'm not trying to claim I was in constant danger or anything like that. But I could have been chucked into prison and done away with at any time and no one would have been any the wiser. That's what I'm driving at. It's the job of the Comintern to co-ordinate the work of the national Communist parties. That isn't easy see, at the best of times. Now it's getting worse. And it will go on getting worse. Month by month. Year by year. When the capitalists get the wind up, fascism will come marching in. It's as simple as that, girl. And what can that mean except that we are heading for one great big God-almighty clash? It's got to come. I'm not complaining. But some people are going to get smashed to little bits. I'm telling you this first hand, Amy girl. So what could old Pen do except send a few pretty postcards? And I bet more than half of them never got through?'

They walked on in uneasy silence.

'Things happen here too,' Amy said. 'Nowhere ever stands still. Not even here.'

Pen laughed easily as though she had made a joke. He had begun to relax visibly and behave as though merely being with her was balm to his soul.

'Anyway,' he said. 'They want me back. I think my travelling days are over. For the time being anyway. So it's back to the valley, kid, with a whole heap of organising to do. And I can tell you this, Amy fach, there's nowhere in the whole bloody wide world I'd rather be.'

He spoke as if he knew the warmth of his words would please her. Amy's reaction was pert and unexpected.

'In that case what are you doing up here?'

He laughed at the sound of her old inimitable frankness.

'Economics for Infants, kid,' he said.

Amy had paused to open her umbrella. He seemed to be on the point of taking her arm and demonstrating his delight in her nearness. Instead he turned up the collar of his overcoat with a stoical disregard for the rain.

'Nominated to attend,' Pen said. 'I jumped at it I can tell you. A quick glance at the map and I saw that as the crow flies this *Coleg y Castell* couldn't be far from you. I'm a romantic at heart, see, and I reckoned I was due for a bonus. They call it a five-week course, mainly for the Unemployed, in Economics, The Scientific Method and something our wordy Warden has chosen to call Affirmative Living! What's that, do you think? Well, it includes Art, Welsh culture and Musical Appreciation. That's Education for you. For Adult Infants. Funny lot we are. Thought you might come up for a meal to tell you the truth. We're allowed guests, you see, up to a point. You know we've got men up there who can hardly talk English! There's a quarryman from the hills there, somewhere, Bethesda is it? Or Ebenezer? One of those Jewish names. Got a chest like a punctured bellows. One of the worst I ever heard. He's got his own little trick though. He waits for a pause in the discussion and then out it comes like the bleat of a short-winded sheep. "But what is Life, Mr Chairman?"'

Pen attempted his own version of the slow-moving Gwynedd accent. He was disappointed that Amy did not find it as amusing as he did himself.

'There's a chap called Tasker Thomas,' he said. 'He drops in on a Tuesday to conduct a weekly seminar he calls "The Christian Solution". For some reason he makes a bee-line for me. I do everything I can to avoid it. I even volunteer for washing up. But he won't begin without me. If I'm washing up he brings half a dozen in to finish the job so that I can take part. The more I go for him, the more he likes it. You know him then, don't you? Do you reckon he's all there?'

He sounded so genuinely mystified that Amy allowed herself to smile. Pen was encouraged.

'The fiddling ways he and his kind have got to patch up the old capitalist system. It's incredible. A patch here and a patch there when the whole fabric is falling apart. Last week he was going on about that bloody little Indian fakir Gandhi. Personal friend of his, he said. And what did that amount to? One cup of tea and a bun in some Methodist Mission. Anyway I told him straight. You're not going to solve this world's economic problems comrade by giving out a set of toy spinning wheels with packets of Shredded Wheat. He's a nerve-racking bugger. A revolution means doing away with one social order, Mr Thomas, and building up another, I told him.'

'That's what you say,' Amy said playfully.

'That's what one sixth of the world says, kid, and that's only the beginning.'

Pen shook his head pityingly as he thought of Tasker Thomas.

'"The revolution is like the kingdom of heaven, old friend." I mean, what the hell does that mean? And what the hell does he call me "old friend" for? I'm not his old friend. "I'm not your old friend", I said. "I'm your class enemy." And then he laughed like a school kid giving the answer to a penny puzzle. "It's inside you, old friend", he said. "It's inside you."'

They stood outside the stone wall that surrounded the churchyard. The rain became heavier and Pen took shelter under the slate roof of the lych-gate. He smiled at her engagingly. Amy avoided his bold stare by taking some interest in the architecture of the church. It was a long low building with a modest bell-cote at the far end, housing a single bell. She could not avoid seeing how overwhelmingly pleased he was with her presence. He nodded at her encouragingly.

'You're here anyway,' he said. 'You're here.'

He pushed open the stiff iron gate. He stood aside with a bow inviting her to inspect the site. From the shelter of her umbrella, Amy considered him closely.

'What is it you want?' she said. 'You still haven't told me.'

'You of course.'

For a moment it seemed possible she would turn back. She glanced at her wrist watch before stepping under the lych-gate to close her umbrella and shake it.

'This church is very old,' she said. 'I've seen it from the train but I've never been in it.'

In the porch they stopped to read a brief history of the church typed out by the Rector and hung up in a glazed oak frame. The type was fading and not easy to read. Pen stood close to Amy for the first time and held her arm to maintain his balance as he leaned forward to scrutinize all the notices. He read the list of sidesmen and the members of the Women's Guild responsible for the flowers.

'Saint Madrun,' Amy said. 'I've never heard of her before.'

'Big scholar, isn't he?'

Pen read the Rector's typescript.

'"In England we tend to associate the church with a village ... but in Wales the early churches were quite removed from human habitation. This marked isolation is a noteworthy feature of Celtic Christianity." There you are, Saint Amy. Now you know.'

Amy placed her umbrella upside down in the rusting stand as neatly as any faithful parishioner. She had ignored Pen's frivolous remarks while she concentrated on absorbing information.

'"In the Middle Ages the whole church was decorated with frescoes of Heaven and Hell."' She was reading with more serious intent. '"Traces of colour can still be found on the east wall."'

He had begun to stroke her arm with tender reticence, when she turned away to open the heavy door. The hinges gave a sustained creak as she pushed the door open and stepped inside. Amy looked about her with exaggerated interest. When Pen tried to take her arm again, she moved into the nave. She walked down towards the altar studying the inscribed stones cemented into the walls.

'Look at this one, Pen.'

She was whispering to draw his attention to an eighteenth-century inscription on white marble.

'It says the incumbent was also a benefactor who restored the church and his remains are buried under the altar.'

Pen spoke more loudly than usual.

'What are you whispering for? Afraid of the ju-ju or something? Do you think ju-ju is the same as Duw, Duw? There's a good question.'

'Hush.' Amy smiled at him forgivingly.

'You don't believe in all this mumbo-jumbo,' Pen said. 'So why tip-toe and whisper? There aren't any fairies here. You can see for yourself.'

Pen waved an arm to indicate the emptiness of the pews and the cold interior of the church. Amy wanted to rationalise her attitude.

'One has to have a certain respect for the past,' she said.

'Does one, hell!'

'Pen!'

'Okay, okay. I didn't come here to argue about this kind of stuff. It's all irrelevant anyway. The whole of this part of the world. I can tell you that. Fine for holidays. For day-dreamings and time-wasting. Ideal for the Tasker-Thomases of this world. But not for you, Amy. Not for you and me.'

He took hold of her hand and they sat down together in the nearest pew under the stone pulpit. Amy was trembling slightly. She spoke as though to account for the fact.

'It's so cold and damp in here,' she said.

'I want you with me,' Pen said. 'That's why I wrote. I can't keep going any longer without you. That was the real hell about it if you want to know. The sheer bloody loneliness. If you only knew how much I used to think about you. In those ghastly little lodging-houses and all those bug-ridden beds I used to send myself to sleep trying to remember the warmth and reality of your body. My Amy.'

He sank to his knees on the stone floor so that he could embrace her thighs and rest his head in her lap. His eyes were closed. His hands began to feel her body with hungry gratitude as he murmured her name over and over again.

'Pen,' she said. 'Let's talk. You said you wanted to speak to me.'

Her voice sounded weak. She tried to lift his heavy head with both hands. He looked up and opened his eyes wide. They shone with an unfamiliar fervour in the light from the church window.

'With my body I thee worship,' he said. 'This is the place, isn't it? It's for good this time, Amy. Marriage. By whatever rites you choose. You can't refuse me. You can't refuse yourself. We've got to be together. This is the source of our power. This is where the real future begins.'

She could muster no more than a token resistance to his embraces. Their bodies' need for each other bent them into awkward and ludicrous shapes and angles on the narrow pew. Amy held on to his physical strength as though she were afraid of drowning in a flood of emotional release. Sustained by his strong arms she sank to the floor with her head and her fair hair hanging to one side in the attitude of a willing victim. It was the coldness of the church flagstones against her flesh that brought her abruptly to her senses. She struggled against him.

'Not here,' she said. 'Not here. This is a gravestone. What are you trying to do? Destroy me? This is a place of death.'

He stretched himself above her, his face gleaming with triumph and pride in his masculinity and its power.

'I'm not death,' he said. 'I'm life. And you know it. That's why you're here. I'm the life you need, Amy. Just as much as I need you.'

'Not here.'

She scrambled away, suddenly and desperately ashamed of her partial nakedness. She muttered angrily as she adjusted her clothes.

'What if somebody had come in? What if anyone had walked in?'

She found her beret under the pew and replaced it on her head. His laughter infuriated her. Out of her own uncertainty and fear she seemed to be scrambling about for scraps of evidence she could put together in a formula of self-defence. She had to assert a measure of control over a situation that could so easily deteriorate into some unendurable form of humiliation and defeat.

'You bring me here. To this place. Here.' Her words tumbled out, mumbled, ill-considered. 'Talk about marriage. One of your tricks with women. To get your way. And to do it in a place like this. So that you can have your way with me. I understand, you know. I know how men like you talk when they get together. I'm not a complete fool. I know what you're doing.'

Pen began to shake her. Every word she spoke fuelled his anger. He picked up his tattered overcoat and wrapped it tightly around himself. Then he took her roughly by the arm as though she were under arrest and whispered fiercely close to her ear through his clenched teeth.

'You're so damn clever,' he said, 'and you don't understand anything. Not one damn thing.'

He pushed her roughly in front of him down the nave.

'You are a silly little petty-bourgeois bitch and I ought to knock the hide off you. In the aisle and all. I'll walk you down the aisle. Backwards.'

'Don't you dare.'

'A silly little petty bourgeois bitch instead of a decent working-class girl. Can you understand that, Amy Parry? Stuck in your nice little digs. A pretty little schoolteacher in her pretty little clothes. Singing in the pretty chapel choir no doubt. Marking your pretty little books all night and smoking your pretty little cigarettes and collecting your pretty little pay packet from the government. Reward for good behaviour and faithful service. You'll get a clock at the end of it to tick away what's left of your time!'

In the porch she struggled free from his iron grasp because he was ready to release her. Imposing his physical strength on her had restored his basic good humour. He was ready to laugh again.

'Better a cock than a clock,' he said. 'I can tell you that for a start, Miss Parry.'

She found her umbrella and raised it ready to attack him. She screamed in his face.

'Shut up! Shut up! Do you hear me!'

Pen raised both his fists and shook them. He was full of approval.

'That's it, kid,' he said. 'Good working-class stuff. You shout your head off and then maybe we'll get to understand each other on the right level. Down with petty-bourgeois inhibitions. Good dialectic. Come on now. Get it all off your chest.'

100

'You're not going to treat me like a – like a –'

'That's the style. We've got to fight before we –'

'I don't want to. I don't want to fight with you. I don't. I don't.'

Slowly Amy brought her voice under control. It seemed as if she believed she was about to leave him.

'I don't want to talk to you, I don't want to see you. Is that clear?'

Pen nodded sympathetically.

'It's been a long time,' he said. 'A hell of a long time.'

He took her arm confidently and Amy allowed him to lead her outside. The air was fresh and cold. The shower of rain had passed. In the fitful sunlight the shadow of clouds flitted over the angled gravestones. Beyond the churchyard wall from a field which had been recently ploughed the wind carried the cry of an isolated lapwing. The graveyard was well kept: the grass regularly scythed and the gravel paths kept neat and clear. Pen spoke to Amy with urgent and yet solemn confidence as they walked together closely between the tombs.

'We're together. That's what matters, kid. And what I'm trying to say is that we should stick together. I can't find all the words I need to argue the case. And they call me an orator, if you please. What I'm saying is this, Amy. With you and me, it's what our bodies say that matters. Start there. I understand that much. And march shoulder to shoulder as equals, no, as one, to collect the future because it belongs to us anyway. Do you see what I mean? It's there for the taking. Socialism isn't a dream. It's reality. The only bloody reality worth having. And it starts with our flesh and blood, kid. That's the way to look at it. This thing between us, this love, this lust, this desire, I mean you can call it what you like, this us that is more than the sum of the parts, it's got to be understood in the context of the class struggle. It's just got to be. It's as simple as that Amy. Now you don't want to be stuck in a backwater for the rest of your life, like an umbrella in a lost luggage office!'

He snatched her umbrella from her hand and waved it triumphantly over her head until he saw her smile uncertainly, not sure whether to laugh or cry.

101

'Together there's nothing we can't do! The dynamo of revolution!'

They stood before a stone hut built against the stout wall that marked out the consecrated circle. The door was open. Scythes and sickles hung on the wall and a long wooden bier. Inside, there was a manger covered in cobwebs and a cobbled area mostly covered by hay harvested between the graves the previous summer. Amy shook her head. She was unwilling to go inside.

'It's not possible,' she said.

Pen was confident and assertive.

'Of course it is.'

Gently he took her hands.

'Nothing wrong with this little stable,' he said. 'This is ancient poverty. Best place to start. At the bottom with the pigs and the peasants. The trick is to take your poverty and wrap it round you like one of those magic cloaks. A magic Celtic cloak if that's what you fancy.'

He bent his head to move inside. With complete assurance he took possession of the place. He led her into the hut, closing the door on the outside world and putting the bier against it. Light filtered in through cracks in the door. Amy began to tremble. Their isolation in the unfamiliar twilight drew her closer to him. He made their bed from the hay and spread his coat and hers on it.

'It's a long time . . .'

Amy muttered incoherently, with much to say and yet incapable of speech. Pen was saying something about the darkness underground in the pit and how it had affected his eyesight. She tried to listen. With great sympathy and strength he drew her down towards him.

'Of course it is, my love. My little love. But you mustn't worry.'

He helped her to remove her suspender belt. She was so soothed by the tenderness of his ministrations, she began to touch his face with her fingertips with a nervous sightless insistence, learning its contours all over again, lingering most fondly over the high cheek bones. Pen himself was talking in a low steady voice a slow litany that would help to keep his own emotions under control.

'Waited . . . We've waited all right. We've waited, haven't we, Amy? Every day, every week, every month, a lifetime already wasted away from you Amy, I can tell you that. Away from this . . . and this . . .'

He whispered less as his hands persuaded her whole body to become less tense. She only spoke when he entered her.

'Be careful, Pen. Please be careful. Don't make me pregnant. Please . . .'

His voice was still soothing and masterful.

'You have to trust me and we have to trust each other. I'll take care of you, Amy. I'll take care of you, my love. Always. Don't worry.'

11

In the garden Nathan Harris was singing. The raucous noise did not disturb the robin perched familiarly on the metal crosspiece of the fork Mrs Rossett had left on the edge of the onion patch. The single apple tree was in blossom and the sun shone on a clod of upturned soil. Nathan's hands in grey mittens rested stiffly on the long handle of a spade with a narrow blade. He was pleased with his limited effort. His second best hat was balanced on his grey curls. He wore a scarf and two cardigans under his tweed overcoat. In an interval of silence as he straightened his back slowly, he heard the delicate flutter of the bird's wings. It had landed on the upturned soil within inches of his immobile feet. His parchment pale face creased into a broad smile. He made coaxing noises with his lips. The robin's attention was riveted on a glimpse of earthworm wriggling into the soil.

Amy emerged from the kitchen carrying a mug of cocoa.

'Now then, Mr Harris,' she said. 'You must drink this while it's hot.'

With some difficulty he turned and shuffled the short distance to the garden seat near the apple tree. The seat was strewn with cushions, scarves and coats to keep him as warm and comfortable as possible. There was also a Greek New Testament small and light enough for him to hold. He held on tightly to Amy as she helped him lower himself into a corner of the seat.

'These old cricks.'

He gasped with relief when he was finally in position.

'Are you going to join me, Miss Parry? For our cocoa break.'

He took unconcealed delight in her presence. Amy brought her own cup from the kitchen. She picked up the Greek New Testament and sat down alongside him.

'What about *The Critique of Pure Reason*?' she said. 'Four pages before lunch. In the original.'

'On a day like this?' he said. '"The heavens declare the glory of God: and the firmament sheweth his handy-work . . . In them hath he set a tabernacle for the sun: which cometh forth as a bridegroom out of his chamber . . ." It doesn't matter how old you are, when the spring comes.'

Amy placed his mug of cocoa carefully between his cold hands. His eyes followed what she was doing with mute gratitude. Slowly he raised the mug to his lips and sipped noisily at the liquid.

'What do you think of the idea of a class war, Mr Harris?'

Amy framed her question carefully. She could have been initiating the kind of speculative discussion that gave the arthritic cripple particular pleasure.

'Well now,' he said. 'That's a big question.'

'There is a struggle going on, isn't there?' Amy said. 'No one can deny that. When we look around the world. It dominates the politics of our time. Everywhere except here, that is. Pendraw has its own troubles, goodness knows. But in terms of the class struggle, it looks like an irrelevent backwater.'

Nathan's hat trembled perilously on top of his curls as he nodded encouraging Amy to speak.

'I know it's complicated by all sorts of factors,' she said. 'But you've lived in the South. You've seen it all at first hand. It is a class struggle, isn't it? The workers have to fight to avoid being exploited. And the only way they can win is by taking over the means of production, distribution and exchange. That's true, isn't it?'

'That's the theory,' Nathan said.

Amy was suddenly impatient.

'But is it true?' she said.

She spoke as one who urgently needed an answer.

'You've lived in the middle of it all,' she said. 'Where the real action is. It's too comfortable here, isn't it? For somebody like me. With a good job. A secure position. I'm not doing anything. I'm not suffering in any way at all.'

Nathan Harris smiled at her affectionately.

'Miss Parry,' he said. 'There is no virtue in suffering for its own sake. I can tell you that from first hand.'

Nathan smiled at her affectionately.

Amy laid her mug on the grass and clasped her hands together.

'It's so difficult,' she said. 'to say what one really means.'

'Well, let me tell you this.'

He was eager to bring her comfort.

'There is a struggle going on here and you are an important part of it. Everything is relative you see. We do what we can as the day allows us. Everything is relative. To some great authority sitting in Peking or Moscow or London, anything happening in Pendraw is less than a storm in a teacup. Beneath their notice. But Providence is marvellous. It picks on the most obscure stable to bring a saviour into the world. We never know which rock a new Moses may chance to strike. Or what little stream will grow into a great river of new life!'

In spite of himself his voice had reached an oratorical pitch. He brought his arm down and rested it carefully on the metal arm at the end of the garden seat.

'Will you listen to me? An old man preaching under an apple tree.'

He breathed deeply and narrowed his eyes to stare directly into the brightness of the blossoms.

'You see the effect you have, Miss Parry?'

They sat together in silence drinking cocoa and enjoying the peace of the small garden. Mrs Rossett's cat stalked through the open kitchen door. The robin flew into the apple tree. The cat arrived at the garden seat and began to rub its fur against Amy's legs.

'Things can happen you know,' Nathan Harris said. 'Even in a place like Pendraw with all its bickering. And my goodness, it has more than its fair share. I was telling my sister Annie this morning, in the South we had industrial strife. And plenty of it. But at least it was all in the open. And what's in the open has a chance to blow away! Now here you see things are buried and hidden. And what is hidden can fester. Now if you poison the soil you destroy all power for growth at the very root.'

Amy made no comment. She seemed to be considering the minister's version of the differences between two societies as she finished her drink.

'The class war,' Nathan Harris said. 'And the class struggle. There is a distinction to be made there. War means weapons and wiping out an enemy. Killing. Slaughter. To achieve power and maintain it. Now what we have to ask, in our tradition, is what has this to do with the suffering Saviour on the cross or the struggle against selfishness and sin?'

Amy offered to relieve him of his empty mug. Momentarily he held on to it to keep her near.

'You are an example of unselfishness,' he said. 'Like all good women. If you will let me say this, Miss Parry, as a friend. You suffer enough. When I think of Mr Val Gwyn . . . But I shan't say any more. You will forgive an old cripple for intruding.'

He had been slow to see what he took to be her resentment.

'I'll just rinse these mugs,' Amy said.

His face wore a childishly worried look but it lit up again when he heard the rapping of the front door knocker reverberate in the house.

'Visitors!' he said. His mouth opened with pleasurable expectation.

Amy left the mugs in the kitchen sink and went to open the door. Eddie Meredith stood on the pavement with a suitcase at his feet. Across the street the elementary school caretaker's children were in their favourite positions at the protective wire, watching their encounter.

'Amy,' Eddie said. 'I must talk to you.'

Her response was formal and defensive.

'I thought your term had started,' she said.

'It has.'

He saw that she was staring at the children across the road.

'Can I come in?'

His tone grew increasingly urgent. They moved down the passage which smelt of wax polish to Amy's room. Through the single window they could see the crippled minister sitting expectantly under the apple tree, his head raised like a blind man's listening hard to identify an approaching footfall. There were books on the table for the lesson Amy was preparing.

'What on earth's the matter?' Amy said. 'Is it the end of the world?'

Eddie shifted his suitcase out of the doorway. Amy watched him with muted disapproval.

'Well, in a way it is for me,' he said. 'That swine of a father of mine.'

He glanced at Amy as if he hoped she would rebuke him.

'My aunt left me two hundred pounds,' Eddie said. 'To be handed over on my twenty-fifth birthday. Or at an earlier date if my sainted father deemed it appropriate. All I need is less than half of it for my trip to Germany. And the old bastard won't pay up.'

'Oh dear,' Amy said.

'It's worse than "Oh dear".' Eddie seized hold of Amy's hand. 'You understand,' he said, 'Berlin is the place, I've got to get there. It's where everything of any importance is happening. The experiments. The new style. You know how much the theatre means to me, Amy. It's my life. I know I must sound impossibly self-centred to you. I'm aware of it. You see, I know I have it in me to create. I must have my chance, and I know exactly where I need to go to get it.'

Amy was looking through the window. She was concerned about Nathan Harris.

'What do you expect me to do about it?' she said.

'Lend me a hundred pounds,' Eddie said.

Having spoken he seemed to acquire a fresh sense of the largeness of the sum.

'Lend me fifty.'

107

He sat down without being asked in the mahogany arm chair. Deflated, he stared at Mrs Rossett's family photographs in silver frames that stood on either side of the glass dome covering waxed fruit on the sideboard which took up so much space in the room.

'That's three months' salary, Mr Meredith,' Amy said. 'I just haven't got it.'

He was beginning to look at her hopefully again. She determined to disabuse him before he stared to ask for smaller sums.

'I send a pound a week to my aunt and uncle in Llanelw,' she said. 'It isn't much but it helps them to live a little more comfortably.'

She seemed to consider whether it was necessary to elaborate and then decided it was not.

'You'd better come and say hello to Nathan Harris,' she said. 'He'll be wondering who called. He likes to see visitors.'

Eddie was reluctant to rise to his feet.

'Amy,' he said. 'What am I going to do?'

Amy shook her head, sympathetic but with nothing to suggest.

'Will you talk to my father? Have a word with him. He thinks you are fantastic. He's right too.'

'That sounds absurd,' Amy said.

She was in the doorway, ready to lead the way to the garden.

'He thinks you've got a fantastic voice. Offer to sing a solo with his choir at the Salem Concert. Something like that. The choir is about the only thing that means anything to him. I think that's a marvellous idea, don't you?'

'No. I don't.'

He made no attempt to get to his feet.

'Amy. What shall I do? What shall I do?' He beat his fists on his knees.

'You'll think of something. Now come on.'

As they passed through the kitchen, Eddie was seized with another spasm of indignation.

'He's getting five percent on it,' he said. 'My aunt died when I was fourteen. She thought the world of me. Imagine, he's been getting five percent on my money for the last seven years! I mean if he gives me just the interest, that would be more than enough to see me through.'

His mouth hung open when he saw that Amy was smiling.

'The thing is, basically, the man is a miser,' Eddie said. 'And worse than that. He doesn't believe in education. Oh, he'll go around the place with newspaper cuttings in his wallet about his brilliant son and his scholarship to Oxford and all that. But that's just nothing. It costs absolutely nothing to bask in reflected glory and you can go on doing it for ever as long as the sun shines.'

'Stop moaning,' Amy said. 'You're bound to think of something. If they want something enough, people usually do.'

Nathan Harris raised a crooked arm in greeting when he saw who the visitor was.

'Here's a brilliant young man,' he said in his penetrating voice. 'And one of us! What do you think of this Public Meeting business?'

'What Public Meeting?' Eddie said.

He hung back uncertain whether or not to offer to shake hands.

'"What Public Meeting" he says!' Nathan Harris sounded as though he were enjoying a joke. 'Quite an event, Mr Eddie Meredith,' he said. 'Quite an event in the history of our little town I can assure you. Our right honourable and illustrious leader, Member of Parliament no less. Coming down from the clouds to cut our little Pendraw Gordian knot! A Cottage Hospital or a Memorial Hall? A democratic decision. And the process to be presided over by the great democratic leader himself. What a privilege!'

Nathan Harris's irony was exhausted.

'Well I suppose we must give him the benefit of the doubt. Along with the rest of them. It will be interesting to hear both sides put their case in the open.'

There was an awkward silence. Eddie hung back on the narrow garden path. Amy found herself at a loss for something appropriate to say. Nathan Harris concentrated his benevolent attention on the young man on the garden path.

'I hear you are going to Germany,' he said. 'I congratulate

you. It's as much as I can manage to get to the front door.'

He was obliged to enjoy his own joke. The awkward silence descended a second time.

'I was in Germany once,' Nathan Harris said.

It was sufficient to stir a flicker of interest in Eddie's sulky face.

'Before the war, of course. I was a young man then. In Marburg. Trying to write a thesis. I nearly starved to death.'

'Mr Harris!'

Amy looked at him with alarm before she smiled.

'Not *The Critique of Pure Reason*?'

'Oh no.' Nathan Harris chuckled happily. '"The Mystical Element in Luther's Conception of Faith",' he said. 'I never got to the bottom of it. Mind you at the time I was full of it. Thought I'd found the key that everybody else had mislaid.'

His stiff frame shook as he laughed at himself until his hat slipped forward and the rim rested on his aquiline nose. Amy stepped forward delicately and restored the hat to the crown of his head. Eddie could contain himself no longer.

'It's so unjust,' he said. 'That's what I resent most about it.'

Nathan Harris secured himself in the garden seat and looked at the young man enquiringly.

'My father won't allow me to use my own money to go to Germany,' Eddie said. 'Unless I have it, I won't be able to go!'

There was a note of desperation in his voice. Nathan Harris looked at him anxiously.

'It's expensive,' Eddie said. 'Far more so than in your day. And I need to travel. I need to see things. For my research. There are no scholarships or grants available. All I have is this invitation from Pastor Otto Hartman, and a few letters of introduction. I need to pay my way.'

Nathan Harris gave Eddie's problem his concentrated attention. Eddie smiled charmingly.

'I shouldn't be bothering you,' he said. 'Either of you. But to whom can one turn to unburden oneself, except to one's friends? I realise I must sound horrifically childish. But I do have a sense of mission. One is so loath to say these things, but I have this intuition that something is waiting for me over

110

there, some momentary revelation that will release the dumb force that drives me. Teach me to speak. To say the things I was meant to say.'

For the first time Amy appeared to be listening to him with sympathetic interest. Nathan Harris stirred like a man emerging from a trance. He had an useful suggestion to make.

'Tasker Thomas,' he said. 'Get him to speak to your father.'

Eddie looked doubtful.

'I don't know.' he said. 'Tasker might put his back up. My old man is impervious to rational processes once his back goes up. I don't know that he's ever reached the stage of being capable of rational process anyway, if it came to that.'

Nathan Harris was ready to correct him.

'He's been moved by Tasker's preaching,' he said. 'Mr H. M. Meredith. Your father. Excellent organist. He has been moved by Tasker's preaching. He told me so himself.'

Eddie schooled himself to show polite gratitude.

'It's very kind of you to bother about my little troubles, Mr Harris,' he said. 'I'm truly grateful. I'm sorry if I've been too emotional about it. But...'

He made a gesture that implied an artist could only be forgiven for too intense a preoccupation with the practice of his art.

'If you'll excuse me,' he said. 'I have a train to catch. Thank you again for your time and your trouble.'

Amy escorted Eddie back to her room where he picked up his suitcase, giving a profound sigh as he did so.

'It's hopeless,' he said.

Amy touched his arm sympathetically.

'I'll speak to Tasker,' she said. 'Perhaps he and I could go and see your father. We'll do what we can.'

'Bless you.'

Eddie seized her hand impulsively and kissed it. At the door he stopped to turn before opening it. He had cheered up and was winking roguishly at Amy. He bent to whisper in her ear a naughty secret.

'The old boy is crazy about you,' he said. 'I don't blame him either.'

'Don't be so stupid,' Amy said.

'It's not so stupid,' Eddie said. 'Think of it as a film. Welsh version of *The Blue Angel*. Cripple minister infatuated with lovely young teacher. I can see it all now. Victorian setting, I think, don't you? He falls on his knees by the fender to pick up her slippers and press them to his lips.'

'You idiot,' Amy said indignantly.

She made a stern effort to stop herself laughing.

'Get back to your books,' she said. 'If your great German expedition amounts to nothing more than toy theatres and tinsel it's not worth the bother.'

Eddie's mood changed quickly.

'Amy. Dreams are what we live by. We can only bear just so much of reality. It's so bloody awful most of the time.'

He gazed at her like a child waiting for some sign of affection and forgiveness. Amy opened the door.

'Go on,' she said with a friendly smile. 'Hurry up and catch your train.'

12

Tasker's voluminous raincoat gave an episcopal grace to the way he dismounted from his bicycle. It was a tall machine and as he stood at his ease to survey the workhouse buildings from the open gateway, there was a striking distance between the extremities of the handlebars gripped tightly by his hands and his feet that had touched the earth again. All he beheld was neatness and order. Even the grey stones of the workhouse looked as if they had been recently scrubbed. In the residential section, the windows of the first floor shone brightly enough behind their freshly painted grills to reflect the clouds moving at their own leisurely pace across the sky. A row of women were engaged in weeding the flower-beds between the gravelled courtyard and the high wall that surrounded the cowsheds and pigsties. Tasker passed the palm of his hand lightly over the top of his head allowing his fingers to make contact with the hair which grew like a fluffy halo around his sunburned pate. His raised arm prevented him from registering the almost subterranean approach of a small figure carrying a large rake. When the inmate spoke, Tasker's hand was still in the air in a gesture of crooked benediction.

'They won't let you keep that. I can tell you that for a start.'

The little man pointed his rake at the bicycle. He seemed to resent its size. He was no more than five feet tall himself. He wore a gaberdine overcoat tied around the middle with a clean length of binder twine, and a hat with the brim turned down which hid much of his long face.

'I wouldn't have put a foot in the place if my house hadn't burnt down. I can tell you that. Up at six. Washing in cold water. Supper at half past four and off to bed at seven. That's it for you. In a nutshell. You may as well know. It's not the worst, so I'm told. But I wouldn't say it was the best either. Since you've got a bike, it would pay you to go and look around before you make your mind up.'

'Well, thank you,' Tasker said. 'Thank you very much for the tip.'

The small man with the rake was so intent on expressing himself that he gave himself no time to take in the smile of amusement on Tasker's face.

'I don't know if you read the papers,' he said. 'They're always a week old before we get a look at them. But there was a man I know up before the magistrates last month. Put a brick through the window of the jewellers in Lower Bangor. And do you know why?'

'To "pinch" something?' Tasker made the tentative suggestion with his eyebrows roguishly raised.

'Nothing of the sort. He told the bench, he wanted to be arrested. Sent to prison for a change. Heard that the food was better there than in the workhouse. And that's a fact!'

The small man bent his head right back so that he could glare up directly into Tasker's eyes. It was only then that he realised the visitor was not the type to be in sufficiently reduced circumstances to be asking to be taken in.

'I've seen you before somewhere,' he said. 'And with a collar around your neck.'

Tasker was laughing with exaggerated goodwill. He wanted to put the man at his ease.

'Now then, old friend,' he said. 'Remember the adage. "It's not by its beak that you buy a woodcock!"'

'What's the name then?'

Tasker's benevolent manner encouraged him to be bold and forthright.

'Tasker Thomas.'

The small man leaned more heavily on his rake and rubbed his chin against a knuckle. He muttered the name over to himself: but it was clear that it meant nothing in particular to him. He was at a loss but loath to abandon the pleasure of an unexpected conversation with someone from outside.

'I'm a Baptist by rights,' he said. 'That's where I feel really at home.'

'Isaacs! Get back to your work!'

Eddie Meredith's father, the workhouse Master, stood on the steps outside the reception office to exercise his authority. Isaacs had strayed beyond the territorial limits of the task allotted to him. Without questioning the order the little man tugged his hat over his eyes and marched away to resume the weeding and raking of the gravel path which led to the rear entrance of the Casuals Section. H. M. Meredith stalked across the courtyard with his right arm outstretched in welcome. He could also have been hurrying to head off any unauthorised inspection of the premises by such an unorthodox minister. The workhouse Master looked like a man at the mercy of a permanent inner anxiety. Eddie's cherubic dimples had shrunk into creases running down both H. M. Meredith's thin cheeks: the resemblance between father and son had become minimal. What was left of his hair was plastered down close to his skull. He took as much pride in his own appearance as in that of the institution over which he presided. He wore riding breeches with highly polished leggings and a gold tiepin glittered behind the knot of his silk tie.

'It may sound harsh,' he said as he offered Tasker his hand. 'But it's the only language some of them understand.'

114

His manner was nervously brisk. He embarked at once on a line of purposeful conversation.

'This place is spotless, as you can see,' he said. 'We take a pride in our Union. I prefer the word "Union", you know, to "Workhouse". I'm a Carmarthenshire man myself. Now what part do you hail from, Mr Thomas?'

He put the question as if the information would provide him with a vital clue to Tasker Thomas's true identity. Tasker was already engaged in a broad survey of the premises. He waved a hand in the direction of the Casuals Section.

'There's room over there for what we might call natural extension,' Tasker said. 'Make room for Casualties as well as Casuals.'

He smiled to show that he was poised to make imaginative suggestions. The Master responded with a salvo of stern facts.

'Casuals are required to break a given quantity of stones to pay for their night's lodging and a nourishing meal,' he said. 'Those are the Rules. And in a place like this you are lost if you don't abide by them. The Rules are the Law and the Prophets.'

He thrust his head forward to sense Tasker's reaction.

'I may sound hard, but I'm not really hard at all,' Meredith said. 'Just, but not hard. Now the Matron, that's my wife of course, she's as soft as putty. Much too soft. Take last night for example. Only last night.'

The Master interrupted their progress to the main building, to enlarge on the story with narrowed eyes.

'We've got a girl in here with water on the brain. Lost both her parents last winter. A tragic case. Now Matron heard her crying as she did her rounds last night. Crying in the women's ward. That's where the girl sleeps you see. So what does Matron do? Takes her into her own bedroom. Into our quarters. Which are cramped enough even with Eddie away. In the next bed to mine. Well, I had to put a stop to it. "It's wrong to be soft in this job Nel," I said. "And it's worse than wrong." Now that looks harsh and I admit it freely. But it is one of the basic principles of good government. You must have discipline and you can't have favourites. As I say to the

115

Board of Guardians, and they back me up all the way, fair play to them, if you're running a place like this you must stamp on the first sign of indiscipline.'

With lips still parted, he gazed at Tasker's broad face, waiting for his frankness to be appreciated.

'What happened to the girl?' Tasker said.

In the exposition of general principle the Master had forgotten about her.

'With a case like that,' he said, 'you can't do much about it. Except keep her warm and clean.'

Tasker sighed deeply and shook his head.

'We are such weak creatures,' he said. 'We all need help in one way or another.'

Meredith glanced suspiciously at the minister. Tasker was an unconventional figure. He was ordained minister of the denomination to which Meredith adhered as a conspicuously faithful member; but he was also a champion of dubious causes.

'The Strait and Narrow,' Meredith said. 'Nothing else for it in a place like this. And for all I know in the outside world either. But I am not in charge of that, thank goodness.'

They stood together on the verandah in front of the Reception Office. The bottom half of the window had been left open so that Meredith could keep an eye on the row of women weeding the flower beds in the shadow of the high stone wall.

'Mustn't let him get near the women's side.'

Meredith was whispering a confidence. Tasker looked confused.

'Who?' he said.

'Isaacs bach,' he said. 'You wouldn't think it to look at him, but he's got some very nasty little habits. Chiefly indecent exposure. Let me say no more than that. A Master has to have eyes in the back of his head if he wants to do his job properly. It's a strain sometimes I have to admit. There are things you would like to do, relaxations and such like you would like to introduce; but bring in too much choice, Mr Thomas, and before you know where you are you are in the middle of chaos and disaster.'

At last the note of nervous urgency in the Master's rasping

voice tapped the great reservoir of Tasker's sympathy with the human condition. He gazed with compassion at the row of pens and pencils in Mr Meredith's waistcoat pockets.

'You have great responsibilities,' Tasker said.

This acknowledgement was made in Tasker's warmest manner. To the Master it sounded sufficiently like a well-earned tribute to enable him to relax a little.

'I'd like to show you the Board Room,' he said. 'It is the nearest we can come to a show piece. Nel keeps it like a pin in paper. It's just on our left here, Mr Thomas, if you will allow me to lead the way.'

On the walls of the Board Room hung portraits of a succession of Mayors of Pendraw, most of them in their robes of office, and of chairmen of the Union Board of Guardians. A green baize cloth covered the long table and the chairs set around it were highly polished. The Master was pleased with the resonance that the reverberation in the room added to his voice.

'Civic dignitaries help to give us some status,' he said. 'Their presence reminds us of our worth. It's not all lysol and carbolic.'

He was quick to register Tasker's interest in the enlarged photograph of Alderman Llew, the current Chairman of the Guardians, in his robes of office as a former Mayor of the Borough of Pendraw. Tasker studied the lachrymose eyes that stared back at him suspiciously. Below a thin mouth, a white beard had been trimmed to enlarge the man's chin and curled upwards with a curling tongs.

'A relic of his more public days,' Meredith said. 'Now he cherishes the shadows. You've met him, I take it, Mr Thomas?'

'Only briefly,' Tasker said. 'I heard his wife had been unwell. I went up to the house but I failed to see the lady.'

Meredith pursed his lips and shook his head.

'His secret cross,' he said.

The dark whisper reverberated in the deserted Board Room.

'I'll say no more. But he has enemies in this town, Mr Thomas who will use anything against him. Anything.'

Meredith's lips twisted as he emphasised the word.

'That Doctor DSO, DSO or not, will stop at nothing. He is what we in Llanelli in the old days used to call an Intestinal Inquisitor.'

He smiled rigidly as he waited for Tasker to be amused by the phrase. He was disappointed to observe that his visitor had barely heard it. The man had lifted his gaze to the ceiling as if he were preparing to tune in to the melodies of an invisible world. Meredith leaned closer to make an intuitive, empathetic lunge towards a more intimate level of communication.

'I'll admit this to you, Mr Thomas. My true vocation is music.'

Tasker made an effort to listen sympathetically.

'As you know, Mr Thomas,' Meredith said. 'I officiate at the organ at Engedi on alternate Sundays throughout the winter months.'

His fingers began to move to demonstrate his unquenchable urge to play.

'But it isn't enough. This office I hold requires dedication that can be hard on a man sometimes.'

This sentiment in itself was sufficient to remind him of yet another aspect of duty. He fumbled in his pocket for a referee's whistle which he placed briefly between his lips as if to rehearse the action of blowing it.

'Excuse me, Mr Thomas. Only a moment.'

He rushed out to the verandah between the Board Room and the office. He left the door so that the visitor could continue to observe the perfect way in which the Master ran the institution. He blew three piercing blasts on the whistle. In no time Tasker Thomas could hear the crunch of running feet on the gravel. There was a race between two of the younger women to do his bidding. A fat girl came into view panting with triumph and pushing back her unsuccessful rival.

'It's me, sir.'

She looked up eagerly at the Master.

'Alice. You go down to the kitchen gardens. Ask John Jones for two nice lettuce. For the Master's table. And two thin shallots. He knows how I like them. And something from the greenhouse. And a nice bunch of fresh flowers. See how quick you can be. The rest of you get on with your work.'

The Master paused to survey his domain with a careful frown before he returned to attend to his guest.

He was disturbed to discover Tasker sitting comfortably in the armchair at the head of the table reserved for the Chairman of the Board of Guardians. He filled it with so much quiet authority that the Master was temporarily induced to accept him in that role.

'Mr Meredith,' Tasker said with a great benevolence. 'You and I must collaborate. Co-operate for the good of the community.'

Tasker's powerful forearms rested on the green baize with an immovable confidence that could be enjoyed only by a man with vital contacts in high places. Cautiously, Meredith sat himself down at the other end of the long table. He bent forward to partake of a friendly exchange.

'Forgive my curiosity, Mr Thomas. Please don't mind me asking. But aren't you related to the Iscoed family?'

Meredith pronounced the name of the wealthy family with a proper degree of awe.

'Only distantly. Very distantly. Very distantly. My maternal grandfather and the first Lord Iscoed were first cousins.'

'Well, there you are.'

Meredith spoke as though he had proved something of value to his own satisfaction.

'If all wealthy people were only half as devoted to good works, this country would be a far better place.'

He was pleased with his summing up.

'And if I could ask you something else . . .'

Meredith leaned confidentially over the table.

'Miss Parry from the County School. She has an excellent mezzo voice by the way. Was she not some kind of secretary to the Honourable Eirwen Iscoed?'

'I believe she was.'

Tasker straightened in his chair. He made it clear this was not the line he wished their discussion to follow.

'The need for a Cottage Hospital,' Tasker said.

Meredith immediately began to shake his head.

119

'Not here,' he said. 'Not here.'

'Well, that's the problem I would like to discuss with you,' Tasker said. 'There is a strong current of opinion in favour of converting the Casual Wing of this establishment.'

'It wouldn't work. It wouldn't work.'

Meredith was growing more heatedly vehement.

'Now that's exactly the kind of information we need. You are in a very strong position, Mr Meredith. Now shall I tell you what I would suggest? Prepare a paper. Cool and logical. Setting out the objections. Number them in order of importance. If you need any help in drafting the document I would be only too pleased to help. Now that will clear the air. We must have these things well out in the open. Then we can move ahead with our search for an alternative site. I can say this, Mr Meredith, without betraying a confidence. The Iscoed family are interested. I can say no more than that at the moment. Except to add that I am hopeful of diverting a small tributary to the great river of their benevolence in the direction of helping to establish a much needed Cottage Hospital for Pendraw and the surrounding district.'

'Are you really?'

The information had a calming effect on the Master of the Workhouse. He was able to show that he was deeply impressed.

'Collaboration,' Tasker said. 'We must make that our watchword!'

'Collaboration.'

Mr Meredith repeated the word like an incantation.

'There is a new spirit abroad in our little town,' Tasker said. 'One cannot but feel it. Anything can happen. Mighty works of the spirit occur when the wind of heaven blows.'

Meredith listened eagerly. Where there was fresh information to be gleaned, he was ready to be first in the field.

'Now in this generation I firmly believe the spirit will express itself through social channels. In that unpolitical and unscientific sense, you could call me a socialist.'

'Ah yes.' Meredith wagged his finger to show how much he enjoyed the subtle distinctions.

'But the denominations must wake up,' Tasker said. 'They

must keep their lamps trimmed and full of oil or they will be caught napping.'

'Absolutely.'

Meredith was in complete agreement.

'That's something I've often said myself, Mr Thomas. We have to keep up with the times.'

Tasker placed his hands on the table and rose to his feet. The main purpose of his visit was at an end.

'We understand each other,' he said.

The Master repeated the phrase like a password.

'We understand each other, Mr Thomas.'

Before they passed through the doorway Tasker paused and laid his hand lightly on Meredith's shoulder.

'You have a very gifted son, my friend,' he said.

The Master smiled broadly as though he were receiving a prize. Then he saw an opportunity of making a light-hearted joke.

'We are a gifted family, Mr Thomas,' he said. 'Shall we put it that way?'

'I'm sure you would agree that he has particular talents that should be encouraged.'

'Agreed. Agreed.'

It was a generalisation to which Meredith could see no immediate objection. Tasker was closing his eyes tightly as he sought for more specific inspiration.

'We live in an increasingly materialistic world,' he said. 'And an increasingly competitive world. I sometimes feel in this little country of ours we use up valuable spiritual substance in excessive competition. It's a grave weakness of the Eisteddfod if I may venture to say so. And of the education system. Too much competition can give rise to greed for material success and petty glory and a corresponding fear of failure. Do you see what I mean?'

Mr Meredith looked a little impatient as he nodded. He waited to learn what these theories had to do with the future of his only son.

'Too much greed and too much fear and what kind of a Wales and what kind of a world will we have on our hands, Mr Meredith? Now your son is possessed with the powerful combination of high ideals and artistic talent.'

'We have never had to force him,' the Master said. 'Never. Mind you, I'm not saying there weren't moments when I had to keep his nose on the grindstone. His mother would never have done that you see. Much too soft-hearted.'

Tasker's shoulders lifted as he prepared to take the next hurdle.

'The real feat, the real triumph,' he said, 'is to hang on to those high ideals and not lose them in the struggle to reach the top. Now Eddie understands that. And that is why it is so important for him to meet and work with people of like mind, of shared ideals, in other lands. Now then, dear friend, why not allow the young man to travel to Berlin? Pastor Otto is a good friend of mine. He'll do everything he can to help keep Eddie's expenses to a minimum.'

'Berlin.'

The word seemed to stick in the Master's throat.

'Germans.'

These were names to forget, not to repeat.

'I fought them,' H. M. Meredith said. 'I fought them for two and a half years.'

He stared wide-eyed at Tasker Thomas. He could not forget the unsparing efforts that grey enemy had made to kill him. Tasker made a great effort to sweep aside all doubts.

'But links like these with Pastor Otto will make sure all that will never happen again.'

'Germany.' As he uttered the word, the Master seemed to be witnessing all over again the forces of the most powerful industrial state in the world being mobilised for the express purpose of killing him or maiming him for life.

'When I think of the comrades I lost,' he said.

'That's just it, comrade!' Tasker said. 'I was in it too, you know. We must stretch out the hand of friendship and creative good will and make sure it will never happen again. Think of your Eddie as an ambassador of the gospel of good will, going out to make the world a finer place to live in. "And whosoever shall compel thee to go a mile, go with him twain".'

Meredith's head bent under the impact of such a combination of scriptural injunction and progressive thought. When he raised it, he had quietly shifted his ground.

'He has the latest ideals,' Meredith said. 'I have to agree with you there. With the speed of change it isn't easy for men like me brought up in a hard school to keep up with the ways of modern times. But to be truthful, our Eddie is also a little spoilt. And I can tell you why. In so many words. His mother and I always felt we had to indulge him a little to make up for bringing him up in a Workhouse. Our home was confined by the walls of this institution and we didn't want him to think of it as a prison. So we erred if anything in the opposite direction. So as a result and we are to blame to some extent he has grown up clever but also in some ways selfish and unregarding. Also to some extent I blame that high wall.'

The Master stood on the verandah pointing at the wall at the end of the courtyard.

'I'm not up in psychology and that sort of thing but I have heard Eddie say himself that when he was a boy he always wanted to escape over that wall.'

Tasker pressed his hands together in a manner reminiscent of a Hindu greeting.

'Dear brother,' he said. 'Will you let him go?'

They walked solemnly side by side across the courtyard. For a brief moment Isaacs bach's small figure appeared at the end of his length of territory at the corner of the building. He leaned forward on his large rake in an attempt to overhear what those set in authority over him were saying.

'With your blessing,' Tasker said.

Meredith clenched his fists behind his back.

'You are most persuasive, Mr Thomas,' he said. 'And don't think I am ungrateful for the interest you are taking in the boy. It does a father's heart good to see men like yourself ready to help our young along to a better understanding of this troubled world of ours. Next year.'

He pronounced the two words generously. Tasker looked puzzled.

'Not this year, but next year perhaps. When he has proved himself at Oxford, you see. And when he has proved that he is mature enough to go his own way.'

Tasker looked disturbed and disappointed. 'He was looking forward to it so much,' he said.

'And besides,' Meredith said. 'I haven't brought this up.

123

But Nel, you know, is in delicate health. And she is dead set against him going. Put it like this. Can I allow my son to break his mother's heart?'

Meredith pressed his fist triumphantly into his chest. Tasker was at a loss to find an adequate response to his question. Suddenly the Master turned his head. He caught Isaacs watching them before the little man could shift out of sight. The Master's ear remained cocked until he heard the noise of the rake scraping the gravel.

13

The late afternoon sun sent a flood of elegiac light through the War-memorial window at the end of the school hall. The stained glass depicted idealised figures in khaki uniform contemplating an angel of victory around whose feet *Dulce et decorum est pro patria mori* was painted in the artist's idea of Celtic lettering. The dais served as a narrow stage on which senior pupils in borrowed gowns were rehearsing a morality play under the benevolent supervision of Mr Samwell the Welsh master. From the rear of the hall, Amy watched him lean his leather-patched elbows on a window sill above a cold radiator and suck away wisely at his empty briar pipe while the cast went on repeating their lines. Under the stained glass they fidgeted inside positions they were meant to hold with allegorical stiffness. The girl playing Miss Truthful Conscience had a particularly monotonous voice; it suggested resignation rather than accusation.

'The bitterest sorrow in life, dull creature
Is to forfeit your soul through the flaw in your nature!'

Mr Samwell took his briar pipe out of his mouth to smile, examine the bowl, sniff at it briefly, before tucking it away, bowl upwards into the breast pocket of his tweed jacket. He was inclined to divide his attention between the players and

Miss Amy Parry. The play had been edited and adapted by John Cilydd More, but it remained difficult to present with inexperienced schoolchildren. Although Amy's function was to help with the songs which occurred at intervals throughout the play, Mr Samwell was grateful for her moral support and eager to accept any production suggestions she might feel inclined to make.

'Heads are my trophies!'

A sudden bass roar from the dais enlivened the proceedings. The head of a gangling youth who had long been crouched behind the upright piano waiting for his cue, shot into view. He was King Death in the play and had been allotted the part by virtue of his deep bass voice.

'Heads are my trophies! And none can withstand me.
Rich men, poor men, all fall before me!'

Mistress Truthful Conscience began to giggle. She blushed as though she had broken wind and covered her mouth with her fingers. The giggling fit fanned out among the rest of the cast. The figures shook in their appointed stations as though they were about to collapse from some defect in their inner structure. Mr Samwell reached for his pipe and pointed at them accusingly.

'Look here,' he said. He had a soft agreeable voice that suggested some reluctance at any time to exercise authority. 'We can't have the whole cast giggling every time King Death shows up. It simply won't do. Will it, Miss Parry?'

He turned to gain Amy's support for his gentle strictures. He was smiling and she smiled, and this allowed all the players including King Death himself to burst out laughing. Mr Samwell glanced at his pocket watch.

'Well, I think we can leave it there for today,' he said. 'You have all learnt your lines very well, haven't they, Miss Parry?'

Amy felt obliged to speak. She paced easily up the block floor carrying the script of the play behind her back.

'The songs are coming along well,' she said.

'Good. Good.'

Mr Samwell beamed at her appreciatively. He was about to wave his hand when Amy said: 'If I could see the Miser and the Miser's Wife, Monday dinner-hour. Here in the Hall.'

When she had finished, Mr Samwell completed his wave and the cast dispersed. The King of Death nodded cheerfully at his teachers as he took long strides across the hall. He had a small head on a long body and a heap of red hair made him even taller. When he smiled he screwed up his eyes behind the thick lenses of his spectacles and a row of bad teeth came into view.

'Good casting there,' Mr Samwell said.

He was inclined to make this kind of gnomic utterance under his breath. Amy encouraged him to speak his mind more plainly.

'Why do you say that, Mr Samwell?'

'King Death.'

He spoke more freely when he heard the clatter of the boy's heavy boots grow distant in the corridor.

'Two of his uncles hanged themselves.'

Amy grimaced disapprovingly. In case she should think his remark in bad taste, Mr Samwell launched out on an exposition of the youth's family background.

'Now is it an inherited tendency or is it a by-product of an environment of agricultural depression?' he said. 'Does one form of depression exacerbate the other? There are families that can manage quite happily on remote farms among the peat bogs. There are others quite a lot better off materially who seem to succumb to a rash of suicide. Yet another facet of the old problem of nature and nurture.'

Mr Samwell tapped his teeth contentedly with the stem of his pipe. Talking to Amy was an agreeable exercise he was happy to prolong.

'It's the system surely,' Amy said.

He was instantly attentive to any opinion she would care to express.

'People put up with things, instead of doing something to change them,' she said.

She took off her graduate gown. Underneath she was wearing a smart but severely cut brown dress. As though to delay her departure Mr Samwell pointed his pipe at the deserted dais.

'Difficult stuff for children, isn't it?'

Amy stared at the narrow acting area.

'So little room up there,' she said. 'So little room for action.'

Mr Samwell looked at her anxiously.

'It's too static you mean? Do you think I should get John Cilydd More to come and take a look? After all, it is his version.'

'I don't know,' Amy said. 'It's very wordy. Perhaps if he cut some more it might help.'

'Ah.'

He spoke as though she had reminded him of something.

'What are these "Interludes" when all is said and done?' he said. 'Nothing more or less than dramatised sermons. Well, now it is my opinion for what it is worth that in this modern age, people are losing the taste for sermons. Regrettable in my view. But we have to face the facts. So what we are doing is a museum piece in more than one sense. But the Head is very keen on it. And so is Mrs Pierce.'

The mere mention of the headmaster's wife was sufficient to make them both smile.

'He persuaded her you see,' Mr Samwell said, 'that it would be a feather in the school's cultural cap if we put on a little known eighteenth-century piece. With the earthier bits taken out of course. I told him it would be the first performance in two hundred years. Not that I could be one hundred percent certain, but he wouldn't know any better.'

Mr Samwell was very pleased with his humorous comment. Amy was listening to him patiently and he had every reason to believe she was enjoying their conversation. In the corridor they would have to go their separate ways. The men's staff-room and the women's were at opposite ends of the school building.

'Oh, by the way.'

Mr Samwell paused in his progress. He raised his voice.

'Our Sunday School outing is going to Llanelw next month,' he said.

His voice echoed in the empty corridor. Amy turned politely to listen.

'I believe that is your home town,' Mr Samwell said.

He felt in his pocket for his pipe.

'And Mrs More's of course.'

'Well, we both went to school there,' Amy said.

'The trip is on a Saturday,' Mr Samwell said. 'If you would care for a seat in the charabanc, and Mrs More of course, if she feels up to it, I would be happy to arrange it. I'm Superintendent of the Sunday School this year for my sins. As you know we Baptists are a small denomination here in Pendraw. There will be plenty of room in the bus. It's cheap too. And it would give you a whole day at home.'

'It's very kind of you to think of us, Mr Samwell.'

Her hesitation had begun to embarrass him. His pipe was in his hand and he waved it in a display of benevolent disinterest. He was no more than a thoughtful colleague, naturally inclined to consider the welfare of a young member of the staff. They heard loud footsteps. Mr Samwell turned to see the boy who played the King of Death approaching.

'What is it, William Henry?'

For once he seemed glad to exercise schoolmasterly authority. The boy waved a long arm towards Amy.

'Miss Parry,' he said breathlessly. 'There's a man at the top of the yard with a van. He's asking for you.'

'For me?'

Amy reacted with weary disbelief. She was a conscientious teacher with many unexpected calls on her attention: but this was late on a Friday afternoon after a strenuous school week.

'He's from the South, Miss. Come all the way in that van, I shouldn't wonder. I said I'd do my best to find you.'

Amy became aware how closely she was being observed by both colleague and pupil. In the pale light of the corridor her cheeks grew red. They were openly thirsting for some explanation. She had sufficient self-control not to supply one. They would never presume to put their curiosity into words. On the other hand if she wished to preserve the exalted image she enjoyed in the school, some explanation had better be forthcoming.

'Ah,' Amy said, as if a sudden solution had presented itself. 'It could be my cousin. He attends *Coleg y Castell* sometimes. For conferences and meetings.'

Mr Samwell was ready to learn more, even if it were only about the nature of the conferences in *Coleg y Castell*, but Amy was already pressing an eager William Henry into service.

'Would you take these things up to the Women's Staff Room for me, William Henry? And my gown? Would you be so kind?'

William Henry was only too happy to oblige her. He galloped off down the corridor and they could hear his heavy boots clambering up the distant flights of stairs. Amy twitched the cuffs of her smart but severely cut dress. Mr Samwell watched her with open admiration.

'As I say,' he said. 'There would be a seat for you on the bus if you wanted one.'

'Thank you Mr Samwell,' Amy said. 'It's very kind of you to think of me.'

'If you could let me know,' he said.

He was apologetic for detaining her. Her departure would leave the school corridor unbearably empty.

'I shall have to close the list by Monday week.'

Outside Amy stood blinking in the brilliant sunshine. She was taken aback to see a butcher's van parked alongside the new bicycle shed. In the bright light she could make out bloodstains that had not been washed away since the van's most recent visit to the slaughterhouse. Above it the white stencilled lettering *J. A. Bevan. Family Butcher, Hendrerhys, Glam.* was clearly legible from a distance. At first she could see no sign of Pen. She discovered him seated on the running board leaning against the high mudguard, enjoying a cigarette and quietly observing the school caretaker's wife taking her washing down from the clothes line strung across their kitchen garden. She was a well built woman and plainly curious about him and his van. When Amy approached he transferred his gaze to the cromlech that stood conspicuously in the field above the school, surrounded by gorse.

'What on earth's this?'

Amy smiled as she made her blunt enquiry. The caretaker's wife picked up her clothes basket and bestowed a sly smile upon them both before she retreated around the house to her back kitchen.

'Transport,' Pen said.

They were free spirits who could dispense with the irksome trappings of formal behaviour. To be frank and spontaneous seemed essential to their relationship. Pen folded his powerful arms and pointed his cigarette in the direction of the cromlech.

'Funny old place, this,' he said. 'Doesn't seem part of the real world at all. On the outside of everything. Left behind by History.'

'Is that what you think?' Amy appeared confident and self-possessed. 'Is that what you think of us?'

'Aye.'

He grinned and stretched himself before he threw away his cigarette and concentrated on appreciating her person.

'Theoretically,' he said. 'Dialectically, that is.'

'Why do you bother to come here then?' she said.

'I've come for you,' he said.

He stood up. His loose fitting double-breasted suit was heavily creased by the journey. His black hair that had been so carefully brushed and brilliantined that morning was now just sticky enough to preserve a film of dust like a record of his long journey. He spread his hands over the red shirt he was wearing. A refraction of light as he moved made his eyes green and luminous and as purposeful as a cat's: any state of inaction was no more than a preparation for attack. His presence pleased and disturbed her.

'Me?' she said.

'Why didn't you answer my letter?'

The touch of urgency brought a gravel edge to his voice. He would have liked to speak at length but there was no time to be eloquent.

Amy had no immediate excuse ready. She moved back when he came too near her.

'I've told you,' she said. 'You must give me time.'

'That's one thing we haven't got,' Pen said.

His dogmatism annoyed her.

'You are always saying things like that,' she said. 'Nothing is ever that simple, I can tell you.'

He was determined and relentless.

'Oh yes it is,' he said. 'In the world as it is, it's about the only thing that is. You're the woman I want. And I'm the man you want.'

'For God's sake,' Amy said. 'Keep your voice down.'

There were a few pupils still about, late making their way home. William Henry raised his hand in a cheerful wave.

'I have a position here,' Amy said.

Mr Samwell was crossing the yard to collect his bicycle. Amy turned and squinted at the sky above the cromlech so that she would not be obliged to acknowledge Mr Samwell. He was wearing a neat hat, a belted raincoat and carried a small leather attache case that looked potentially important. His bicycle clips were already in place above his ankles.

'A position,' Pen said. He seemed to find the word amusing. 'Lying down or standing up?'

As he wheeled his bicycle away, Mr Samwell raised his hat gravely to Amy although she was not looking at him.

'Who's that?' Pen said. 'What's he got in that bag? Packets of tea samples?'

Amy resented his attitude.

'What you don't realise, Pen Lewis, is that this is a very tightly knit community. Just like your precious valleys.'

'Oh, I know all about that,' Pen said.

'No you don't.'

Amy raised her voice angrily.

'You like to think you know everything,' she said. 'But you don't. I said tightly knit, not close knit. There's that to begin with. And my position is exposed enough as it is.'

'Peace and all that?' Pen said. 'Old Tasker's stuff. And Val Gwyn's romantic nationalism. Waiting for Owain Glyndwr to turn up.'

'There are plenty of people in this town absolutely aching to find fault with me,' Amy said.

'Well, you don't want to lose any sleep about a little thing like that, do you?'

'It's not a little thing,' Amy said. 'Not to me. It's my career and it's my life.'

She had turned to stare at the van in a way that suggested she had taken a deep dislike to it. Her attitude as much as what she was saying at last made him uneasy.

'Don't let's start misunderstanding each other,' he said. 'There's not time for that.'

'There is time,' Amy said. 'There is time. I'm not going to let you rush me.'

'It's no life for a healthy and intelligent young woman to be stuck in a backwater like this. That's all I'm telling you.'

He smiled but Amy did not respond. Her arms were folded tightly across her stomach like an additional form of restraint that would prevent her from uttering bitter and hurtful words that could never be retracted. Pen became more conscious of her predicament. He tried to wipe away a smudge of oil on his cheek with the back of his hand.

'Is there somewhere we could go?' he said. 'I'm parched for a cup of tea.'

Amy looked again at the van. The machine was not only an embarrassment, it was an emblem of devotion. She began to take into account the effort he had made to drive all the way from the South just to see her. She smiled slowly.

'What am I going to do with you?' she said.

He grinned at her happily.

'Do you need me to tell you?' he said.

'You are my cousin,' Amy said.

'Am I hell, I'll tell you what I am.'

He reached out an arm to grab her impatiently. She stepped back nimbly out of his reach.

'That woman's looking,' Amy said. 'From the bedroom window.'

'That's somewhere I would like to be, I can tell you,' Pen said.

'We'll go down to my digs,' Amy said. 'Mrs Rossett will make my cousin one of her high teas. She's marvellous on cakes and scones.'

Her spirits rose as she took charge of the situation.

'Then you can rest,' she said. 'After your long journey. While I decide what to do with you.'

'Me?'

Pen frowned and shaded his eyes against the light.

'Who can I ask to put my cousin up for the night. It's a ticklish question.'

'You don't have to bother about that,' Pen said. 'I can sleep in the van.'

'There's plenty of room in Marine Terrace,' Amy said. 'In Cilydd and Enid's house. But I can't tell lies to them. Enid writes long letters to Val. And Val knows you're not my cousin, to say the least of it.'

'Why tell lies at all?' Pen said. 'Everybody's got to know about us sooner or later.'

Amy closed her eyes.

'If only things were as simple as you seem to find them,' she said. 'What a wonderful world we'd be living in.'

Amy's nose wrinkled fastidiously as she opened the rear door and peered into the dark interior of the van. It was empty except for Pen's kit-bag and bedding.

'I can smell meat,' Amy said.

'What the hell do you expect in a butcher's van? I tell you, I can sleep in there. I've slept in much worse places.'

'I've got a meeting at half-past seven,' Amy said.

'A meeting?' He looked dismayed.

A note of teasing crept into her voice.

'Oh we have meetings too you know. Not as important as yours of course. But they occur all the time. Even in a backwater.'

'Do you have to go, Amy? Do you?'

He was relieved when she rewarded him with a smile of calculated benevolence.

'Let's feed you first,' she said. 'You look very hungry.'

14

Amy held Pen's head between her hands and brought her lips close to his ear.

'Lie still,' she said. 'Just lie still on me.'

She held her breath to listen for the smallest sound. In the scullery Mrs Rossett's cat was miaowing disconsolately, wanting to be let out. The rest of the house was silent. Pen's body lay between her thighs. To relieve her of as much of his weight as he could he gripped the grotesquely carved mahogany arms of the chair in which she was sitting. The remains of their high tea had not been cleared away. One scone lay unclaimed on the grease stained paper doily. Mrs Rossett's second-best china was edged in deep blue. Uncosied, the teapot was enthroned on a stand of oriental design. Above the starched white cloth the spout surveyed the debris of a modest feast with a glazed calm. Mrs Rossett herself had departed on some errand of her own, but there was no telling when she might return.

'Lie still, Pen.'

'That's easier said than done,' Pen said. 'For cousins with an inclination towards incest.'

Amy began to shake with the effort of suppressing her laughter. Pen moved his head and opened an eye wide to inspect the ornate sideboard against the wall. It was loaded with ornaments, photographs in silver frames and in the centre a bowl of wax fruit under a glass dome.

'What a place . . .'

He slid down so that his head rested in her lap. Amy could barely hear the things he muttered, but she smiled happily at the sound of his voice.

'To think of you living in this petty bourgeois mausoleum. I wouldn't keep a parrot in a place like this, I can tell you. Not to mention a canary. Are you going to take these off?'

'No. I'm not.'

Pen made a noise of comic discontent.

'I must be the biggest bloody fool north of Nantyglo. Roaming all over Wales like a love-sick gibbering adolescent in a bloody butcher's van. And for what? Would you like to tell me?'

Amy ran her fingers gently through his black hair.

'To be near me. Just be content with nearness. Just for now.'

'I suppose this is what they call love. Bloody hell. Driving two hundred bumpy bloody miles in order to grovel at Amy Parry's feet. I must be out of my mind.'

Amy laughed aloud and then checked herself to listen

again for any sound in the house. Relieved at the total silence she began to stroke his head again.

'I ought to wash your hair,' she said. 'And scrub your back while I'm at it. Like a collier's wife.'

Pen sat up to look at her.

'Well, damn,' he said. 'That's all I'm asking, girl!'

Amy pulled down her dress and leaned forward to argue with him, her hands primly folded on her knees.

'But you're not a collier, are you? And you never will be if the Owners can help it. You're an unemployed agitator. Doesn't that sound terrible? Penry Lewis, the well known unemployed agitator from Cwmdu.'

'And part-time organiser if you please,' Pen said. 'Let's have a bit of respect due to rank, shall we? A key role I may add. So what the hell am I doing sitting on my arse on the floor of a petty bourgeois parlour in petty bourgeois Pendraw?'

'Making love to me,' Amy said.

He raised his eyebrows and looked around the room with sceptical disdain.

'This place has been deliberately designed to make the human body feel incapable of copulation. Just look at it! The sideboard nudges the table and the table nudges the chair and the chair turns my legs into mahogany pit props.'

He pulled a face to show how stiff he was. Laughing gaily, Amy helped him to his feet. He took hold of her, feeling her shape with both hands to make her understand that it restored his waning belief in his own physical being.

'Oh,' he said. 'The demands I want to make on you, Madame Amy. Oh the demands, my pretty, the demands.'

Amy held on to his arms to restrain him.

'Okay,' he said. 'Okay. Over and above sexual ones. We belong together. Two halves of one whole as they say. What is the logic of physical desire, sweetheart? Practical love.'

'Now be calm, Pen.'

'I am being calm, damn it! Practical love extends itself into a Life Invention with capital letters with or without capital. I'm not going to be modest. Not with you in my arms. We are going to transform the whole wide world!'

'Is that all?'

He resented the way she was grinning at him. He detached himself from her, making her sit in the armchair so that she could follow his argument more closely.

'Now you listen to me. This rotten capitalist system is about to fall to bits. I'm convinced of it. And when that happens, they're going to turn very nasty. Get it? Now the trick is that we get nasty with them first. The socialist revolution has got to be just round the corner and ready to pounce. And the first lot to pounce will be the organised unemployed and their spearhead will be the party of the proletariat. That's why the South is so bloody vital and important and why this petrified parlourised backwater counts for bugger all. Can you see that?'

Amy offered no answer. She frowned as she considered deeply what he was saying and her lips pouted like a child's. Looking at her, Pen restrained his own customary flow of eloquence in order to make an effort to understand what she could be feeling.

'I know you like your job. Or like to hold a job of your own anyway. I appreciate that. I really do. You're a girl who likes to stand on her own two feet and I love you for it. I must do, mustn't I? Or I would be attending a co-ordinating committee in Newport at this moment instead of grovelling here in front of you.'

'Grovel?' Amy said. 'I like that. You wouldn't know how to.'

Pen had begun to pace the confined space in front of the fireplace. When the hearthrug got in his way, he kicked it angrily as if it were an objectionable domestic animal. He would abandon the pleasure of theoretical discourse in order to present Amy Parry with what he considered the most desirable course of action they could take.

'Now get this, Amy. I'm not asking you to put your pretty little head on a block. Or make any sacrifice at all. Far from it. By Christ, the future I am offering you is positively respectable. Now listen.'

Pen paused as though he were about to reveal secret information.

'We've forged a new link with Labour.'

Amy was swift with her comment.

'My goodness,' she said. 'I thought they were the enemy. Tammany Hall and all that.'

'Listen. Let me tell you something. Politics is about interests, not morals. If it could help to bring the revolution sooner, I'd make a pact with Old Nick himself. But that's not the point at issue, comrade. I've got my little Labour link, and he owes me one bloody great favour. And I'm going to collect. A job for you.'

Amy sounded deeply shocked.

'Pen Lewis! That's terrible.'

'Little creep wants to get into Parliament. Can't sleep at night longing for it. Tea on the terrace. Winding up Big Ben. I'm going to put him in the Talking shop. So he can go to sleep in the bosom of the mother of parliaments. What's wrong with that?'

'I'm not joking, Pen.'

'Neither am I. Interests not morals. Remember?'

'But surely a creature like that represents everything we're fighting against. Canvassing. Corruption. All that sort of thing.'

'Who's "we"?'

Pen sat at the oval table and smoothed the cloth with the palm of his hand.

'Val, for example,' Amy said.

Pen sighed briefly.

'Yes,' he said. 'Poor old Val.'

He saw how angry Amy looked and raised a hand to pacify her.

'No,' he said. 'I mean it. He's a fine chap. Really nice. No, I mean it. But you could fill a charabanc with nice chaps and drive them straight over the edge of a cliff.'

'It's not so long ago he wrote a marvellous article about it.'

Amy lowered her head. She looked distressed. Pen screwed up his eyes and shook his head as he pondered how he could best distract her. He put the last scone in his mouth and tried heavy handed humour.

'I think it's time I took your political education in hand.'

'My education?' Amy pointed indignantly at herself as though her B.A. degree was pinned to her dress.

'Oh aye.'

137

He smiled at her cheerfully.

'You've been wrapped up in this Welsh language cocoon, see? Like a pretty little pupa. If that's the right term. An arrested stage of development is what it amounts to. Not your fault but it means you've never had a chance to understand the real world ... What's the matter?'

A cloud of vexation was almost visible around Amy's head.

'I don't like being lectured to,' she said.

Pen slapped the palm of his hand on the tablecloth.

'Aye,' he said. 'Well, who does if it comes to that?'

Amy did not respond to his attempt to be jolly. The silence became so complete, they could hear a grandfather clock ticking in the next room. Pen rubbed the surface of the cloth with his finger. He seemed conscious of time passing and the difficulty of what he could say next. He sighed and then muttered gloomily.

'I suppose it's this Val business still, isn't it?'

Amy said nothing.

'I'm making a bloody mess of it, aren't I? It's because I'm crazy about you in a way I've never been about a woman before. That's why I'm making this extra effort to be honest. Can you see that?'

He was encouraged by the ghost of a forgiving smile on her face.

'I belong to Wales too, you know. To a real living Wales that's being wiped out by the bloody Tories and the City of London and bloody English capitalism at its worst. The Wales that really matters. All you've got up here is a fossilised zoo. A home for the aged and decrepit mixed up with a children's playground. Come on girl!'

Pen jumped to his feet.

'Listen, Amy. If the working class is going to inherit the earth in my lifetime, I want to be there. And I want you to be there with me. You've got to be there. Take the risks that have to be taken and learn what it is to be fully alive.'

He took her by both hands and jerked her to her feet.

'There's no other way of life worth living. Honestly.'

His passionate embrace set a seal on his argument. She held on gratefully to the strength of his body. With one eye open she caught a glimpse of herself in the sideboard mirror before she raised her head to receive his hungry kisses.

'Now listen, Amy,' he said. 'I might not have the guts to make this offer again. Listen, if there is any power element in our relationship . . . kid, you can have it all. I hand myself over to you, lock, stock and barrel.'

Amy's fingers stroked his cheek. Her tenderness seemed a combination of maternal concern and proprietory pride.

'Only one small reservation . . .' He smiled and kissed the tips of her fingers. 'Just remember that I have my little part to play in the proletarian revolution.'

'You old Red,' Amy said. 'You need a clean shirt. I'll wash this and iron it for you.'

'Oh, jiawch . . .' Pen laughed delightedly. 'You've got the April thesis, girl! "Time to cast off the soiled shirt . . . time to put on clean linen" . . .'

She had to struggle to release herself from his embrace when she heard Nathan Harris's penetrating voice at the front door.

'Pen,' she said. 'That's Mr Harris. Quick. Put a comb through your hair or something. Tidy yourself up, will you?'

She was already engaged in restoring her own appearance. Pen watched her appreciatively as she straightened her silk stockings and her dress.

'Come on,' she said. 'Don't just stand there.'

She examined herself carefully in the sideboard mirror. She knew how laboured Nathan Harris's movements were. There was time for her to open the door and meet him with a bright smile in the corridor.

'Hendrerhys! Hendrerhys!'

Nathan was uttering the name like an incantation. He left the front door so that he could admire the writing on the side of the van outside. He shuffled sideways to return Amy's smile.

'I know the place well,' he said to her. 'Preached many times at Penrhewl and Hebron, Hendrerhys. "Hebron afternoon and evening" Hebron people. The very salt of the earth, my dear. The warmth of them. The genuineness. In the face of all that adversity and wicked poverty . . . that tremendous unity of the spirit.'

139

'You haven't met my cousin, Mr Harris. Penry Lewis from Cwmdu.'

Nathan Harris's bones could almost be heard to creak as he made an effort to move quickly to Amy's room. Pen stood on the hearth rug with his hands in his pockets. He took them out to feel about for a packet of cigarettes. When he found one it was empty. He crushed it in his fist and turned around to consider tossing it into the cold fireplace.

'Cwmdu!' Nathan Harris said. 'I know it well. I was a minister in the South you see. I don't know whether Miss Parry told you?'

Amy whispered her brief explanation like an apology.

'I'm afraid he doesn't speak Welsh, Mr Harris.'

Speaking English, Nathan tried to sound sympathetic rather than critical.

'Oh the loss to that valley,' he said. 'It cuts me to the quick just to think of it. Think of the music locked up in those names! Hendrerhys, Pwll Hywel, Gelli Fynaches, Blaen-henwysg, Pwll Berw. The floor of the valley is paved with golden traditions. Every rivulet babbles in the old tongue and the feet of bards and patriots and true lovers of Cymraeg have trod every inch of those hills for generation after generation.'

'Aye, well...'

Pen grinned ruefully and crushed the cigarette packet smaller in his fist.

'We manage,' he said.

With quick sympathy Nathan adjusted himself to the young man's attitude.

'Well of course you do. Anyway, welcome to Pendraw, Mr Lewis. Welcome.'

Nathan was able to bow his head and raise his arms as a sketchy indication of the kind of graceful gesture he would like to have made.

'Could not have come at a better time, could he, Miss Parry?'

Nathan smiled roguishly and Amy did her best to conceal that she had no clear idea of what he was driving at. The minister was ready to take off on another flight of eloquence, this time in English. He seemed amused by the exercise himself, like a man who takes part in an unrehearsed charade as a gesture of good will towards a mixed assembly of family and strangers.

'The spirit of reformation is blowing through Pendraw! And it is a most exhilarating experience. I've never seen anything quite like it, to tell you the truth. And I can remember the Revival mark you and that is close on thirty years ago. Before you were born, my children. It is like a Revival. But this time on a very practical level. Practical Christianity, you could call it. A spirit of willing co-operation in every sphere. And our Miss Parry bless her. She is in the thick of it.'

Amy shook her head modestly. She lowered her head to avoid looking at Pen in the eye.

'I tell you, Mr Lewis, there are people working together in Pendraw these days that weren't even talking to each other last winter! Isn't that a fact, Miss Parry?'

'Yes it is.' Amy nodded a little too vigorously.

'And in a way, you see, it's dear old Tasker at the heart of it all! He has brought a new spirit into the place. You know like the voice that breathed o'er Eden, although I know that verges on metaphorical blasphemy. But you can feel the change in the air. Isn't that so, Miss Parry?'

'Oh yes.'

'I've never seen a man rise so nobly to a challenge. A new kind of minister, you see. Not a pulpit-bound old fogey like me you see, preaching out of force of habit. No. He's a man who leads by example. Shining example too. Have you met Tasker Thomas, Mr Lewis?'

Nathan spoke as though the first thing Amy should do would be to take a visiting relative to be introduced to the new hero of the community.

'Aye,' Pen said. 'I've met 'im. Crossed swords with 'im. Dialectically, you might say. At *Coleg y Castell*.'

'Oh?'

Nathan lengthened the exclamation as if to give his eyebrows time to rise to their maximum height.

'Is that so?'

'Pen is a socialist,' Amy said.

She made the explanation as tactfully as she could.

'Is he now?'

Nathan shut his eyes tight with an effort to recollection.

'What did that man say now, that English politician, what's his name? "We are all of us Socialists now."'

A smile spread over his face as the phrase came back to him.

'Yes,' Pen said. 'Well I'm a Communist, see. That's one better isn't it?'

Nathan observed him with deepening interest and a measure of disquiet.

'You have quite a following down there,' Nathan said. 'In Cwmdu and Hendrerhys.'

There was still a tinge of nostalgia in the way he uttered the place names.

'Moral leadership,' Pen said. 'That's what I'd call it. You take a lead, don't you? And then the masses follow.'

Nathan remained silent to consider the proposition before indicating that he could not fault it. Amy spoke.

'I'm taking Pen to see the sights, Mr Harris,' she said. 'Mrs Rossett has given us a lovely tea. I thought I'd take Penry to Glanrafon. Enid and Cilydd will be there.'

'Yes indeed. There's a family worth meeting.'

Nathan was eager to show his agreement. His sister had gone out and it was up to him to show the visitor every possible hospitality.

'Have you had enough to eat, Mr Lewis? Would you like something more?'

Pen smiled broadly and tried to catch Amy's eye.

'I call to mind the words of my old minister,' Nathan said, 'when his dear old Siân used to ask a guest if he would like another cup of tea,' Nathan raised an arm stiffly to mime a gesture of the old minister. "Don't ask, woman! Give!"'

He did it humorously enough to allow them all to find some relief from social tension in laughter.

'Now don't let me stand in your way. Off you go to enjoy the beauty of the evening. How is the Interlude going, Miss Parry? I'm looking forward so much to seeing it. Not a revolution, you see, Mr Lewis, but a revelation!'

He paused briefly to give Pen and Amy an opportunity to

appreciate his little joke. They stood awkwardly in the corridor waiting for him to finish talking.

'And maybe it is a revolution too. In its own small way. Thanks to Tasker. There's a creative spirit abroad you see that follows inevitably in the wake of that spirit of reform I was telling you about. But listen to me talking. Let me speed you on your way.'

He raised his arm as Amy and Pen went through the front door in a final salute to the word *Hendrerhys* blazoned on the side of the van.

'Shall I close the front door, Mr Harris?'

He nodded slowly. He could see Amy smiling in the warm sunlight and it was a sight he was loath to part with. He still wore his overcoat and outside it his scarf which was of exceptional width. It hung much lower on one side than the other. For a moment it appeared as though she might come back in to help him take off his coat.

Outside, Pen was engaged in cranking the starting-handle of the van. He jumped back with a curse as the engine misfired and Amy closed the door hastily. She could still hear the retired minister's voice as she climbed into the van. The parting benediction became wistful because of the distance it was obliged to travel.

'God bless you both!'

Pen found a cigarette. He lit it before concentrating on driving the van in the direction Amy pointed to. In the school playground across the road, two little children ran to the tall wire fence to see what was happening. Amy sat well back in her seat until they were clear of the town. The van was bound to attract attention: but only the most curious observer could make out who exactly it was sitting in the shadow of the interior. Twice Amy had to raise her hand to indicate which road they should take as they travelled westward. Once outside the town, she sat forward and gazed eagerly ahead ready to enjoy any adventure.

'It's not so bad, Pen, is it? At least it goes.'

The noise was so loud she had to pat the panel with her hand for him to understand it was the van she was talking about. To please and excite her he made it go as fast as it could. The van shook and rattled and the bonnet cover bounced up and down. Amy laughed and clapped her hands. He slowed down when he saw steam beginning to rise from the radiator. The reduction in the noise enabled them to talk to each other in loud voices.

'What was all that about reforming the town then?'

Amy was delighted by his curiosity. He smiled at her uncertainly, aware that she wanted to tease him.

'Made you sit up didn't it, comrade?'

'Well, it's difficult for a chap like me to tell with an old codger like that. I mean, is he speaking the truth or just exaggerating for effect? I mean, preachers do exaggerate, don't they?'

'It is true,' Amy said. 'Pendraw is in the grip of a reform movement. All sorts of things going on. The old Guard are powerless to stop it. Tasker Thomas will be the Man of the Hour.'

'They can't take him seriously, can they? In *Coleg y Castell*, most of us thought the man was a bit of a clown to tell you the truth.'

'He gets things done,' Amy said. 'And no sacrifice is too great for him. He sleeps in a hut at the bottom of the garden so that two families from the slum cottages can live in the Manse. Enid and John Cilydd want him to move into their house on Beach Road. Tasker says he will if the weather gets bad. There are people around who are beginning to call him a saint.'

Pen gripped the steering wheel tight and shook his head.

'They'll get him,' he said.

'Who's "they"?'

'The people who operate power. This is Liberal territory isn't it? They'll get him.'

'The Liberal Association is split down the middle,' Amy said.'

She spoke airily to demonstrate her knowledge of local politics.

'Well, that's it, isn't it? A temporary power vacuum filled in by a fakir. It's as simple as that. It's all irrelevant, see?'

He grinned at her happily. His confidence in his ability to read a political situation was fully restored.

144

'A temporary aberration. A throwback among a super-stitious people to tribalism and the power of the witch-doctor. That's what it is. Neither here nor there, Miss Parry, in an industrialised world. We've got more important things to think about.'

'Oh, have we?'

'Aye. You and me and the class war for a start. Hey, where are we going?'

They had come to a country cross roads. Guiltily Amy pressed her fingers below her lips.

'That's the way to Glanrafon,' she said.

She pointed back over her shoulders.

'I lied again. I'm not taking you there.'

She looked radiant, her eyes wide with youthful frankness.

'I don't want to go to Glanrafon. I want to be with you.'

Impulsively she laid her hand over his gripping the steering wheel. It was a form of compact.

'I want to show you somewhere special. A private place. Enid introduced me to it. Now I'll show it to you.'

'Which way then?'

He was as gruff as a man sworn never to be carried away by any fortuitous surge of emotion.

'Left,' Amy said. 'Couldn't be any other direction for you, could there, comrade Lewis?'

'Down there?'

Pen looked doubtfully at the surface of the lane. A high ridge of turf grew down the centre between two rough tracks.

'Don't worry. I'll show you where to leave Billy Bevan Butcher's van. Then I'll blindfold you and lead you by the hand through the woods.'

The steering wheel spun in Pen's hands as he struggled to reverse the intractable vehicle into a gateway overgrown with brambles. Amy stood in the lane with her hands behind her back, watching the tyres surmounting the exposed roots of a great sycamore tree. There was little she could do except observe the operation. When he switched off the shrieking engine, she sighed with relief and raised her hand to touch a branch of the sycamore which grew so low that it almost constituted a barrier to any traffic down the lane which led directly to a sandy cove. Pen looked for two large stones to block the rear wheels of the van. Amy passed through a broken gateway to take a path that led up into a dense wood. In the warmth of the evening a thrush was singing. She rested the palm of her hand against the sheen of a beech bole and lifted her head to listen. The thrush was taking advantage of the evening quiet to weave its elegant phrases through the tree tops. As much of the sky as was visible was a cloudless blue tinged with golden light. When he caught up with her, Pen had more to say about Tasker Thomas.

'I wiped the floor with him,' he said.

He saw Amy's head was raised looking for the where-abouts of the thrush. He pointed easily at the branch where it was perched and continued with the observation he had begun to make.

'For a so-called educated man, his reasoning powers were nil. So how can a man like that make his way in the political sphere? That's the point.'

He was slow to realise that they stood on the threshold of a private world and that she was offering to share it with him. There was wood sorrel nestling at his feet and not far from where they stood, a ragged azalea bush was in full bronze flower. They were at the end of a garden that had run wild. At the bottom of the dingle a thin stream made its way to the shore. On the opposite bank there was a tulip tree and more varieties of rhododendron and azalea. The path along which they walked was still black and damp with leaf mould in spite of the warm weather.

'Mysterious, isn't it?'

Amy fingered the tassels on the neck of her dress and spoke in a low voice. As he listened to the muted reverberation of her voice he seemed to appreciate how much she was the centre of it all. The slanting rays of the evening sun picked out a wide-eyed girl with gold hair in a pale dress, ready to lead him into the heart of a shady wood that was also a garden. When he touched her she took hold of both his hands.

'Do you want to hear the story?' she said.

She cradled his hands confidently in hers as if she derived particular pleasure from containing their strength.

'Up there, there was a big house. A mansion.'

146

Obediently Pen gazed at the barrier of well grown trees behind them. They towered above the narrow glen. Below they could hear the faint lapping of the tide inching through the rocks to reach the sandy cove. Like a little girl who plays at being a school teacher, Amy gave his hands a shake to gain his complete attention.

'This Englishwoman inherited a fortune and ran away with a sea captain from Cadlan. That's the next village down the coast. They lived for a while in Italy and then he chose this spot and they bought all the land and built a mansion and called it Porth Ceiriadog.'

'What's that supposed to mean?' Pen said.

He sounded critical and mildly impatient.

'Enid says it means "Beloved Bay" or something like that. Anyway for some reason, he went back to sea. Got bored I expect. And he was drowned. She was completely shattered, poor old thing and took to living like a recluse. Dressed all in black with a veil over her face and never went out. All she did was have a refuge built on each of the two islands just outside the bay. Every week she had servants row over to leave food and fresh water there for any possible shipwrecked mariners. They stopped doing it after she died because they said the stuff was encouraging the rat population and the rats were eating the puffin eggs. Sad, isn't it? Even before she died the house was falling into decay. They pulled it down a few years ago. But you can still see the walls of the kitchen garden. And the woods are gorgeous still. And the grotto's still there, where she used to sit on fine days and stare at the sea.'

He leaned over to kiss her lips almost negligently. He studied them in isolation as if he were at a loss to account for their colour and the attraction of their ripe youthful shape.

'You are not a bit sorry for her, are you?' Amy said.

She held him back from kissing her again. He grinned at her.

'Ask yourself where did all that money come from,' he said. 'The money to build that house. The fortune she inherited. The slave trade? A sugar plantation? Cotton mills?'

Amy was displeased with his manner and his matter of fact reaction.

'Money didn't stop her suffering, did it?'

She turned her back on the path to the ruined garden and began to saunter towards the sea shore. Pen followed her, taking off his jacket and swinging it over his shoulder. She spoke to him without turning round.

'You just don't believe in being romantic,' she said. 'On principle.'

'Put it this way,' he said. 'If religion is the opium of the people, romance is the candy floss.'

'I may as well not have bothered to bring you here.'

Amy sounded petulant in spite of herself.

'Oh, it's very nice,' Pen said.

'Nice!'

She turned to face him looking so fiercely beautiful that he smiled with pleasure. She spread out her arms inviting him to consider as much of the bay and the headland as had come into view. He did not take his eyes off her.

'We have everything here!' she said. 'And you should jolly well appreciate it! Islands. Ruins. Lighthouses. Castles. Gardens. Wishing wells. I mean, when the sun shines is there anywhere in the entire wide world to compare with it? Come on, you miserable *Hwntw*! Admit it.'

Beneath them the sandy cove was golden brown in the sunlight. The shallow tide was cool emerald as it crept in among the larger rocks nudging the lazy lengths of seaweed and leaving a curved line of speckled foam on the smooth edge of the sand. In the wood behind them the glitter of a small waterfall caught the low rays of the sun.

'Very nice indeed,' Pen said.

He dropped his jacket and folded her in his arms with elaborate care.

'But you've got to start with Reality, see.'

He gave her a gentle squeeze to emphasise the point.

'I'm serious about you. So I can't go wasting my precious time with romantic clap-trap. That stuff is just an extension of capitalist deception into the field of personal relationships. I mean that. It's the language you use to deceive people. I don't want to deceive you, do I? I want to tell you the truth.'

'Go on then. Tell me the Truth.'

Nursing her in his arms, he thought hard as he contemplated the view.

'Well, rhythm, isn't it?' He spoke softly, kissing her hair. 'The basis of everything. Matter and motion.'

'What about me?'

She deliberately made her voice small and childlike as if to represent the cry of a solitary living thing lost above a vast ocean of movement.

'Ah yes. You.' He kissed her lips with reverent care and then smiled. 'You are my external stimulus,' he said.

'Well thank you very much.'

She thumped his chest with the side of her clenched fist.

'That's very nice, I must say. I'm flattered beyond words.'

She half-laughed her protests when he picked her up, ready to carry her away. She pointed urgently at his jacket on the ground. He was strong enough to turn and bend his knees so that she could reach down and pick it up. Seized with a desire to make him laugh, she draped the jacket like a shawl over his head and drew it tight under his chin. In the shelter of the rocks closest to the trees he set her down as carefully as a child and knelt in front of her to regain his breath. When he recovered he spread himself over her deliberately exaggerating his masculine strength.

'Kidnap,' he said. 'That's what I had in mind. We should be half-way back to the South by now. Instead, here I am trapped on a Lotus Eater's Isle. Or cave. Or whatever it is. And it's all your fault. I hope you realise, Amy Parry, that you are messing up my life.'

'What about mine?'

She watched him calmly as he began to undress her.

'Aye, well, that's it, isn't it, kid?'

Pen seemed to be mocking his own accent and pushing aside any form of rational discussion as he concentrated on a more delicate task. He had folded his jacket to make a pillow for her head.

'What about mine? My life?'

Amy persisted in trying to talk. She lay still, but her eyes were not properly closed. There remained a critical edge to her submission which in itself inspired him to temper strength with tenderness. The tenacity of his collier's hands became the central expression of his love and devotion. They could soothe more effectively than his harsh voice. She could not question them. Her own fingers rested briefly on his belt, neither helping nor preventing him from unfastening it, but still faintly claiming some control over the process.

While it lasted, his love-making was a form of knowledge that seemed to offer new life for them both. He knew how to be gentle when that was all she wanted. He could husband his great strength. He knew how to relate the hardness of his own body to the softness of hers and how to use his power when she let him understand her overwhelming need to be mastered and possessed. So much intensity opened out a prospect of another level of existence where their natures would be transformed. At the very least something of one would for all time become part of the other. They mingled each other's names with unintelligible sounds so that ordinary terms of endearment became signals of profound understanding. The shadows of the rocks and the evening light had closed in upon them like a conspiracy of nature offering to hide their half-naked bodies. As her hands searched the contours of his body for the source of his strength a phrase took shape that seemed to bring her reassurance.

'It is beautiful, isn't it? It is beautiful, Pen?'

He remained silent. Her words were incantations to accompany the creation of a private world. The darkening headland thrust out to sea and the sound of her voice was like the restlessness of the waves that surrounded it, alive with the iridescent light of a sun just sunk below the horizon. Her hands caressed the shape of his head. She had to speak to keep at bay all thought that could threaten her exalted state.

'We could stay here for ever. Just the two of us. For ever. In our own world. Here. I mean it. For ever. Pen. I brought you here to give it to you. It is beautiful. Isn't it?'

She drew herself apart to make him more aware of their surroundings; to make him see the entire landscape as part of their ecstasy, recreated by the power of their love. Pleasantly exhausted, with his hands behind his head Pen studied the strange light on the sea.

'Aye, of course it is.'

He rolled over to consider the same glow of sunset on her face. His slow smile showed the depth of pleasure he found in exploring each detail.

'But it's you I'm after, kid. You know that, don't you?'

She began to shiver and he helped her dress with as much tender care as he undressed her. He placed his jacket over her shoulders. She clutched at him as though he were the only rock that could save her from being swept away.

'It's so beautiful,' she said. 'Why can't we live here for ever? Why not Pen?'

He was reluctant to accept the seriousness of her proposal. They walked together to the edge of the sea. They had to discuss their relationship on a rational basis. Whatever words they used would be weighed as heavily as rocks that could only sink to the floor of their consciousness and lie there immobile for ever.

'My work isn't here,' Pen said.

She clung to him refusing to let him move.

'Mine is. Mine is, Pen.'

She waited for his response. When she released her grip, he walked away, his hands deep in his pockets and his shoulders bent as he trod the soft margin of the sea. In the twilight the romantic landscape was being transformed into a configuration of obstacles, matter specifically designed to keep them apart. Salt tears welled up in her eyes, making her blink as though a sudden wind had sprung up over the sea. When she called out his name, a seagull flying high towards the edge of the headlands echoed the sound. When he turned to look at her he had become a dark figure in the distance, too far away for her to make out the expression on his face.

15

On an unseasonably cold evening the rain trickled down the long windows of the assembly hall at Pendraw. The warmth generated by the people crowded inside was clammy and comfortless. Not all the wooden seats were occupied because so many men preferred to stand or shift about in their damp raincoats in search of friends, acquaintances or any form of diversion. The chief speaker was long overdue. The platform was deserted. It was framed in a temporary proscenium arch which was still embellished with bedraggled mottos and emblems after a recent eisteddfod. Behind a battered table on the stage were ranged five empty chairs. Like a man who knows he is liable to be confronted by persons he would prefer to avoid than meet, John Cilydd shifted around the fringe of the assembly, his coat open, his hands in his jacket pockets and his hat still on his head. At the rear of the hall his uncle Gwilym seized him by the sleeve to eye him through pince-nez with an air of distinct disapproval.

'He's twenty-seven minutes late,' Uncle Gwilym said.

He consulted the gold watch secreted in the right hand lower pocket of his waistcoat.

'Don't blame me,' Cilydd said.

The hubbub of the hall allowed his uncle to ignore the comment.

'Now look who's here,' Uncle Gwilym said.

His elder brother Simon was poking his head in through the double doors. With one foot he held the door open as he took off his bowler hat and passed a gnarled hand over his bald pate. As a farmer and a countryman he could approach an urban convocation with the kind of detachment that only served to deepen his interest. He looked pleased to discover his brother and his nephew so conveniently at hand. Here was a place to set aside the sibling rivalries that governed their relationship when they met at Glanrafon in their mother's presence. Gwilym was widely known as Gwilym Glaslyn, a bardic name, and as the author of a weekly column in the local journal. There could be no one better qualified to put Simon in the picture and comment on what was going on. His nephew too could be considered as a reasonable social asset. A solicitor after all was a figure of some importance and Cilydd's triumph at the National Eisteddfod spoke well of the family of which Uncle Simon after all was the senior male representative.

'Well,' he said. 'What's happening?'

He was entitled to be informed. He glanced from his brother to his nephew and back, demanding a display of firm but unobtrusive family solidarity.

'He's twenty-seven minutes late,' Gwilym said.

Uncle Simon raised his eyebrows and smiled patiently to show that he was less obsessed than his town-dwelling brother with mechanical punctuality.

'In my view,' Gwilym said, 'it's up to the organisers to do something. If they don't, this meeting will degenerate into a shambles.'

The trace of agitation was sufficient to encourage Simon to demonstrate imperturbable calm.

'He'll be here,' Simon said. 'And then in no time at all he'll have them all in the palm of his hand.'

Gwilym shifted sideways to give the other two an interrupted view of the platform.

'Just look at it,' he said. 'An absolute disgrace. So untidy. Just look.'

He pointed angrily at the largest motto, 'The World's Age to the Welsh Tongue', drooping from the top of the proscenium arch with the indignity of a piece of wallpaper peeling off a wall.

'This is supposed to be a special occasion,' he said.

Sentences for a paragraph in his weekly column were clearly forming in his mind. His brother watched him with a smile intended to show amused interest: the small eyes were more zealously intent on picking up every sign and signal above the general noise. No one possessed a more penetrating understanding of local affairs than his brother Gwilym. But Gwilym himself was still preoccupied with general principles.

'Indifference and inertia,' Gwilym said.

'Eh?'

153

Simon had failed to make the necessary link between circumstance and observation. The smile transformed into a grimace. Gwilym raised his voice.

'The twin evils of our time,' he said. 'Indifference and inertia. And they make themselves manifest in every sphere.'

The remark was addressed more specifically to his nephew. There was after all a sense in which the two most intellectually gifted members of the family should make a continuing effort to illuminate a subject with the sparks they struck off each other.

'He's dodging it,' Cilydd said.

Both his uncles bridled.

'You are talking about a man who never dodged anything in his life,' Gwilym said. 'You are talking about a politican famous for his courage!'

Cilydd was relentlessly realistic.

'He doesn't want to get involved,' he said. 'He made a noise as if he were going to drop in and cut the Gordian knot with one slice of his celebrated sword, but only a brief study of the situation would tell the old fox that he couldn't do it, without mortally offending one faction or the other. Further reflection would also reveal that your mighty Alderman Llew was on his last legs. If only on the question of age. Whereas Doc Davies DSO, however unpleasant a character, was hale and hearty and collecting growing support in the Liberal Association. And so on. Do *I* have to tell *you*?'

Cilydd seemed satisfied when he saw that both his uncles were shocked and shaken. Uncle Simon was obliged to speak, as the senior member of the family present; but he could find nothing new to say.

'When he arrives,' he said, 'in a matter of minutes he will have the whole lot of them in the hollow of his hand.'

It was a confession of faith. Cilydd's chin sank on his chest as he gave it more consideration than it was worth. An expression of distaste spread over his face.

'He can't count on that,' Cilydd said. 'Not anymore. People don't stay stupid for ever.'

Both his uncles were appalled as the essentially sacrilegious nature of his remark sank in. Uncle Simon's broad chest heaved as he made the effort of dredging up an impressive memory.

'I recall twelve years ago,' he said. 'In the Pavilion it was. The old wooden pavilion. Three thousand people. They sang until they were hoarse. He was an hour and a quarter late then. The cares of high office.'

Uncle Gwilym's face lit up.

'That's what they should be doing,' he said. 'Find someone to lead the singing.'

He trembled like a compass needle as he peered about for someone in a position of sufficient authority to whom he could make the helpful suggestion.

'I could be wrong of course,' Cilydd said.

He spoke with mischievous deliberation and clarity and watched their faces as they waited with mounting eagerness for an act of contrition.

'People could still be as stupid as ever,' Cilydd said. 'All it needs is a little war somewhere to set the jingos jumping.'

He stared with particular impudence at his Uncle Gwilym.

'But that wouldn't help our hero would it?' Cilydd said calmly. 'He's all for Disarmament these days, isn't he? But he could drop that quickly enough I suppose. If high office called and all that sort of thing. He's against bombing from the air, I hear. You must find that very encouraging.'

Uncle Gwilym's pale face was flushing a dark red. He screwed a clenched fist into the palm of his other hand. He sounded as indignant as though he had been insulted by his wayward nephew.

'Loyalty,' he said. 'That's an important element in politics, as it is in everything else. "Be *loyal*", as Ezra More used to say to us. "Be *loyal*, boys, in everything you do!"'

'Maybe you're right,' Cilydd said.

His air of lofty detachment did nothing to soothe his uncle's feelings.

'Why don't you two go and sit down?' he said. 'Just over there, look. Two very good seats in the third row. If you're close enough, he might even wave at you. After all, we are distantly related.'

Taller than his uncles he was able to point out to them the two vacant seats.

'Not there,' Uncle Gwilym said. 'Not there.'

He appeared outraged at the suggestion.

'Why not?' Cilydd said.

'Just look! Can't you see. That lot sitting there. Doctor DSO's caucus. Just spoiling for a fight.'

'Can't you all be loyal together?' Cilydd said. 'When the great man comes marching in. Raising his arm in salute. Like Mussolini.'

Uncle Gwilym hissed a speechless protest. A harassed looking individual in a wing collar and formal suit limped into view carrying a single sheet of paper in his hand. A momentary silence fell as he used the sheet of paper to shade his eyes while he scanned the audience like a lost mariner in search of some sight of land. A swelling murmur of discontent swept through the hall as the man limped out of sight again without giving them any news.

'The idiot.'

Uncle Gwilym muttered through his clenched teeth. His brother Simon leaned closer to overhear what he was saying.

'No gumption. Can't he see how a little hymn-singing would help in a situation like this? Cohesive and calming. He's an incompetent idiot.'

'Uncle,' Cilydd said. 'where do you stand?'

'Where do I stand? Everyone knows where I stand.'

Cilydd grinned. 'Impartiality of the press?' he said.

'Alderman Llew has done a great deal for this town,' Uncle Gwilym said. 'And for the community as a whole. He may be ageing and failing but no one should forget that.'

'Which gets priority, his Memorial Hall or the Cottage Hospital?' Cilydd said. 'And if the Hospital, where is it to be?'

'These are delicate matters,' Uncle Gwilym said. 'And they should be treated delicately.'

He was prepared to give a lucid and yet subtle exposition of the complexities of the situation. His elder brother's little eyes gleamed hungrily. Uncle Gwilym's concentration was broken by a flurry of activity in the ill-concealed wing space on the left of the stage.

A messenger had arrived in a leather coat and leggings, with motorcycle goggles still resting on his heaving chest. He was followed by four elderly men as he handed the limping official an envelope he had extracted with difficulty from the depth of his leather jacket. It was clear to those in the audience who could see that the message had been scribbled on the outside of the envelope. The limping man's lips moved slowly as he deciphered the handwriting. At last he had something to say and a silence descended on the hall for the first time that evening.

'My dear friends, we have disappointing news.'

Some vestige of an ancient aspiration to excel as an orator made the man tempt his audience's patience with prolonged pauses. Uncle Gwilym snorted his own small measure of disapproval. He hissed.

'Out with it, man!'

'Our much loved and illustrious member of parliament and great leader has been taken seriously ill. At this very moment he lies in his London home, under medical care.'

The noise which broke out was a mixture of concern and consternation. Uncle Simon was deeply disturbed by the news.

'Dear God,' he said. 'Dear God.'

His mouth hung open as though he had just learnt of a catastrophe. Cilydd directed his smile at Uncle Gwilym who was straining his ear for further information.

'Shall we call it a diplomatic indisposition?'

Cilydd spoke so quietly his uncle was able to ignore him.

'Where has that message come from?' said Uncle Gwilym. He demanded information.

'Ah well,' said Cilydd. 'No further than from the alderman's bedside. You can just imagine those honeyed excuses flowing down the telephone line. In a matter of seconds he has the old lion purring like a pussy cat in the hollow of his hand. Thus our illustrious leader slips out of an awkward little situation.'

Uncle Gwilym tried to ignore Cilydd's remarks. He pointed at an identifiable figure bobbing up and down in the third row close to the two seats Cilydd had suggested his uncles could have taken.

'Just look at him! There's your Doctor DSO for you. Itching to take over.'

The doctor did appear to be acting in defiance of the man on the platform who was waving the envelope in an attempt to gain silence and attention. The doctor was trying to settle on an agreed course of action with his staunchest supporters. At last a lull in the uproar gave the man on the platform a chance to speak.

'I am going to suggest my dear friends, before we disperse, that this meeting sends a cordial message of good will to our illustrious member, telling him to hurry up and get better.'

His homely manner gained him a ragged round of applause. He warmed to his task.

'We can send a telegram direct to our stricken leader's bedside ...'

'Who's going to pay for it!'

The spontaneous witticism released pent-up protest from all parts of the hall. The limping man lost what little control he ever had over the proceedings. Amid mounting shouts for order, the doctor's supporters demanded silence so that their man could be heard. The Doctor's attempt at a parliamentary manner was unsympathetic. When he spoke, his chin reached out as aggressively as a fist.

'Look here!' he said. 'There are crucial matters to be settled to-night! Whether the member of parliament is here or not. I propose we proceed forthwith to discuss them in an orderly manner.'

This was cheered only by his supporters. He was not a popular figure. He responded by glaring combatively all around him.

'I am a professional man and I have no political axe to grind!'

This defiant statement was met with assorted expressions of incredulity.

'My sole concern is the public health of what amounts to a disease-ridden district!'

He made it sound like an insult. The response was deafening. There were three lone official figures on the platform waving their arms like tree branches in a high wind. The majority was asserting itself. Each time the doctor stood

158

up and attempted to continue with his speech he was greeted with synchronised shouts of 'Sit down!' 'Sit down!' There were even shouts of 'Don't dictate to us, Doctor DSO.' When he finally gave up, there was a lull in the excitement. Attention settled on the crippled figure of the Reverend Nathan Harris propelling itself with painful stiffness into a standing oratorical position alongside the seat he occupied next to the aisle. His penetrating voice rang out like a fire bell.

'I would like to offer a compromise proposal! Now we are all here assembled, we may as well have our money's worth!'

The measure of applause he gained with his mild joke was also an acknowledgement of the staunch effort he had made to get up and speak.

'I haven't asked his permission to put his name forward. But I propose the name of a man we can all respect to chair this meeting. He doesn't belong to my denomination: but I'm not going to hold that against him! I propose we call on the Reverend Tasker Thomas to step forward and chair this as an open meeting. And bring his own agenda with him. Does anyone second that little composite proposal?'

Cilydd took off his hat and waved it about as he called out his readiness to second the proposal. Both his uncles stared at him with embarrassed disapproval. But enthusiastic expressions of support were coming already from all corners of the hall. In a mild emulation of revolutionary zeal, men encumbered with long-belted mackintoshes and overcoats clambered on the stage, their faces red with unexpected exertion and the pleasure of defiance. They took possession of the table draped with the red dragon and in spite of the protests of the original organisers, lowered it to the level of the floor. Tasker was already being pushed and pulled to the front by eager supporters. There was cheering and Cilydd forced himself to join in. His uncles were less pleased. Gwilym took hold of his sleeve and shook it in an attempt to warn and restrain him.

'Now don't you get involved,' his Uncle Gwilym said. 'There are plenty of people in this town that are not going to like this.'

Cilydd had to struggle against the weight on his sleeve to

go on clapping. Tasker was facing the people half-seated on the edge of the draped table. His informality delighted the crowd. He looked so benevolent and friendly, the cheering grew louder. Uncle Gwilym was able to raise his voice.

'Can't you see what's happening? Playing into the hands of the opposition! Just look at the doctor. Just look.'

He made his brother stretch his neck to get a better view of the forthright doctor who was leaning back in his chair, arms folded, obviously content to let events take their course. Cilydd shook his arm free and gave way to an outburst of exasperation.

'What does it matter? So long as the job gets done.'

Uncle Gwilym was ready with an explanation, but Tasker had already begun to speak. He sounded as genial and intimate as though he were addressing an adult Sunday School class.

'If this was a sermon, I would have to start with a text, wouldn't I? Now I'm willing to bet every one of you could guess what that text would be. Every single one of you!'

It was a risky start. There was a momentary pause while an assembly accustomed to eloquence adjusted itself to a style that appeared so casual it verged on the sloppy. Those like Cilydd, most in sympathy with the speaker, devoted themselves to smiling and nodding as though they had the power to invoke a suitable response from the entire gathering. His uncles shifted away from Cilydd's side. They were distancing themselves from so committed a figure while still keeping him under surveillance. The atmosphere of revolutionary enthusiasm had temporarily transformed their nephew's appearance. His cheeks were not only flushed; they were filling out. His mouth was open and had a wet boyish eagerness about it and his hair fell over his forehead. It was hardly a suitable image for a reliable and restrained small town solicitor.

'Since this is a secular occasion let me give you my text in a piece of doggerel that I'm rather fond of.'

Tasker smiled as though he were completely confident that everyone present would become just as attached to the doggerel as he was.

160

'To love mankind in general, friends, is far less labour
Than sharing blessings with your next-door-neighbour...'

Again there was an awkward pause as the audience took individual and collective measure of the couplet. Cilydd was one of the first to respond with a loud obliging laugh. This was taken up. Tasker ventured to repeat the couplet with changes of emphasis and almost winked with knowing warmth as he saw people repeating the words as a first step towards learning them by heart.

'Well now then, friends. Pendraw, "jewel of the coast", depends on its scenery, um? Not on its scenes.'

The meeting now seemed in the mood to respond cheerfully to every sally he chose to make. It could relax and enjoy whatever divertissement he provided before getting down to business: while Tasker could make the most of a happy accident that gave him direct access to the hearts and minds of so many natives of the district. To launch a new era of harmony and cooperation, all he seemed to need to do was exercise paternal wisdom and display consistently disinterested moderation.

'Now, my good friends, I know we all agree that the politics of grace play far too small a part on the great stage of the world! Very well. Let us give it a try nearer home. We need a Cottage Hospital. Everyone agrees with that, of whatever political persuasion. Everyone. We need work for our unemployed. Everyone agrees with that too. Now you may well call me a naive and impractical Christian preacher, but I say that if the government now provides grants for public improvement what is there to prevent our building that hospital and at the same time giving work to our unemployed men?'

The response was applause and cries of approval from all parts of the hall. Uncle Gwilym shuffled back to Cilydd's side, bursting to utter his words of warning.

'What did I tell you?' he said. 'Just look at the doctor DSO. He's absolutely delighted. This is exactly what he wanted.'

Caught up in the excitement Cilydd did not hear the doors

behind him creak open. Mrs Rossett poked her head inside. She was plainly overawed by the press of people and the overwhelming preponderance of males in such boisterous mood. Glad to be unobserved she tip-toed within reach of Cilydd and tapped him gently on the elbow.

'Did my brother speak?' she said.

Cilydd nodded enthusiastically. Mrs Rossett leaned forward to listen to Tasker.

'Isn't he marvellous?' she said.

She could have been referring to her brother or to Tasker Thomas.

'So natural,' she said. 'So unpretentious. So refreshing.'

A fresh gust of laughter swept through the assembly hall in response to a parsonical quip from Tasker. The meeting now was prepared to respond to his easy-going style. More women were slipping into the hall through the doors that Mrs Rossett had left open. Tasker raised his arms in a gesture of welcome.

'Do come in! There is plenty of room! Don't be afraid of these masculine cohorts, dear ladies. They are gentle at heart, I can assure you. Let us face the Truth together and share the great tasks that lie before us.'

Mrs Nefin Jones, the acting district nurse, was too short to see over Mrs Rossett's shoulder.

'He's right, you see,' she said. 'He's right.' She turned around to address anyone who would listen. 'Women are entitled to be seen and heard,' she said. 'Just as much as anyone else.'

16

In the confined space between the hall-stand and the door, Mrs Rossett extended both hands towards Enid.

'Well now, then,' she said. 'My dear Mrs More. Let me walk with you. I would enjoy it. I really would.'

'I always seem to call when Amy's out,' Enid said.

She sounded troubled. Mrs Rossett was eager to console her.

'It's her aunt,' she said. 'At Llanelw. Or rather should I say her uncle. He isn't well and he makes great demands on her aunt. Not a patient patient! So Miss Parry feels obliged to go and help her aunt as much as she can. For ever catching trains these days, poor girl. She never has a moment.'

Mrs Rossett found a coat and hat in the closet under the stairs. While she put them on she continued to chatter cheerfully.

'My dear, you'll think this quite ridiculous, but do you know I have been quite seriously considering acquiring a dog.'

She bent her knees to study her appearance in the small mirror of the hall-stand. Under her hat she adjusted the two black curls on either side of her smiling face.

'For one reason only. Just to take it for walks. Aren't we such absurd creatures, we poor women? We allow our entire lives to be circumscribed by the most inane conventions. Nathan says why don't I take the cat for a walk? Well why not just take myself for a walk, I say. He has such a wonderful sense of humour.'

'Things are changing,' Enid said.

She was making a visible effort to stop worrying about her friend and establish an agreeable relationship with Mrs Rossett.

'Aren't they just!' Mrs Rossett's eyes widened with enthusiasm. 'I was telling Nathan this morning. If all this goes on we won't be able to recognise the place. Or ourselves. It's the transformation from within, Nathan said. That is the thing that will make a permanent difference. That's what he said to Mr Lewis.'

Enid looked puzzled.

'Miss Parry's cousin,' Mrs Rossett said. 'From the south. He's a Communist.'

'I don't think I've ever met him,' Enid said.

It was a defensive murmur. Mrs Rossett raised her voice to neutralise any possible embarrassment.

'Nathan is very broad-minded,' she said. 'Having been a

minister in the South, you see, he knows exactly how to deal with the type. Man to man and straight from the shoulder. Mind you, Miss Parry's cousin seemed very intelligent. And he was very well mannered. But as Nathan says, they are very able debaters. Sharpest wits in Wales, he says, and well beyond it. If they took the trouble they could sweep their way through Parliament. But as Nathan says, economic reform is important: but only religion can do anything about changing human nature.'

They set out down Eifion Street with the confident resolution of allies. Things were about to change and even the way they walked would bear witness to the fact. Mrs Rossett greeted the people she knew with an encouraging warmth. Every inhabitant of the town would become a partner in a great adventure. As for herself all her life she had had to contend with a height that made her unduly conspicuous. She had met the challenge by a studied degree of deportment which now stood her in good stead. Her ordinary demeanour was illuminated with an aura of serenity. Under such protection Enid was able to carry her burden of pregnancy through the streets with greater ease. Evans the printer lingered on the step of his front office in order to be in a position to greet them both warmly.

'Now there you have a man who has changed,' Mrs Rossett said. 'And against all odds. Against the force of heredity if not the force of gravity.'

She was amused by her own notion.

'Do you know,' she said, 'my grandfather came across his grandfather in the Gulf of Guayquil. They were both on the South American run out of Glaslyn. And do you know what was the first thing they did? They had a furious argument about infant baptism. And my grandfather said, "Look here, Owen Evans, they've got enough volcanos in this part of the world, without you adding to their number."'

It had been raining but as they walked through the town the sun burst through the clouds and the streets were filled with such dazzling light it was difficult for passers-by to recognise each other. Mrs Rossett helped Enid step around the puddles in Station Square. She drew her attention to the birds in the trim trees singing after the rain. When they reached the embankment road, Mrs Rossett took Enid's arm. The damp world around them was bathed in the glamour of the sunlight. In the shallow water on the landward side of the cob, families of ducks and swans were drifting to and fro in front of an expanse of reeds. The two women paused to admire their gliding progress in and out of the transient light.

'Let us learn from the harmony of nature,' Mrs Rossett said. 'Do you know, I went for a walk to the edge of the sea last night. There was the most wonderful sunset. And I thought to myself that millions of creatures must have thought that before me. There it is. The gate of heaven. A great golden door in the sky. And then I thought how perfect this life could be if only we could set aside all the nagging little obstacles that set us in such a state of enmity towards one another. And then I listened to the waves, my dear. And I could hear their music perfectly, rolling over and over, "Live in harmony, live in harmony".'

She waved a hand to illustrate the rhythm of the phrase.

'Isn't that exactly what Tasker is telling our little town?'

She pointed at the town centre they had left behind them. Smoke from many chimneys was suspended in a light that was drying out the slate rooftops.

'Is it such a difficult lesson to learn?' Mrs Rossett said.

'Not if we are left alone to learn it,' Enid said.

Mrs Rossett was disturbed by the unexpectedly sombre note in Enid's voice.

'My husband has heard that the Air Ministry are making enquiries about Saints Island,' Enid said. 'They want the whole area as a new ground for training and development.'

'Developing what?'

'Aerial bombardment,' Enid said. 'What else?'

'But I thought that was outlawed. By the League of Nations,' Mrs Rossett said.

'Isn't it a terrible irony?' Enid said. 'John Cilydd couldn't get over it. On the very island where we want to rebuild the Abbey as a centre of international peace and reconciliation.'

'Does Tasker know?'

Enid shook her head.

'It's hardly likely,' she said. 'Cilydd heard it at the Assizes this morning. A barrister from Chester is an MP. He's going

165

to put down a question in the House of Commons. That can only mean that the first steps have already been taken.'

'How terrible,' Mrs Rossett said. 'How terrible.'

'There will have to be a Defence Committee,' Enid said. 'The churches will have to take a lead.'

'Bombing is terrible,' Mrs Rossett said. 'Little children should be able to look up at the sky without being afraid of what falls out of it.'

'Public opinion is a strange thing,' Enid said. 'Public opinion. Public policy. Public outcry. Very soon we are going to have a campaign on our hands. And once you have a campaign it has to be conducted like a military operation. A fight. And that's the end of peace and harmony.'

Mrs Rossett stared wistfully across the harbour.

'It all looks so peaceful,' she said. 'You know what my brother Nathan said the other night, after the public meeting. He was so excited. So full of delight. "If I could use my legs, Annie", he said, "I would dance on that table". I felt the same myself. To be there and see him change the nature of the place before our very eyes.'

Mrs Rossett bent to make an earnest attempt to gain all Enid's attention.

'Pendraw has always had a bad name for bickering,' she said. 'It's a funny thing isn't it? How a place can gain that sort of reputation. Like churches, of course. And villages. Some enjoy peace and tranquillity and some are for ever bickering and back-biting. Poor old Pendraw has always been inclined to the latter category. Strange isn't it? Nathan has all sorts of theories about it. He would like to write an essay on the subject. But the poor boy's fingers ... he can't hold a pen.'

Mrs Rossett's face broke into a beatific smile.

'Our Miss Parry, bless her. She told him once he could dictate to her and she would take it down. But he would never trespass on her time. Or her good will.'

Mrs Rossett turned her face to the breeze from the sea and breathed deliberately. They sauntered along the wide pavement at a confidential pace.

'She's such a likable person.' The idea of Amy brought a fresh smile to her face. 'And she thinks so highly of you. Her best friend.'

166

Mrs Rossett lowered her voice as if she were in danger of being overheard.

'"The best brain of our year!" she said. "And the best character too. Enid always stands up for what is right."'

Enid was blushing.

'Am I embarrassing you?' Mrs Rossett said. 'I don't mean to. But it's so wonderful sometimes to be allowed to speak aloud to say just what one is thinking. That's not always possible. At least for someone like me. A widow and so on. No real function in the world except to look after a crippled brother. Childless and useless. Except to keep a house tidy. And make meals of course. If I talk too much you must stop me. Do you promise?'

Enid nodded. She seemed to be measuring the distance from where they were to her own front door.

'One looks into the future and hopes for new harmonies,' Mrs Rossett said. 'And yet one never ventures to interfere or even speak. Because whatever one says it sounds just like the daydream of a silly widow sitting in front of her kitchen fire and stroking her cat.'

They stood opposite Enid's front door and seemed to be considering crossing the road. The door was painted dark green. A dim light was visible through the basement window. Mrs Rossett looked admiringly at the tall house in the middle of the terrace.

'What a sacred place a home is,' she said. 'This one in particular.'

Tenderly she squeezed Enid's arm before releasing it.

'You are expecting a child,' she said. 'What a wonderful moment in time. Like a picture of the annunciation. After all, only a woman can carry the hope of the world.'

'There's a light in the kitchen,' Enid said. 'John Cilydd must be home.'

'Go to him my dear. Go to him.'.

Mrs Rossett spoke in a low reverential tone, as though she were being privileged to take part in a romantic ritual.

'Won't you come in?'

Enid made the polite invitation. Mrs Rossett quietly shook her head.

'I wouldn't dream of imposing myself,' she said. 'But I

wish you both so well. Believe me. From the bottom of my heart.'

17

A sea mist had captured the island. The survey they were conducting had been brought to a halt. Tasker led the way from the trestle tables set up in the shelter of the walls of the ruined abbey. Above the mist, he said, there was a blue sky and a warmer world and the higher they went the closer they would come to it. He strode ahead up the steep hillside. His stout legs were bare and a khaki groundsheet hung from his shoulders like an abbreviated toga. His arms were free for oratorical gestures.

The island hill was not high enough to escape from the mist. As they gathered around him, the company dedicated to peace and international fellowship could hear the muted wailing of invisible sea birds above the mist and the weirdly dislocated crash of waves against rocks. Some of the foreigners looked uneasy. Tasker raised his hands in a gesture of friendly benediction. Drops of moisture clung to the red hairs on his legs. There was dampness everywhere. He was intent on raising everyone's spirits.

'They simply couldn't use a place like this as a target,' he said. 'The bones of twenty thousand saints would rise in protest. Of course they would. That is what the Past is good for, friends, to protect the Present. And that is what we are good for. When the world sees this abbey being rebuilt with the voluntary labour of young men from all over Europe – the very same young men who would be first to die in another war – rebuilt and dedicated as a Centre of Peace and Co-operation, how could it not be inspired by example! They want us to believe that our old Europe is completely submerged in capitalistic greed and nationalistic hatreds. When I say "they" I mean those powerful men who worship the idols of power and greed, the golden calves of profit and imperialistic power! What have we to offer? Nothing less than a world "where there shall be neither Greek nor Jew, circumcision nor uncircumcision, Barbarian, Scythian, bond nor free, capital nor labour: but Christ, Christ is all and in all".'

John Cilydd became aware of fingers tugging at the sleeve of his old raincoat. Eddie Meredith was drawing him back from the edge of the group into the cover of the mist. Eddie's black curls were covered with damp gossamer. His lengthy tattered raincoat was buttoned at the neck and hung down like a loose cape. The rugby jersey he wore underneath was striped in black and yellow and the white shorts had pockets in them. There were holes in the canvas sides of his gym-shoes and most of the buttons on the raincoat were missing. When he winked he looked like a disobedient cherub. Even as he allowed himself to be lured away, Cilydd continued to listen to Tasker's voice through the mist.

'The strength of our Faith . . . in the last resort we have nothing else . . .'

'Eddie!' Cilydd whispered hoarsely. 'Eddie. What is it?'

When the group on the hillside was no longer visible through the mist, Eddie turned to lead the way with sure-footed grace down a sheep path between the bracken and the gorse. Cilydd was obliged to break into a trot to keep him in sight.

'Here!'

Eddie did not bother to whisper any more. He had found his way to a track which lay between banked hedgerows. This was an unusual feature on an island where fields and farms were marked out for the most part by low dry-stone walls. Cilydd refused to follow any further without being told where they were going.

'What is the point of this?'

He spoke as sharply as a schoolmaster as he wiped the moisture from his spectacles. He was wearing a black beret at an angle. The effect was a little comical: a professional man attempting to enter more fully into the spirit of camping and life in the open air,

'You are about to be initiated!'

Eddie grinned as he pointed at Cilydd, confident of his ability to charm.

'A poet has to be initiated. That's self-evident.'

Eddie stalked ahead into the mist. Cilydd followed him reluctantly.

'It's a change anyway.'

He could hear Eddie's voice. The young man spoke with an assurance garnered from successes on playing fields and in examination rooms. The future seemed to belong to him as of right.

'This damn fool business of getting up at six in the morning. And prayer meetings for goodness sake. It's like a children's crusade.'

Eddie waited for Cilydd to catch up with him.

'Some of these local disciples of old Tasker give me the willies.' Eddie said. 'That awful twit of a chemistry teacher from Llandudno. Have you smelt his socks?'

'He means well,' Cilydd said.

Eddie poked an accusing finger at him. 'There you go,' he said. 'Making excuses for him. Bores like that should be exterminated. He's a pompous bore. What's the matter?'

'The mist,' John Cilydd said. 'I wish it would lift. I've got to get back. Enid will be worried. I should never have come really. She insisted.'

Eddie showed some sympathetic understanding by remaining silent. They walked on at a slower pace.

'You can't believe half the things old Tasker bumbles on about, can you?'

Cilydd looked troubled.

'Is he capable of real leadership?' Eddie said. 'There are times when I doubt it. He doesn't really understand the world we are living in. Not really. He still thinks in terms of mighty preachers swaying multitudes. I mean, this ridiculous obsession with his maternal grandfather. What would old Freud have to say about that? I'm not saying it wasn't incredible, the way the old preachers could mould the minds and behaviour patterns of multitudes. But that's gone for ever. Manipulation from now on belongs to machines and to the invisible hands that control the levers. How can a man who is just an inch and a half off the ground for most of the time ever come to grips with things as they really are. Don't you agree?'

He was eager to force Cilydd to agree with him.

'If that's what you think, why did you come?' Cilydd said.

'Ah!' Eddie leaned provocatively against the hedge bank. 'All sorts of reasons,' he said.

Cilydd was prepared to cross examine him.

'I'm asking you a serious question,' he said.

'Fiddling about with the abbey ruins won't stop the Air Ministry,' Eddie said. 'I'm quite sure of that. Neither will Tasker's antiquated pulpit eloquence. Whether he huffs and puffs in Welsh or English.'

'Then why did you come?'

'I'm not sure about pacifism either,' Eddie said. 'I know it's logical and rational. But human affairs are not conducted on a rational level, are they? What we need is a blood sacrifice. On the Irish model. I think I can see the sense of that. So long as it's not my blood, of course.'

Eddie smiled and stared confidently at Cilydd, completely certain of his own charms and attraction.

'You still haven't answered my question,' Cilydd said.

'Ah well, I'll tell you exactly. To be with you.'

Cilydd went pale. Eddie turned on his side and began to use both hands with delicate precision to expose wild flowers growing on the bank.

'Your poetry means a lot to me,' Eddie said. 'Honestly now. Maybe because it hit me in late adolescence or whatever they call it. It had an impact anyway. Here's the stuff for me, I thought. Make the old language jump free of the shackles of nonconformist prudery, hypocrisy. An authentic pagan note. Make Welsh sound like Shakespeare. "Where the bee sucks there suck I, In a cowslip's bell I lie . . ." Back to the original sensuous source of poetry.'

Eddie was pleased with what he had found to say. They were alone together in the sunken track and intensely aware of their immediate surroundings.

'This is rare.' Eddie parted the wet grass again to let Cilydd have a clear view of a wild flower with white petals.

'And here's another one. Squeeze the juice on the eyelids and you have a cure for blindness.'

Cilydd leaned against the hedge bank, clutching the flower.

'I've always loved superstitions,' Eddie said. 'They belong to a world older than saints' bones. They're in my blood. I wish I could put it all into words like you.'

He closed his eyes, putting his hands behind his head and stretching his body against the bank. Hesitantly Cilydd did the same. His face was pale. He shivered inside his raincoat. Their eyes were still closed when they felt the first warmth of the sun on their faces.

'There you are, you see!'

Eddie straightened and at one bound he was standing in the middle of the track grinning at Cilydd.

'He did it!'

Cilydd lay against the bank relieved to hear Eddie talking.

'Who did what?'

He was prepared to relax and join in the young man's fun. The mist had rolled away. Insects emerged as though at a given signal. The damp leaves of the sunken track were being transformed into a garden by the hum of bees.

'He made the mist roll away,' Eddie said. 'My friend the Wizard. Because that was what you wanted. One friend always obliges another.'

Eddie came closer as though he had a new secret to impart. He raised a foot to brace himself against the bank and gazed intently at the impression left by his body on the bruised grass.

'You and I are going to collaborate,' he said.

'Are we?' Cilydd smiled and looked more at ease.

'Yes we are,' Eddie said. 'I'm younger, I know, and I haven't got your poetic gift or anything like that. But I understand that place better than any of you. I was born and brought up in it. Pendraw is a nasty little muck heap. That is to say, a muck heap stuck in a dreadful boring deadly rut. That's where they should drop their bombs. Right on it.'

'Nowhere is that bad.'

Eddie became indignant when he saw Cilydd was laughing at him.

'You should have been brought up in the Workhouse like me, Mr More. Get a worm's eye view of the heap. You see things as they really are. Like my old man. I've spent a lifetime watching him. Bullying the inmates. Playing the organ in chapel. Sucking up to authority, especially his precious alderman. Terrorising his wife. Preventing his son from doing anything he wants. And above all, going through that ghastly *Glaslyn Herald* every week looking for his name. Going through every line of the damn thing and ready to explode if he doesn't find an epithet of praise attached to his sacred name.'

Eddie was acting out extravagant despair, lurching about the track with such violence that Cilydd moved towards him, ready to sympathise and bring his comfort. Eddie turned towards him with a theatrical snarl.

'Do you expect me to squander my little ration of living, trying to sort out a place like Pendraw?'

'You are either over-reacting or over-acting,' Cilydd said. 'I'm not sure which.'

Eddie's frowns were replaced in the twinkling of an eye by a disarming smile.

'I am, aren't I?' he said.

He took hold of Cilydd's arm and leaned forward in a conscious gesture of boyish frankness and charm.

'What is a muck heap good for?' he said. 'Creative compost. Nothing more or less. Lovely raw material. And where there's muck, there's brass! Heaps of it. Just waiting to be dug up by me and you.'

'Why us?' Cilydd said.

'Because we are special!'

Eddie began to prance about, eager to display his athletic prowess by bounding up the banks on either side of the track. Cilydd trod more carefully. He was not used to the camping style of trudging about without socks.

'We're no different from anybody else,' he said.

Eddie perched precariously on a large stone and raised his voice.

'That's where you're wrong, Poet More! I may be worldly but I understand this sort of thing better than you do. There is a world shortage of vision and originality. Just think of the laws of supply and demand and then think of the gift you have. Shall I say what I think?'

173

Cilydd was amused by his antics.

'I don't see how I can stop you,' he said.

Eddie closed his eyes and made his voice sepulchral.

'I see two enormous millstones around your stiff poetic neck,' he said. 'The first is the highbrow millstone, and Welsh highbrow to boot. That doubles the weight. That's bad enough, but the second millstone is even worse. Idealism. Blind uncompromising impractical idealism. That's the name for it. So in the great race through the flood waters of life you'll just have time to put in two or three strokes, win a crown or chair or two, before you sink to the murky bottom, lost without a trace.'

'Well thank you very much.'

Cilydd was still laughing when Eddie leapt off the stone and raced up a path to a moss covered stile. There was a rusty iron gate across the track. Beyond, brambles grew between hazel and elderberry, completely blocking the way to the well.

'You need me, my friend! You really do.'

Eddie was able to use the stile as a stage for more theatrical gestures.

'As you can see, I am a showman. And a showman has to know what people want. And what they want is unlimited black puddings and football pools and an endless supply of Sunday newspapers. So what chance has poor old Tasker got? Do you know what? I had the most marvellous idea last night for a murder mystery. People love murder mysteries. Set in Pendraw of course. A preacher comes by with a portable pulpit. Children begin to disappear. The townsfolk blame everyone. And all the time it's the preacher that's guilty. What do you think of that?'

'Terrible,' Cilydd said.

Eddie ignored his comment.

'I would play the character myself of course,' he said. 'Six parts Tasker and four parts H. M. Meredith.'

'That's a bit hard on Tasker,' Cilydd said.

He leaned against the rusty gate, his fist under his chin. He seemed to be examining the surroundings of the well more closely than he was listening to Eddie. Brambles on the far side had been cut quite recently to clear the entrance to the

174

hermit's cell in the rock. At the top of the rock a Celtic cross had been erected in the nineteenth century to make visitors more aware of the sacredness of the spot. The well itself was surrounded by a low stone wall. Steps had been cut into the slope from the stile where Eddie was standing. It was the most convenient approach to the well.

'He is infatuated with youthful innocence!'

Eddie was eager to manipulate the reverberation in the hollow. He danced about on the steps with exaggerated agility, his raincoat ballooning behind him. He spread out his arms when he was certain that Cilydd was watching him.

'Like me. Youthful innocence,' Eddie said. 'He was a bit gone on me, you know. I think he still is.'

'You fool.'

Cilydd moved down the steps. He seemed excessively careful of where he put his feet. His face was flushed with an emotion that could have been anger or excitement.

'I wish you were.'

Eddie's voice was little more than a whisper but he could hear the words distinctly. Cilydd stood rigidly still on the slope. With sudden energy, Eddie turned and ran at the rockface. He spread his arms and legs in spider fashion in an attempt to climb the twenty odd feet. Cilydd watched him anxiously. Less than half way up he lost his hold. With a dramatic cry he jumped down to land safely on the cleared space in front of the cell. He rubbed his knee, turned to grin at Cilydd and crawled into the crack in the rock. He cupped his hands over his mouth to create a more ghostly echo as he spoke.

'Let the Poet step forward! And leave the solicitor and Commissioner for Oaths behind! Oh, under that black beret what authentic fires burn!'

'Shut up!'

Cilydd hurried down the last steps.

'Keep your voice down, will you? The whole island will hear you.' Eddie emerged from the cave. He crept up behind Cilydd and whispered in his ear.

'There is something we have to do.'

'What?'

'Initiates fill their mouths with well water. They walk

around the well three times. Kneel, wish and then swallow the magic fluid. Pagan transubstantiation.'

Cilydd had begun to study his surroundings with even closer interest.

'Wells,' he said. 'Hidden springs. Why do they fascinate so much?'

'We can do it together,' Eddie said. 'As a mark of friendship.'

'Does one have to?'

'To please me. And you will please yourself.'

Cilydd watched Eddie kneel and part the surface of the water, staring down into its depth. Eddie looked up imploring Cilydd to do the same. When their mouths were filled with the water, they walked hand in hand three times around the well. Eddie drew him down so that they knelt, facing each other, their eyes closed. Cilydd almost choked before he swallowed. He pressed his hands against his throat.

'What did you wish?'

Eddie's eyes were open. His childish curiosity was more than he could contain.

'I'll tell you exactly what I asked for,' Eddie said. 'To go to Germany. And for you to come with me.'

'That's impossible,' Cilydd said. He sounded both impatient and uneasy.

'Nothing is impossible,' Eddie said. 'Not to us it isn't. If we work together.'

Cilydd was already shaking his head. Eddie's voice was intense with rebellion.

'Why not? We are free or we are nothing. That's what I think. If we get buried alive in a hole like Pendraw, it's nobody's fault except our own.'

They were absorbed in each other: alongside the well, two figures uncertain whether to engage in combat or embrace. Eddie placed his hands carefully on Cilydd's shoulders. They seemed to need the stillness and the silence in the hollow alongside the well merely to consider each other. They were in close contact and yet there remained a small distance between them. Eddie was about to speak when their communing was broken by a resonant call high above their heads.

'Brothers!'

At the first sound, Cilydd dropped his hand from Eddie's shoulder. His head shot up and his mouth hung open. Tasker was standing in front of the Celtic cross with his arms outstretched. His legs were foreshortened by the angle of vision and looked stouter than ever. The khaki groundsheet still hung from his shoulders. His sparse red hair was wet and plastered close to his skull.

'Oh God.' Eddie lowered his head to mutter angrily to himself. 'Trust him to spoil it.'

'The smoke is rising from the gorse on the watchout!'

The phrase was perfectly enunciated. Any phrase he chose to use could sail through the air whether addressing two or a multitude.

'The tide is right, John Cilydd. Your boat is ready to leave and we, alas, must lose you. But only for the time being I hope.'

His smile was like a benediction and Cilydd was obliged to smile back.

'Jesus!' Eddie found some relief by hissing the word under his breath. It did not matter so long as Tasker could not hear him.

18

The tide crept stealthily around Enid's toes leaving bubbles of foam above them as they sank deeper into the sand. She looked rooted to the spot by the weight of her pregnancy. From where she stood, even in the bright sunlight the sea was a substance of elemental power stretching empty to the horizon but shifting with an endless and insatiable hunger. She turned away and waved to Amy who stood with her hands on her hips further up the shore. For more than two miles the beach curved towards a high blunt headland that seemed the only piece of land capable of withstanding the strength of the sea. Closer at hand an isolated rock the height of a tree stood as solitary as a watch tower on the open shore. From where Amy stood a surface of firm sand stretched like a narrow highway between the pebbles towards the rock. They had both turned their backs on the settlement of boarding houses and hotels built in granite and yellow brick at the western extremity of the promenade.

'Are you all right?'

Amy took Enid's hand and drew her away from the edge of the sea.

'Are you having one of your nightmares again?' Amy said. 'Or is this just a common or garden trance?'

'I was thinking,' Enid said. 'Salt in the blood. Where does it come from except from the sea?'

She made no complaint as they walked towards the rock, but everything about her suggested the physical discomfort of her condition. The veins stood out on her pale legs. Her eyes watered constantly and her hair fell listlessly about her face. Amy glanced at her wrist watch.

'I don't see any sign of a boat or a sail or anything,' she said. 'Why on earth did he go, if he didn't want to?'

Enid smiled patiently. She was conserving her strength for the final effort to reach the rock.

'The trouble with men is they never grow up,' Amy said. She clearly derived satisfaction from the finality of her verdict. 'In one way or another they long to go on playing all their lives,' she said. 'Or dreaming. And what is dreaming except playing in the mind? With girls it's so different. You start menstruating and there you are.' – Amy drove a fist into the palm of her left hand – 'bang in the middle of reality.'

Enid smiled, again without speaking.

'Are you all right?' Amy said.

She showed great concern for her friend's condition. Enid was ready to set her mind at rest.

'Mrs Nefin Jones says women would be better off carrying through the winter and giving birth in May. Like mares.'

'Let's sit down somewhere.'

Amy looked around for the most comfortable position.

'I want to get as far as Cilydd's rock,' Enid said. 'I call it Cilydd's because he likes it so much. It's our favourite walk.

178

Through the gorse and the wasteland beyond the golf course. It's the place to catch the first sight of a sail.'

'I may as well say what I think,' Amy said. 'With you so near your time, he shouldn't have gone. I told him in so many words. "What if the weather changed and you got stuck on that stupid island?' He didn't like it one bit.'

'I wanted him to go,' Enid said.

'I know you did. Only because you thought it was what he wanted. I tell you, Enid More, you spoil him. You really do.'

'It was important for him to go,' Enid said.

'Why? Why was it so important? There's nothing more important than this.'

Amy nudged her and then held her with both hands when she realised how unsteady Enid was on her feet.

'It's important to establish the legal claim on the Abbey ruins,' Enid said. 'The deeds and so on. Important propaganda in the struggle with the Air Ministry when it comes. In the courts and so on. Publicity. He's looking ahead.'

'He could have done all that in the office,' Amy said impatiently.

They both fell silent. A lack of mutual understanding made them both uneasy. Their views of John Cilydd's behaviour differed so widely it cast a shadow over their friendship. Closer to the rock, Enid made a fresh attempt to win Amy's sympathy for her husband.

'It's strange how his life has been haunted by the sea,' she said. 'His father was drowned at sea. Did you know that?'

'No, I didn't.'

Amy screwed up her eyes in an intense effort to appear impressed. Together they concentrated on the gradual climb to the top of the rock from the landward side. Amy held both Enid's hands and drew her up step by step. When they reached the top Enid was breathless with triumph. The view inspired her. On the eastern horizon she saw the vague outlines of the mountains in the afternoon sun and shafts of the same light exposed the horizontal strata running through the two uninhabited islands and the headland that thrust out towards them.

'He was forbidden to go sailing as a boy. So he would come

179

here and sit and dream. On this rock. No wonder he likes it so much. Then when he was fourteen or so he broke the rule and went sailing with three friends. Young pioneers of 1915 in search of adventure and burning with war fever. Looking for submarines! They got caught in the cross current. The boat capsized. They were nearly drowned.'

'Gosh.'

Amy stared anxiously out to sea. The massive calm of the waters seemed less reassuring to her than it had been before.

'Let's sit down shall we?' Amy said, smiling. 'In case we get washed away when the tide reaches us.'

'He's written a poem about it.' Enid spoke in a tone of particular confidentiality. 'But he won't publish it. He's been playing about with it for years. An aesthetic problem, basically. To what extent should he tamper with the facts of the original experience in order to structure the particular message he has to convey. And what message?'

She saw Amy's eyebrows were raised in comical contemplation of the poet's dilemma.

'I'm afraid I can't help you there,' Amy said.

They both burst out laughing. They were friends sharing an old and well-tried joke: and they were both relieved to find their intimacy re-established on its well-tried footing.

'Are you warm enough?' Amy said.

'Yes. I'm fine.'

Amy placed herself between her friend and the breeze coming off the sea.

'It wasn't too much of an effort?' she said.

'Oh no. I love coming here,' Enid said. 'Mind you, I would never have made it without your help.'

Out of the margin of gorse, between the wasteland and the foreshore, two families appeared. The two mothers settled down to prepare a picnic. They domesticated a surface of green sward with a tablecloth while the fathers took the children to the water's edge to paddle and throw sticks and stones into the sea to be retrieved by an excited sheep dog. Amy and Enid were happy to observe their behaviour in silence. Enid shifted from time to time to try and find a more comfortable posture. Amy was at hand to offer her whatever support she could give. Enid pointed at the headland.

'Do you remember you and I catching poor old Sali P and that ghastly Professor Gwilym in the ferns up there? Do you remember how shocked we were? And how priggish?'

Amy frowned with the effort of recall.

'I can remember,' she said. 'But I'm blowed if I can remember how I felt. All I can see when I close my eyes is Sali P's car stuck in the sand and the professor's straw hat on the back seat.'

Enid sighed and shook her head with the sadness of recollection of things long past.

'Amy...'

'Um?'

'What about Val?'

Amy closed her eyes.

'He just has to lie there and suffer,' she said. 'I can't bear to think about it.'

She lowered her head, silent and troubled.

'I have to write,' Enid said. 'I don't expect him to write back for the time being. But I think it comforts him to know what's going on. And he can still say the most wonderful things.'

'Can he?' Amy could not suppress the bitterness in her voice. For her no amount of wisdom could make up for the helplessness of his condition.

'What shall I tell him?'

Enid put the question with great delicacy.

'About what?' Amy said.

'About your Mr Lewis for one thing. Coming here.'

'Tell him whatever you like,' Amy said. 'Or tell him nothing at all. It won't make any difference.'

'I wish you'd tell me...'

Enid tried to shift her position so that she could look her friend straight in the eye. She wanted to demonstrate how much she desired to bring her help and comfort. The effort was painful.

'There's nothing to tell, worth telling,' Amy said.

'I want to help. You know I do.'

'I don't know,' Amy said quietly.

'What do you mean, you don't know?'

'Nobody can help me.'

'That's ridiculous.'

Enid longed to protest more forcefully.

'There are things we have to go through alone. Things we have to submit to,' Amy said.

She struggled to emerge from her mood of despair. She attempted a lighthearted comparison.

'I can't go through the childbirth business for you, can I?' she said. 'I mean, however much I wanted to, I can't have your child. It's the same thing with this love affair business. If it is a love affair.'

Enid found a handkerchief in the pocket of her smock and wiped her eyes carefully.

'Do you love him?' she said. 'That's all I'm asking.'

Amy resisted the temptation to pretend she had not realised it was Pen Lewis Enid was talking about.

'Physically,' she said in a subdued voice. 'Physically he's very attractive.'

Enid was insisting on a truthful answer.

'Yes, but do you love him?' she said. 'That's what matters.'

'Who knows what love is anyway?' Amy made an unsuccessful attempt to sound cynical.

'You do if anybody does,' Enid said. 'You are by nature a very loving person.'

'Am I indeed?'

'Yes you are.'

Their voices were raised as though they were about to quarrel. One of the children at the base of the rock rubbed his eyes as he looked up to listen to them.

'Let me tell you this,' Amy said.

She lowered her voice and brought her face closer to Enid's in an attempt to underline the ruthlessness of her realism.

'So that you can understand just how loving a person I am,' Amy said. 'Physically I long for Pen Lewis. So much sometimes I'm ashamed of it. Especially when I think of Val. But I don't mind so much being torn between them. I mean that's never altogether so unpleasant, is it? To be wanted by two rather fine men. Well, to be wanted by one anyway and to be rejected by the other for the highest ethical and moral reasons.'

182

'Amy,' Enid said. 'Don't talk like that. You're only hurting yourself.'

'I wish I were,' Amy said. 'I wish I were. I wish I could cry. I wish I could scream and shout. But I can't. I'm as dry inside as that piece of driftwood. Salt dry. And I can tell you why. Because I'm so ashamed of myself. That's why. Because I know whatever happens between Pen and myself, the love, the physical magic, whatever it is, will never be to my material benefit. Now do you see what kind of a person I am?'

Enid was longing to embrace and comfort her friend, but she could only free one arm.

'Don't talk like that, Amy darling, please.'

'He can be masterful in a way that turns me into a jelly,' Amy said. 'I admit it. I freely admit it. But I also resent it. I don't want it.'

'But if you love him so much,' Enid said, 'go to him. That's the only answer surely. And I am sure Val would understand.'

'I can't afford to be romantic,' Amy said. 'That's what Pen would call bourgeois self-indulgence.'

'But Amy,' Enid said. 'Love. Real love . . .'

Enid had reached a stage of agitation that smothered her usual ability to conduct a lucid argument.

'Love me, love my politics,' Amy said. 'Struggles, persecution, imprisonment. That's what Pen Lewis has to offer. And poverty. Endless poverty. I can't face a life of poverty.'

Below them the women were calling their children to come and eat. Amy watched them placing the children to sit decorously around the table cloth spread on the ground.

'It strikes a chill into the marrow of my bones, just to think of it,' Amy said. 'I saw it as a child. I'll never forget the misery. And the humiliation. Never again. I would prefer complete loneliness. To be completely alone for ever. A sterile old maid, Mrs More.'

Enid shook her head in a refusal to take the matter lightly.

'You know the way I like my slippers inside the fender of my room in number seven Eifion Street. And my quiet cigarette. And Mrs Rossett bringing me a cup of hot milk before bed. That's the life, Madame More! I'm well on the way to being an old maid.'

'Oh Amy...'

'What's so bad about that anyway? I've always got you.'

With some care she shifted closer to Enid so that she could kiss her fondly on the cheek.

19

The Calvinistic Methodist chapel was the largest in the town. The vestry stood at a right angle to the back of the main building and was a substantial structure in its own right. It was approached through a dark narrow street but the extensive paved forecourt was filled with sunlight. The plain brown wall looked mediterranean in the afternoon sun. The iron gates were wide open and so were the twin doors. The iron railings and the woodwork were painted black and the circular window of coloured glass set high in the wall glittered like semaphore with cheerful signals.

Amy paused in the forecourt to make a final inspection of the petition sheets she was carrying. They were fresh from the printers and the ink was barely dry. Each sheet began with 'We the undersigned' in capital letters and went on to set out in small print the wording of a lengthy resolution against the proposal of the Air Ministry to site a training establishment around Saints Island and the end of the peninsula. She was annoyed to discover a small misprint. It was too late to do anything about it now. The meeting had already started.

In the shade of the vestibule a portly policeman took smiling cognizance of her arrival. He stood with his thumbs stuck in his belt, on a Saturday afternoon a model of disinterested benevolence. Amy tip-toed inside and took up a position behind a long table that normally accommodated

Sunday School books. Cilydd was a solitary figure seated on the bench behind the table. The speaker was Professor Gwilym. He stood at a lectern made of polished pine and frequently consulted his notes through spectacles that he regularly removed when he shifted his gaze from the lecture to the small audience that sat patiently listening to him. Behind him four ministers sat in a row, providing moral support. Tasker was conspicuous among them, both for his open-necked shirt and the informal way he sat sideways in his chair, his arms folded high on his chest and a smile of inexhaustible sympathy and understanding fixed on his large sunburnt face. Between the light-filled rectangular windows, portraits of former ministers of the church hung in their own shadows.

Professor Gwilym was too self-conscious to excel as a public speaker. He had prepared his statement for publication and he was inclined to mumble as he leaned closer to the text to retrieve some imperfectly remembered point which he desired to present in its most elegant form to his present audience. He was nevertheless listened to with respect. The scattered audience was composed of firm supporters of the cause. Furthermore he was an old pupil of the Pendraw County School and the people could regard him as a native returned, garlanded with academic success. He was approaching his peroration. Amy stood on tip-toe with her back against the wall. She saw the professor shut his eyes tightly as he reached for a more emotional approach. He raised a pale white-knuckled fist. It looked like an urgent plea to some higher power to grant him a brief visitation of traditional eloquence.

'I was given the privilege of being born and bred in this glorious peninsula! Its enduring charms need no eulogy from me. This is the pilgrim's peninsula which all through the ages has led to the Island of Saints. This is not only a sanctuary. To our nation all through history this has been a holy place. This is Holy Ground! And now what would they turn it into? An altar for the worship of the bomb. And unforgivable act of desecration and destruction.'

He was encouraged by murmurs of approval in the audience. He began to wag an admonitory index finger in a gesture of warning that developed imperceptibly into a threat.

'If we allow this thing to happen, if we allow an alien power, an oppressive imperialistic government to establish on that sacred soil a school for the training of young men in the refined terrors of aerial bombardment, then I say to you we will have collaborated, actively or passively, it makes no difference, in an act of barbarism that will disgrace us all for ever at the bar of history!'

The spate of eloquence suddenly ran out. Professor Gwilym gripped the edges of the lectern and looked around for somewhere to sit down and recover his equanimity. Tasker Thomas was the first to realise the professor had finished. To lead the uncertain applause he rose to his feet and clapped so rapidly that his large hands seemed to blur into each other. He could have been urging the audience to give the professor a standing ovation. Amy took the opportunity to draw Cilydd's attention to the misprint in the resolution. He shrugged his shoulders to indicate that it was too late to do anything about it. His attitude also suggested a certain dissatisfaction with other aspects of the arrangements for the protest. Still clapping his hands together Tasker moved to the lectern. He was intent on making a personal display of gratitude to the professor.

'Dear friends!' Tasker raised both arms for a silence which had already fallen. 'With all due respect to the reserves of eloquence ranged behind me . . .'

He turned with a beaming smile to indicate his ministerial colleagues. Judging by the expressions on their faces they were not amused by his reference to them.

'After such a well-argued case has been put to us, what remains to be said? To continue making speeches in this vestry, I say this quite frankly, would be preaching to the converted. We are of one heart and one mind.'

Cilydd whispered to Amy that they should each guard a doorway so that the petition forms could be distributed among supporters as they went out.

'We need to go out to the highways and byways and meet the people!'

186

Tasker turned to his fellow ministers. They did not appear to be entirely in agreement with him.

'Use our eloquence and our arguments to bring the majority over to our side,' Tasker said.

There were enough rumbles of approval around the room to encourage his resolve.

'The sun is shining!' he said. 'I move that we adjourn forthwith to the Market Square! Reconvene under the statue of this little city's favourite son. After all, what was he in his day except an apostle of peace and justice?'

'He's rushing things.'

Cilydd whispered urgently to Amy.

'The plan was to wait until Eddie and the students sent a message to say everything was ready.'

He waved a petition sheet to attract Tasker's notice. Tasker immediately assumed Cilydd was referring to their distribution. He lifted a restraining hand.

'Dear friends!' he said. 'Whatever you do, don't leave this meeting empty handed! At the door you will be handed sheets of our Pendraw Peninsula Petition. It is vital that we persuade every single adult inhabitant of each district to sign that petition. Now then, our target is ten thousand signatures in twenty days. Nothing less will do.'

The meeting was confused. Not everyone in the vestry was filled with the desire to go outside and present the cause to a wide public. After an inconclusive consultation with the group of ministers, Tasker disappeared into the body of the chapel. Caught up with distributing petition sheets in the vestry doorway, Cilydd was unable to attract his attention. Amy moved down the steps offering sheets to small groups of soberly dressed men who stood about to chat and enjoy a first cigarette in the bright sunshine. They looked relieved to have escaped from the restraints of the semi-ecclesiastical interior. Professor Gwilym appeared in the doorway. He was making an effort to extract his pipe from one pocket and his pouch from the other in order to conceal the fact that no one was paying him any attention. He smiled broadly when he saw Amy and hailed her first with his pouch and then with his pipe. He moved to engage her in eager conversation.

'You heard me?' he said.

He could not wait for Amy to explain how she had been delayed at the printer's office.

'Not exactly mass conversions,' he said. 'I'm afraid I'll never make a session preacher.'

'It was very good,' Amy said.

The professor waved his hands to show that he was not fishing for compliments.

'Enid's husband tells me we had two County Councillors present,' he said. 'Now those are the people we have to get at.'

Amy was glad to agree. Professor Gwilym glanced quickly around for faces he could recognise.

'I don't see Miss Sali Prydderch,' he said.

'She's with Enid,' Amy said. 'Keeping her company. We persuaded Enid not to come. That was quite difficult.'

Professor Gwilym showed that he found Amy a more than adequate substitute.

'Did you see my letter in *The Manchester Guardian* this morning?' he said.

Amy shook her head apologetically.

'I say "my" letter,' he said modestly as he lit his pipe. 'I composed it, but most of the Common Room signed it. You have to appeal to the English you see. That is, the more enlightened ones. There are more of them than there are of us.'

He wanted her to understand he was making a joke.

'More's the pity of course. But it's a fact of life and we have to live with it.'

As he spoke he had been pressing closer to her so that by now her back was against the railings of the forecourt. The malleable features of his face became darkly serious.

'I wouldn't say this out loud,' he said. 'But in terms of decision, Miss Parry, in terms of the things that really matter, the matters of life and death, as you might say, poor little Wales doesn't count.'

He was transfixing her with a bold stare that demanded respect and even awe for such unsparing frankness.

'And this Welshness, shall I call it, that means so much to us means nothing at all to them. They barely know it exists.

And if they do, they wish it didn't.'

Amy's body sagged helplessly against the railings. With some relief, over the professor's shoulder, she saw Cilydd approaching them. He shook a petition sheet under their noses.

'These are petition sheets,' Cilydd said. 'Not certificates of regular Sunday School attendance. Did you ever see such a shambles? I'm not blaming you. But the whole area should have been divided up and official petitioners chosen by parish. That's what this meeting was for. I explained it to Tasker and he seemed to take it in. You speak to him at some length and he seems to be listening. Now the entire exercise will have to be done again.'

'I'm sorry,' Amy said.

'I'm not blaming you,' Cilydd said. 'But how can you deal with a man who seems to be permanently walking an inch and a half off the ground?'

'Let me ask you something,' Professor Gwilym said.

He spoke with the ponderousness of a man who feels the need to exert his presence.

'Where do you stand, Mr More?'

Cilydd gazed short-sightedly at the professor as if he were identifying an object on the periphery of a sea of problems.

'We'll print your speech, professor,' he said. 'If you would be good enough to translate it, we'd publish it in both languages.'

Resolutely he led the way through the gates and down the narrow street. Amy followed at his heels. The professor had further points to make but he needed all his breath to keep up with Cilydd's urgent strides. Their progress was interrupted by Mrs Annie Rossett. Without her hat she appeared bereft of her customary serenity.

'Mr More!' she said. 'Listen to me. You should know this. There is a gang of ruffians in The King's Head. The town loafers. Somebody is paying for their drinks. Now there is a woman that cleans there who also works for Mrs Edwards the greengrocer's wife. She said they were boasting that they would throw the Reverend Tasker Thomas into the harbour!'

Cilydd smiled grimly.

'I expect it was the drink talking,' he said.

'She was very frightened,' Mrs Rossett said. 'Mrs Edwards was going to come to the meeting. But this woman advised her strongly not to go.'

'We have a coach-load of students due any minute,' Cilydd said. 'I'll see that they give him protection. Don't worry, Mrs Rossett.'

When they turned into the High Street they found it thronged with Saturday afternoon shoppers. Both country folk and holiday visitors were inclined to dawdle and their progress was not easy. Professor Gwilym was determined to put his question to Cilydd. He raised his voice.

'When I ask, where do you stand,' he said, 'what I mean is, in fashionable terms, on the Right or on the Left? Or let me put it this way. Where in relation to Right and Left? I mean we are primarily concerned with a matter of culture. But willy-nilly that drags us into the political arena.'

Cilydd barely heard him. With a show of tact he helped the professor regain a foothold on the crowded pavement. On the street itself, there was a constant battle between vehicles and pedestrians for precedence. Outside the new F.W. Woolworth store they came face to face with H.M. Meredith, the Master of the Workhouse. He wore a yellow rose in the lapel of his jacket and his brown leggings shone in the sun. He had been standing with statuesque stillness until he caught sight of Cilydd and Amy. He barred Cilydd's way.

'What's going on?' he said. 'What's going on?'

Amy held out a petition sheet so that the Master of the Workhouse could read it.

'Would you like to sign this, Mr Meredith?'

'Sign? Sign? What should I sign?'

Meredith scanned the wording of the resolution with deepening suspicion. He was obliged to hold the sheet at arm's length to make out the small print.

'Does the Alderman know about this?' he said. 'You can't organise petitions without letting the Alderman know. It's a matter of common courtesy.'

'Won't you sign it, Mr Meredith?' Amy said. She smiled at him as appealingly as she could.

'Certainly not,' he said. 'And I'll tell you this. I fought the

Germans in one war and I'm quite ready to fight them again should the need arise.'

'My dear man,' Professor Gwilym said. He tried to touch Meredith's jacket in the friendliest fashion. 'This has nothing at all to do with Germans.'

Meredith deeply resented the professor's mode of address.

'It's to do with national defence,' he said. 'That's clear enough.'

'My dear man, it's not *defence* to pour down death and destruction on the heads of defenceless women and children. That's what bombing means. Call it what you like, but it's not defence.'

'I know my own mind,' Meredith said. 'And I know what those in real authority think. And I'll tell you this much' – he addressed himself specifically to Cilydd – 'I will not have my son led astray by the likes of you. Let me tell you that now, plainly, to your face.'

Having made an effective parting shot, his eyes swivelled about to choose the most advantageous direction in which to march off. Ignoring the traffic, he marched imperiously across the street and into the dim interior of a chemist's shop. The professor raised up his arms and intoned sorrowfully.

'"Behold thy gods, O Walia!"'

A sequence of familiar phrases appeared to float before his eyes.

'"So many of us will be tried and so many found wanting!"'

He took off his hat and tilted his face towards the sky. Once more his foot slipped into the gutter.

'"There shall not be left here one stone upon another that shall not be thrown down."'

Passers-by were stopping to listen. Mrs Rossett pressed her hands uneasily against her hair. She seemed to feel the need of a hat to cover it.

'I think I can hear singing,' she said.

It became a matter of greater urgency for them to reach the Market Square as quickly as they could. A farm cart had been drawn up in front of the statue at the west end of the square. The hymn-singing among Tasker's youthful supporters drew people from the market stalls on the opposite side of the square. There was a row of country buses parked between the horse-trough and the public fountain. A white coach was trying to insert itself alongside them. Eddie Meredith stood on the running board calling out brisk instructions to the driver. Inside there were students eager to emerge and join in the fun. Professor Gwilym was overcome with an urge to reach the farm cart.

'I will speak if invited to do so,' he said to Amy. 'It's the time to show which side we are on.'

With his pipe clenched firmly between his teeth he waded forward elbowing his way closer to the extempore platform under the statue.

'Where's Tasker?' Cilydd said.

He looked around anxiously as he muttered under his breath.

'And those ministers. Where are they?'

'Miss Parry! Miss Parry!'

William Henry, the tall boy who played the King of Death in the School Interlude was waving at Amy to attract her attention. He detached himself from the group of hymn-singers to get closer to her.

'We are behind him, Miss,' he said.

He swayed from side to side in front of Amy, eager for her approval.

'What a wonderful man! He will lead us to the Promised Land, Miss Parry. Indeed he will.'

William Henry's fingers tangled with the red curls surmounting his small head. He was as eager to reassure himself as to gain Amy's approval. His exceptional height made it possible for him to look nervously over the heads of the crowd massing in the square. He saw Eddie Meredith pushing his way closer towards them and leaned forward as though it was his function to receive any fresh news. Eddie grasped Cilydd by the shoulder and called out loudly.

'Where on earth is he?' he said. 'We can't have a show without Punch, can we?'

William Henry looked appalled at such a frivolous mention of his hero. His nose twitched under the slack bridge of his thick-lensed spectacles.

'And those ministers,' Eddie said. 'They should be up

192

there with him. Turning pious platitudes into propaganda.'

Eddie grinned cheerfully as he raised his voice again.

'Propaganda!' he said. 'That's education with a cutting edge. Isn't that so, Miss Parry?'

William Henry shifted back into the orbit of the hymn singing. He had a powerful bass voice and the words were suited to what he felt. "Behold He stands between the myrtles, a vision that demands my love..."'

Cilydd was shouting instructions in Eddie's ear. He wanted him to organise the students in a protective ring around the farm cart. A surge forward in the crowd separated them. Tasker had appeared on the cart. He stood there alone, a large striking figure. Cilydd and Amy were pressed more closely together.

'Those ministers should be up there with him.'

Cilydd continued to give vent to his dissatisfaction with the proceedings until Tasker raised his arms in a plea for silence. The crowd responded. The mass of faces turned up expectantly gave him strength and inspiration. This was an unique opportunity to emulate the oratorical feats of his grandfather. A faint noise of traffic and the distant strains of a steam organ in the fairground on the outskirts of the town also seemed designed to spur him on. His face glowed with an elation that promised nothing less than prophetic utterance. With dramatic slowness he turned to point to the statue of the nineteenth-century reformer behind him. His baritone voice soared above the hushed crowd, every syllable as clear and as urgent as a bell in the still air.

'There are imperial powers in this world who build monuments to celebrate their victories and put up statues to honour their generals and admirals and great war leaders! I am proud to belong to a people who chose to put up statues to their preachers, their prophets, their men of God, their reformers, their messengers of peace.'

With a benign gesture he identified himself with the people assembled around him. They accepted the symbolic embrace with an audible sigh of attentive satisfaction.

'"I shall make a sacrifice of myself if need be, to the recalcitrance of my nation." These are his own words, inscribed on his monument. I say to the powers of this world who would establish a Bombing School on this sacred soil and usurp the throne of the Prince of Peace, before you dare to commit this outrage, dare to remove this statue!'

The murmur of approval was on the verge of applause. It was held back because the experienced chapel-goers among the crowd sensed a mere introduction to more telling points that would build up into a satisfying structure of irrefutable conviction.

'Some of my good friends advised me against coming out here on a day like this at the height of the holiday season and making an appeal direct to a busy people. But I told them that the people of this peninsula were my friends. And I told them that not all of them were busy. The ravages of unemployment are eating at the heart of our community, so that old texts seem to take on a new meaning. "Why stand ye here all the day idle?" Matthew 20, verse six. And the answer that you all know. "They say unto him, Because no man hath hired us."'

With a bold gesture Tasker seemed to plunge his arms into the tense silence that confronted him. He would draw out the parable and set it before the people in a new light. Somehow his eloquence would work on their behalf to uncover and give expression to their deepest misgivings.

'Now then, we are told there are responsible people in our community, particularly in this town, who are prepared to welcome a Bombing School and all the pomp and imperial paraphernalia that will go with it because they say it will bring work to the district, business to the town, boost our flagging economy and relieve the nightmare burden of unemployment. Will it? Perhaps it will, in the short term. For a few months. A few weeks. But what a terrible price to pay. There are members of the present government in Westminster who believe Rearmament is the only answer to unemployment. There are people in Berlin and Moscow and Rome and Paris who say exactly the same thing. And up there, the prince of Darkness, Beelzebub, Satan himself and all his black angels and archangels of chaos are rubbing their hands and saying to themselves, "Soon we shall have vast armies on the march ready to reduce our enemy, God's good earth, into a bloody and shattered province of Hell! The whole earth will soon be ours. And one of the first places where we shall gain a foothold will be on that old peninsula beyond Pendraw. We shall take possession of the Pilgrim's Way and pitch our tents in the West so that the Island of Saints will become the Mouth of Hell!"'

The crowd responded with a sound between a gasp and a sigh that seemed to come from one throat. In their anxiety to offer themselves attentively to the thread of Tasker's discourse they took no notice of what was going on in an alley to the left of the statue. Eddie nudged Cilydd in the ribs.

'Look! Just look at that,' he said.

A group of men in working clothes, some of them unsteady on their feet, had taken possession of a coal lorry. Half a dozen had already mounted the lorry and were sitting on the coal sacks, some of them armed with sticks. Even when the engine was started, the driver had difficulty in reversing. There was shouting and bouts of raucous laughter, but still the main attention of the crowd was riveted on Tasker.

'Mr Lloyd George himself has declared that bombing from the air should be proscribed and prohibited among civilized nations. Should we not listen?'

The round of applause was interrupted by the roar of the lorry's engine reversing out of the alley. The men on board began to sing their own uncertain version of 'Rule Britannia'. Others more serious stood on the running board howling out instructions to a driver whose view was almost totally obscured. Their intention appeared to be to skirt the base of the statue, strike the farm-cart and dislodge the speaker. Eddie swore under his breath and began to wave his arms about to attract the attention of the students who had travelled in on the white coach. Tasker went on speaking. His back was turned to the approaching menace and his efforts were concentrated on holding the attention of his audience. But the less committed were already beginning to disperse. As they shrank from the erratic manoeuvres of the lorry, the students moved foward. The result was much pushing and shoving and Tasker's words were lost in the growing confusion. He stood alone on the farm cart, no longer the leader of people dominating the proceedings but increasingly a helpless victim unable to control the forces that were surging around him.

The market square was wide enough to accommodate any number of spectators who wished to remain on the sidelines and watch the developing conflict. Tasker's congregation had dwindled away. His young supporters were divided between active and passive resistance. Some of them were already seated on the ground in the path of the lorry and around the farm cart. William Henry was a conspicuous figure as he drifted around, uncertain which course to take. He sat down briefly and then stood up, clearly looking around for the most inconspicuous escape route. Some of the students were advancing on the driver's cab. Eddie could be seen trying to direct their efforts. To get at the driver they had to try and drag down the men standing on the running board. Cilydd saw a student kicked in the face. Outraged he turned to gesticulate authoritatively at two policemen who stood within hailing distance, their arms folded, watching the proceedings with detached calm. When they ignored his signals he rushed up to them, pointing with his fistful of petition sheets at what was happening.

'Those men are breaking the law!' he said. 'Do you hear me? They are armed with sticks. Causing an affray. And that is probably a stolen vehicle. Do you hear what I'm saying?'

Calmly the two policemen glanced at each other before turning their backs on Cilydd and walking away. Cilydd was beside himself.

'I shall report you both to the Police Committee,' he said. 'Do you hear me? I shall prepare a detailed report. I shall . . .'

Amy pulled urgently at his arm. 'John Cilydd,' she said. 'Look over there.'

Sali Prydderch's tourer had come to a stop with the front wheels on the pavement. Driving into the square at some speed she had been obliged by the crowd of people to make an abrupt turn.

'Something's the matter,' Amy said. 'It must be Enid.'

Cilydd was too obsessed with his indignation to hear her.

'The law,' he said. 'Turning their backs.' He stuffed the petition sheets towards Amy wanting her to take them. 'I'm not going to stand idly by,' he said. 'Just look at that!'

The lorry had moved into forward gear. It was difficult to distinguish between the injured and the passive resisters squatting on the ground. As if under a change of plan the men who had commandeered the coal lorry were now bent on abandoning it and dispersing as fast as they could. But they were surrounded by students and schoolboys. Eddie was on the running board attempting to open the door and capture the driver. Behind him two schoolboys were trying to detain one of the gang by hanging on to his jacket. The man's arms were still free. He swung wildly with his stick and caught Eddie on the shoulder. From the distance, Cilydd trembled as he saw Eddie fall. Amy and Sali Prydderch were shouting to each other desperately.

'Did you hear that?' Amy shook Cilydd's arm. 'John Cilydd! Enid is in labour. She can't stop shivering. She's calling out for you.'

She saw the look of misery and despair on Cilydd's face. 'What's the matter?'

'Eddie,' Cilydd said.

He pointed at the lorry. The cab doors were open. The gang had dispersed. The battle was over. Professor Gwilym was being helped up on to the cart to stand alongside Tasker and offer him his hand. As they watched, Tasker seemed too dazed to take it.

'He's been hurt,' Cilydd said.

Amy was suddenly exasperated by the plaintive note in Cilydd's voice.

'Never mind about Eddie,' she said. 'He can take care of himself. Enid needs you. Come on.'

20

The basement window was two-thirds below the level of the pavement and the street. When the wind shifted, a sudden squall lashed rain against the panes. Cilydd was startled by the sound. It became so dark in the basement that he was obliged to light the oil lamp suspended from the ceiling above the bare table. He drew it down carefully like a man committed to making the minimum of sound. When it was lit, he took off his jacket and placed it over the back of a chair. He consulted his watch in his waistcoat pocket and rolled up his sleeves. There was much to be done. In a dark pantry he found a battered enamelled jug. From the glass lean-to conservatory between the kitchen and the garden he collected a zinc bath hanging on a nail. His attention was concentrated on the square mouth of an open gulley under the sink. He set a box in front of it and sat down with the jug between his knees, his finger nails drumming tinnily against the sides, to study the level of water under the cast-iron grid. His nose twitched like a dog's intent on a hole from which a rat, sooner or later, would be bound to emerge.

The enamelled jug rattled against the cast iron grid as he made his first attempt to fill it. The result was poor. He rubbed his chin as he gazed down at the unsatisfactory quantity of brown water dormant in the channels of the pattern pressed into the bottom of the zinc bath. From the middle drawer of a dresser built on to the pantry partition he extracted a heavy screwdriver hidden by sheaves of pamphlets, leaflets and petition sheets. With this he prised out the cast-iron grid. But the baling process was little improved. The jug was too large for the hole. The tidal water was rising more rapidly. Urgently he rummaged in the basement rooms until he discovered an empty jam jar. He pushed aside the box, knelt down on a folded sack and set to work to protect his property. The high tide and the abnormal rainfall were insinuating sea water into the drainage system of the terrace of boarding houses that stretched in isolation between the embankment road and the promenade. Baling had to be kept up at a steady pace until the tide turned. A rhythm had to be established. He became absorbed in his task attending to each little deluge from the jam jar as if it were related to the downpour outside and in some way a series of revelations concerning the mysterious nature of water. When the rising liquid lapped the edge of the sack he worked more quickly to redress the balance. He did not hear Amy's footsteps on the uncarpeted wooden stairs. She, too, was making an effort to move and speak quietly. She stood watching him in the doorway.

'John Cilydd,' she said. 'What on earth are you doing?'

He was able to answer her without interrupting the rhythm of his baling.

'The joys of fatherhood,' he said. 'Protecting his wife and son from the raging seas.'

'Didn't you know about it? When you bought the house? I thought you were supposed to be a lawyer.'

Cilydd chuckled quietly to show how much he had learnt to appreciate and even enjoy Amy's outbursts of being sharp and forthright. She was his wife's best friend and there had to be some margin of benefit available to him from so close a friendship between the two.

'Well I knew there had to be something keeping the price down,' he said. 'I should have had the whole thing surveyed of course. But I didn't. Strange how all the most important decisions in life seem to be made on impulse.'

He punctuated his reflections by emptying the jam jar. Amy stared with distaste and disapproval at the brown water.

'Flooding and drowning,' Cilydd said. 'The story of my life.'

The expression on Amy's face suggested a lack of sympathy towards self-absorbed poetic speculations. If he was to talk at all it should be about his wife.

'Is she asleep?'

Amy nodded as she bit angrily at the corner of her thumb nail. There was an echo in the basement. They both had to concentrate on keeping their voices down. Amy was also intent on catching any sound that might come from upstairs.

'She was torn.'

Amy paced about the table as she struggled to give rational expression to her misgivings. She looked up at the window and the endless splashing of rain-water on the pavement.

'Thank God the worst is over,' Cilydd said.

His head was lowered over the gulley. He could have been muttering a prayer of relief and thanksgiving.

'It's the smell,' she said.

He misunderstood her.

'It's the sea water,' he said. 'It doesn't smell. It's strange really. It only affects the basements at the lower end of the terrace. Furthest away from the sea. Very mysterious. Surveyor's department baffled. But as old Tasker says, it doesn't take very much to baffle them.'

'I'm talking about Enid. It's a bad smell.'

Cilydd seemed embarrassed. He lowered his head and worked with greater speed.

'She's been through a lot,' he said. 'What she needs now is a rest. That's what the doctor says. Plenty of sleep. It doesn't matter if she can't feed the baby. The nurse will take care of that.'

'It's the smell. It's horrible!' Amy's voice was becoming more assertive. 'It's a sign of poison. I'm sure of it. I don't know what the medical jargon is. But it's evil. I can tell. Her face is burning and yet there's no spark at all in her eye.'

'She's been through so much . . .'

'She's still not right, I'm sure of it. You know what I think, John Cilydd? We ought to take her to hospital. Right away.'

He baled faster as he considered what she was saying.

'There's the doctor,' he said. 'Shouldn't we get him?'

'He's a fool,' Amy said. 'And so is the district nurse. The whole set-up is absolutely disgusting. It could be the middle of the last century. All fatalism and waiting for this or that to take its course.'

Cilydd paused briefly to consult his watch.

'Five minutes more,' he said. 'And then the tide will turn.'

Something about the way he let his watch slip back into his waistcoat triggered off her fury.

'Five minutes? Every second counts. Her life is in danger. I'm sure of it. Anything could happen to her.'

She wanted immediate action from him.

200

'What does it matter about that stupid drain. You get the car out John Cilydd. Now!'

Cilydd scrambled to his feet like a man preparing to ward off an attack. Amy's voice was fiercer than the rain beating against the window. The water from the drain was lapping the toes of his boots.

'It doesn't matter a damn about this stupid floor. The thing is to get her into hospital. I'm convinced of it. I've heard people talking about that smell before.'

She followed him about as he put on his raincoat and looked for an old hat. Anger and anxiety were surging out of her in a flood of words.

'It is an absolute scandal that a town like this doesn't have a maternity hospital. To think a woman has to be dragged twenty-five miles if there's anything wrong with her. What age are we living in? At any time and in all weathers. They have more respect for cattle. The things women have to put up with. Bring it around to the front. And then come upstairs to help me get her down. We've just got to get her there as quickly as we can.'

The row of garages with wooden walls and corrugated iron roofs stood on the waste ground behind the gardens of the Marine Terrace. Cilydd had to struggle against the wind to open the doors. His hat blew away and he had to chase it for several yards before pulling it down again almost over his ears. The moisture in the atmosphere made the touring car difficult to start. He muttered angrily to himself as he swung the handle and jumped back to avoid the kick. The doors quivered and trembled against the bricks and stones he had laid down to hold them open. Even when the car was started every action he took seemed fraught with hazard. In his haste he left the garage doors open and hung on grimly to the steering wheel as the car bounced along the rain filled pot-holes in the track which ran parallel with the gardens of the terrace houses. In low gear he accelerated noisily up the incline that gave access to the embankment road at the promenade end. The weather kept everyone indoors. There was not a single visitor in sight. With care he drew up outside the front door of his house. The name 'Ardwyn' was worked into the stained glass of the fanlight above the door.

He left the engine running and hurried up the stairs in his wet coat and hat. The baby was crying. On the landing he encountered the acting district nurse, Mrs Nevin Jones.

'It isn't right, Mr More,' she said. 'I was telling the young lady. It's wrong to move a patient without the doctor's permission. We are doing all we can, you know. You must be fair to us.'

Cilydd was staring at the glass and rubber instruments the nurse carried in her hands. They were designed to express the milk in the mother's hard breasts.

'I want hot water,' the District Nurse said. 'I want to give the patient hot towel treatment and I don't want her moved, you see. There's a great deal to be done, Mr More. Her temperature's rising. That's not a good thing.'

'Hospital,' Cilydd said.

It was as if it were the only word he could think of. The noise of the baby crying was a nerve-wracking distraction. He frowned and shut his eyes tightly.

'She's got a high temperature,' the nurse said. 'She'd catch her death of cold in that car of yours. Now you listen to me. I know what I'm talking about.'

Cilydd pushed past the nurse to reach the bedroom. Enid was awake. Amy was leaning over the bed trying to comfort her. He was so taken aback by the sight of his wife's delirium and the foul smell in the room that he forgot the oddness of his own appearance with the rain still running off the turned-down brim of his hat and his mackintosh. When she saw him standing open mouthed and motionless in the doorway, Enid let out a scream in a way that he had never heard before.

'Don't let him come near me! Get him out of here! Get the bloody swine out of here! Do you hear me?'

Amy held on to Enid's shoulders to restrain her. She tried to make comforting noises. The acting District Nurse was pushing her way past Cilydd to get in the room and take charge of the crisis. Cilydd himself was a petrified figure, apparently unable to grasp what was going on. Some fever was turning his wife into another person in front of his eyes: a gentle girl transformed into a wild unhinged creature capable of any utterance. It needed both Amy and the nurse to hold her down.

'This is it,' the nurse said. 'Yes indeed. This is it.'

She alternated between muttering to herself and calling out positive instructions.

'Milk fever,' she said. 'At the very least. I want hot towels. I want olive oil. She's delirious you see. Delirious. You can see it for yourself. She has no idea what she's saying. So don't take any notice.'

Enid lay back exhausted from her outburst. Her head still on the pile of pillows as she stared at the ceiling. When she spoke again her voice was calm but unnervingly distant.

'Amy, there's writing on the ceiling. What does it say?'

'Plenty of hot water,' the district nurse said. 'And get Dr Griffiths.'

She wanted to direct Amy and John Cilydd towards positive action, but they seemed mesmerised by what Enid was saying.

'I can't read the letters,' Enid said. 'They're cracking. I can't read them. Read them to me Amy, before they crumble. What are they saying?'

The nurse began to whisper more urgently.

'It's no use listening to her,' she said. 'She's got no idea what she's saying. Now, you've got the car out haven't you, so you can fetch Dr Griffiths as fast as you can. I shall want to give her an enema. But he'd better see her. Be as quick as you can.'

'What language is it?' Enid was speaking in a faint voice. 'I can't read it.'

The nurse put out her hand to push John Cilydd on his way. She held his arm for a moment and shook it.

'Tell him Nurse Nevin Jones thinks it's milk fever.'

'Milk fever?'

Cilydd repeated the words as if he were asking what they meant. He stood rooted to the spot like a man in a nightmare. Again the nurse had to push him.

'The crisis,' she said. 'Tell him to come at once.'

21

Nathan Harris, the retired minister, sat rigidly in his garden chair near the solitary apple tree. Misery more than arthritis fixed him in his captive position with his extra cardigan hung awkwardly over his gaunt shoulders and his elbow protruding over the metal arm of the chair. The cushion that had been placed under it lay on the grass but he made no effort to retrieve it. The attention of his whole being seemed concentrated on Amy who stood on the short garden path as still as a well-behaved child dressed for Sunday School. She wore a black dress and carried a black hat in both hands. She seemed to want to delay putting it on her head as long as possible. One of his deformed hands was extended towards her. He clearly wanted her to speak; to say anything at all. His head was trembling with a visible desire to share her pain and grief.

'She asked me to pray for her,' Amy said.

Amy moved closer to him holding her hat in front of her and staring at him accusingly.

'Why should she do that?'

Nathan Harris's wide mouth opened and shut. He wanted to answer her question, comply with any wish she expressed, give her anything: all he had available to offer was to listen.

'She knew I didn't believe in it. Perfectly well. She was ill of course. Delirious. But not all the time. Not when she said it. "I'm going to die, Amy!" she said. "You will pray for me, won't you?" What was that supposed to mean?'

The minister struggled to hold out his arms. He seemed to long for Amy to fall on her knees and rest her head in his lap so that he could stroke her hair with his crooked fingers as she shook with weeping. Amy stood rigidly erect gaining a sudden strength from her own anger.

'She didn't have to die,' she said. 'It wasn't necessary. Her life was stolen from her. By ignorance. By inefficiency. By a horrible deadly fatalism. I'll never forgive them for it. Not one of them. Not as long as I live. Her life was just thrown away. That's what it amounts to.'

Mr Harris cleared his throat. He was ready to speak but only when it became apparent that was what she most wanted him to do.

'We didn't ask to be born. My mother died when I was a baby. TB or something. It wasn't my fault. How can we be expected to take the blame for faults we never committed as if they were crimes?'

She was glaring at him now, demanding an answer and yet predisposed to reject it whatever it turned out to be. He steeled himself to speak.

'Grief is a terrible thing,' he said. 'I know that. It's like the pain of longing and loss squeezing the life out of you until you can't move.'

His arms lifted again as if inviting her to accept his physical condition as some kind of emblem of her sorrow.

'Until you can't breathe,' he said.

She would not allow him to attribute any aspect of his own present condition or past experience to her. Nothing he said could be in any way acceptable to her. In spite of his sympathy he was part of the order of culpable passivity which she longed to hold responsible for Enid's death.

'Until you feel you are choking.'

He brought his crooked finger dramatically close to his throat. Amy stamped her foot with childish petulance.

'There's nothing wrong with me,' she said. 'I only wish there was.'

She shut her eyes tight and held up her face to the sun.

'I can't believe it,' she said. 'I've seen her in her coffin, and I can't believe it. I've lost the best part of me and I can't believe it. It's like a bad dream. A nightmare. I'm going to wake up and it will be gone.'

She screwed her eyes more tightly as though that alone would transform the situation. Out of the darkness she imposed on herself she heard the minister's voice. Words had occurred to him which he was eager to pass on to her.

'"Surely he hath borne our griefs and carried our sorrows." He will, you see, Amy. He will bear your grief and carry your sorrow.'

Her eyes opened before she spoke with defiant coldness. 'I'll carry my own,' she said.

He sighed and lowered his head. If she wanted to hurt him, he was more than willing to be hurt. Whatever she chose to inflict on him, she would find him a willing victim.

'The whole thing is so absurd,' Amy said. 'A nasty cosmic joke. My goodness, if He does exist, He's got a lot to answer for.'

She lifted her black hat as though she were considering tearing it in pieces. She put the narrow rim between her teeth and then examined it to see whether the bite showed.

'Asking me to pray for her. That's what's so awful. The poor little thing was afraid to die.'

'Most people are, Amy.'

The minister spoke with the authority of long experience.

'Well I'm not,' she said. 'I can tell you that much. Why should I be?'

Both her fists were clenched and she glowed with defiance where she stood in the small back garden. Her anger could not last. Suddenly she was overwhelmed again with grief. Her face crumbled and the tears streamed down her face.

'My poor little Enid,' she said. 'She had a right to live. A birthright. A birth not a death. It wasn't fair. To snatch her life away from her. That can't be right. Can it, Mr Harris? Can it?'

She was begging him to agree with her. She made no attempt to wipe away her tears. They flowed off her chin and dropped on her breast, spreading like stains on the dark material of her dress.

'How are we supposed to understand these things? Can you tell me?'

There was nothing he wanted more than to tell her. One scriptural phrase after another came to his lips and died away before he dared to utter it. She had stopped crying. Her voice had a note of pleading and helplessness in it, but now she stood waiting for whatever he might say like a sullen opponent ready to seize on anything and tear it apart.

' "I have chosen thee in the furnace of affliction",' Nathan Harris said.

'What's that supposed to mean?'

He breathed deeply and ventured a smile.

'It's something I say to myself,' he said, 'when I feel like complaining. It's from Isaiah. I get a lot of comfort out of it. "For the sake of my name I defer my anger, and for the sake of my honour I curb it: I will not destroy you." That's the new translation. And then it goes, "For my sake and my sake only have I acted – is my name to be polluted? Never shall I yield my glory to another."'

'I wouldn't have thought there was much comfort there, quite frankly,' Amy said. 'It sounds pretty awful to me. That is if I've understood it.'

'Well, there you are.'

The minister's spirits were somehow restored. He offered her his large white handkerchief. She accepted it and then blew her nose.

'That's the way it is,' he said. 'You are young and beautiful. I am old and ugly. But it wouldn't do at all for me to worship you. I've got to go on worshipping Him whether I like it or not. Not just follow my fancy. Because in the end, when everything else has faded away, that is what will matter. We must be ignorant, concerning them which are asleep. "For if we believe that Jesus died and rose again, even so them also which sleep in Jesus will God bring with him." We have to hope, Amy. We have to hope.'

Her head was shaking slowly.

'Will you help me up?'

Gripping her hands was painful for him. When he was on his feet it was plain that he longed to take her in his arms and comfort her. She held back, her body suddenly as stiff as his. He released her hands from his cold clutch. With careful politeness she handed him his walking-stick. She stood to one side to allow him as much time as he needed to make his laboured progress back to the house. He stood and stared at her with mute appeal, eager to speak but with nothing more he could say. The pounding of the door-knocker reverberated through the empty house. Contrary to his wont, Nathan Harris expressed no pleasure at the prospect of visitors. For once there was no one he wished to see.

'Would you be so kind as to answer it, Miss Parry?' His manner was gravely formal. 'I am sorry that I have to put you to such trouble.'

Amy opened the door. She was confronted by Mrs Lloyd, Cilydd's grandmother. The old lady was dressed in deep mourning. She stood back on the pavement, her feet well apart. Behind her a black Rolls Royce was stationary, with the engine running. A man in a top hat sat at the wheel.

'Mrs Lloyd,' Amy said.

She struggled to control her voice and to remain calm and self-possessed. Children in the school playground were already watching their encounter. Their stares were fixed on the long black vehicle. The whole town knew of the death of the young wife. Inevitably the funeral would develop into a public event. Both women in black were determined to conduct themselves with dignity and restraint.

'Won't you come in, Mrs Lloyd?'

Amy spoke with measured politeness.

'There isn't time.'

Mrs Lloyd pressed her lips together. Amy could see the trace of a pulse at the top of Mrs Lloyd's square jaw. Under her sandy complexion there was a grey pallor that marked the strain of unexpected bereavement. The natural vigour of Cilydd's grandmother was reduced to little more than a reflex. She gestured urgently at the motor car.

'I want you to come with me, Miss Parry. If you will.'

Accustomed to command, Mrs Lloyd had to bend herself towards making such an open appeal for help. Her blue eyes were fixed on Amy's face. They could be allies. They had to act in consort. The public occasion had to be a fitting mark of general respect for the dead girl. The community had its right to make a demonstration of sympathy if it felt moved to do so. Mrs Lloyd also had an over-riding concern to preserve the honour and good name of the family. In a decently ordered sequence of events this tribute would become an intangible and yet significant portion of the new-born son's inheritance. Whatever either woman meant by the phrase 'for Enid's sake' could only dictate the same course of action. Amy showed that she was ready to respond.

'You had better put your hat on,' Mrs Lloyd said.

The habit of command reasserted itself briefly.

'He's gone to Cae Golau,' Mrs Lloyd said. 'He says he won't attend the funeral.'

Wearily she closed her eyes. Her grandson's uncontrollable grief was more than she could bear. The visible world was an amalgam of obstacles she had to find the strength to overcome. She did not see Nathan Harris at the end of the passage behind Amy raising his hand in a gesture of silent sympathy. Quietly Amy closed the front door of seven Eifion Street. She held Mrs Lloyd's elbow in order to help her into the rear seat of the Rolls Royce. The old woman's deep breathing proclaimed the weight of the emotional burden she was carrying. She leaned forward to make certain the driver knew the best way to Cae Golau. She lay back in the comfortable seat to recover her strength before speaking.

'He objects to the baby being baptised on his mother's coffin,' Mrs Lloyd said. 'I suppose that's what it amounts to.'

Amy took refuge in complete silence. From the corner of her eye she took note of the people who hesitated and stood still on the pavement as the black limousine glided by. They seemed to be rehearsing the way they would line the route and show their respect when the funeral cortege passed through the town. She caught a glimpse of the Master of the Workhouse emerging from a newsagent's in the act of folding his copy of the local newspaper to fit the inside pocket of the raincoat he was carrying on his arm even though the sun was shining brightly. She saw the black armband on his sleeve. He wanted to be seen taking his place among the congregation of mourners even though his connection with the bereavement was distant enough. Everything she saw confirmed that Pendraw was making itself ready for a big funeral. She was startled when Mrs Lloyd's gruff voice broke the silence.

'John Cilydd says they wouldn't listen to her when she was alive, so why make such a fuss now she's dead.'

Mrs Lloyd stared out of the window. The expression on her face suggested detached hostility.

'I suppose people have a right to show their sympathy and

respect,' Mrs Lloyd said. 'It's not just a show. It means something. We have to believe that. If only for the poor girl's sake.'

She seemed unable to bring herself to mention Enid by name.

Discreetly the driver accelerated once they were outside the town. Mrs Lloyd turned her head to engage Amy more earnestly in conversation.

'It has always been the custom in our Connexion to baptise a baby on his mother's coffin. It is a simple dignified custom. The baptism bowl on the lid of the coffin. The sacrament of baptism. Then the burial of the dead. He tries to say it's primitive, barbaric. Those are the kind of words he uses. I can't get through to him. "John Cilydd", I said, "we are all born and we all die." It's terrible of course when a young mother dies or a child dies. Terrible because it's in the wrong order. Not for any other reason. We don't have the right to expect to live for ever. But anything I say he doesn't even hear. I suppose the gap of years between us is too great. I suppose he thinks of himself as being too modern to talk to an old-fashioned old woman.'

She waited for Amy to say something. Momentarily she raised a gloved hand and it was like a mute offer of sharing a form of sovereignty: the driving power of one generation ready to collaborate with the emerging power of another.

'If you could talk to him, Miss Parry,' Mrs Lloyd said, 'he might listen to you. He hasn't even given that little boy a name. He barely wants to look at him.'

'Bedwyr,' Amy said.

Mrs Lloyd looked puzzled. The name was so unfamiliar.

'That was the name they had decided on if it was a boy. You know how keen she was to revive the old names. Bring back the best of the old things.'

Mrs Lloyd listened like a woman eager to understand. The tears that had welled up in Amy's eyes began to course freely down her cheeks.

'She was the brightest,' Amy said. 'She was the best...'

She had so much to say but her mouth was too filled with saliva to speak. Mrs Lloyd leaned over and took Amy's hand in a firm grip.

The lane to Cae Golau was blocked by Cilydd's car. The driver in the top hat turned to receive his instructions from Mrs Lloyd. His face was weather-beaten and his hands were large and calloused, but the expression on his face was sensitive and sympathetic. Mrs Lloyd sat back and frowned disapprovingly at the offending vehicle.

'The Reverend Ezra Lloyd has a great regard for John Cilydd,' she said.

She spoke with a ritualistic monotony.

'I was hoping he would be strong enough to conduct the service. At least the baptism. It has some significance. When you grow up. Who first received you into the faith. "Then will I sprinkle clean water upon you, and ye shall be clean . . . And ye shall dwell in the land that I gave to your father: and ye shall be my people and I will be your God."'

The driver nodded eagerly. Mrs Lloyd was a person for whom he had the deepest respect. His attentive manner could not have been excelled by the most experienced court official. When Mrs Lloyd made it plain she wished to speak to Amy, he eased himself out of the car and walked a few paces up the lane to inspect Cilydd's motor car with polite curiosity.

'He is wild with loss and grief,' Mrs Lloyd said. 'I understand that. I tried to tell him I understood since I have had my share. He wouldn't listen. But believe me, it's afterwards he'll be sorry. And then of course it will be too late. Too late. And he'll regret it for ever. You know where to find him?'

'I think so,' Amy said. 'There was a spot by the stream where they liked to sit. Under the oak tree.'

Mrs Lloyd took her hand again and shook it urgently.

'Find him, Miss Parry,' she said. 'Talk to him. We haven't much time.'

22

Cilydd lay on the moist earth between the oak tree and the
stream. Alongside him Amy recognised the journal that Enid
used to keep. It was open and a gentle breeze kept rustling
the pages. Amy knelt down to close it reverently. She moved
so quietly, Cilydd seemed unaware of her presence. A trickle
of saliva from the corner of his open mouth reached the
mossy ground. Without his spectacles his grey eyes were
glazed and still, fixed on the water in the stream that flowed
on endlessly, catching the light as it bounced over smooth
pebbles and stones. With a small handkerchief, Amy wiped
the corner of his mouth.

'John Cilydd.' Amy whispered his name comfortingly.

'My life is finished,' he said. 'It's over.'

His voice was dry and exhausted. Amy looked at the
condition of his dark business suit. There were patches of
mud drying on the trousers and the sleeves. He had crawled
to the edge of the stream as if the constant flow of water were
the only thing that could preserve his sanity.

'John Cilydd,' Amy said. 'We must go now.'

He stared, mesmerised, at the water.

'It washes you clean,' he said. 'It carries you out of this
world.'

She shook his shoulders, insisting on his attention. When
he looked at her his eyes were as defenceless as a child waking
up from a drugged sleep.

'"Death that takes everyman, why not take me?"'

His quotation made Amy suddenly impatient.

'Now come on,' she said. 'We've got to try and be
sensible.'

Cilydd gave his attention to Enid's journal.

'Did you see it?' he said. 'Did you read it? Listen. Listen to
this.'

In a state of agitation he picked up the notebook but was
unable to pick out the passage he wanted. Instead he read at
random from an earlier section.

'"Home. Wrote to C. Went out in the rain to post it. Had to talk to him and writing was the only way. I wrote reams. Stood in front of the letter-box on the corner of Elwy Street, let it slip from my fingers and heard it bounce on the bottom. On the way back tried to remember what I had written and wondered if I was trying to be clever or negotiate my way into his mind." Listen. Listen. "Speculation is my life blood. I shall go on doing it when the whole world has dissolved into cosmic dust." Listen. Listen.'

'Not now.'

She snatched the notebook from him. She closed it, unable to bear the sight of the familiar handwriting.

'Don't you hear her voice?' Cilydd said. 'In everything she wrote. When I read some of those things I understood for the first time how perfectly she loved me. How privileged I was and how unworthy. I sat here and I thought my brain would burn into ashes. I wanted to speak to her so much, to tell her all the things I should have told her to make up for all my miserable shortcomings.'

He could not control the sobs that were shaking his whole body. Amy could do nothing else except attempt to comfort him. He became calmer in her embrace. His head was on her breast and like a mother comforting her child she stroked his hair.

'Amy. Amy.'

He began to mutter her name. As his body warmed against hers his arms went around her like a lover's. She too had begun to seek some release for her pent-up emotion. He began to mutter fervently and kiss her face.

'You are in my arms,' he said. 'You are both as one to me. You always were. From the first moment I saw you.'

Hungrily he kissed her on the lips and his hands explored the shape of her body. Only then did she push him away from her and scramble angrily to her feet.

'Stop it!'

Apart, they both stared at each other and listened to the quiet of the countryside around them. Cae Golau was out of sight behind the trees. There was an absence of birdsong. In the field beyond the stream a plover rose suddenly and hovered long enough to give its mournful double call before vanishing from sight.

'Listen to me.' Amy breathed deeply, ready to impose her authority. 'Just listen.'

He was looking at her imploringly as if she were his last hope.

'Oh Amy ... she held me together.' He stretched out his hand for her to take. 'She was everything that mattered,' he said.

Amy clenched her fists and pressed them against the pit of her stomach.

'We mustn't drown in our private sorrows,' Amy said. 'A trance of impotent melancholy. That's what she called it. She was always saying things like that.'

A fresh spasm of sorrow threatened to bring Amy to her knees. She spoke more fiercely to control herself and make Cilydd listen.

'Your grandmother wants Ezra Lloyd to take the service,' she said. 'Dragging that old man out of his temperance museum. Do you know why? For one reason only. To make Tasker take a back seat. They never wanted him near the place, did they? Your family.'

Cilydd lowered his head and groaned.

'Pull yourself together,' Amy said. 'Do you hear me?'

'Amy. Amy.' He could have been begging for mercy.

'You take control,' she said. 'Your grandmother will give way to you. You must take charge. Come along. Get to your feet. Stand up.'

She allowed him to cling to her arm.

'You tell her quite firmly that Tasker should baptise that baby. And his name will be Bedwyr. That's what Enid wanted. You know that.'

He leaned on her as they took the path back to the house.

'A wonderful, magical novel'
MARION ZIMMER BRADLEY

From the wintry land of the mountains came Finn, the warrior
whose legacy was both a blessing and a curse.

His mother was a witch and a wanderer upon land. His father –
from what they knew – had risen up like a god from his
kingdom beneath the sea.

And so Finn began his odyssey in search of his birthright:
drawn deep into the secret world of sorcery, braving waters
that would drown a man in dreams, roving among people
who would answer riddles with fresh riddles . . .

'Dark and intriguing, at once wonderful and strange . . . one
of the best fantasies in some time' Publishers Weekly

0 7221 4545 4 FANTASY £4.95

A novel that powers along the trail of a desert – and its terrible secret . . . .

KING
OF THE
GOLDEN
VALLEY

ALAN SCHOLEFIELD

Ex-Navy officer Daniel Coles Wynter, unemployed, receives a letter, forty-six years too late for the person for whom it was intended. The letter hints at a dark scandal involving Daniel's grandfather, an Edwardian motoring ace who took part in the 1910 Pekin-London car race driving his famous Abbot Special halfway across the Gobi Desert to disgrace and infamy . . .

Intrigued by the ill-fated race Daniel and Julie, a television script-writer, find themselves drawn into a drama that is far from dead. Pursuit of the truth leads them into another race . . . for their lives.

"A master storyteller"
New York Times

"Full of romance and surprises, this is a page-turner of a novel"
Publishers Weekly

0 7221 7725 9   GENERAL FICTION   £2.95

Also by Alan Scholefield in Sphere Books:
FIRE IN THE ICE   THE SEA CAVE
GREAT ELEPHANT   THE STONE FLOWER
THE EAGLES OF MALICE   THE HAMMER OF GOD
A VIEW OF VULTURES

By the author of
THIS SIDE OF HEAVEN

Street Song

EMMA BLAIR

Susan's parents had wanted a son . . . and they did little to hide their disappointment with her. As soon as was decently possible they packed her off to boarding school.

If only they could have known . . .

Because in the tradition-bound Scotland of the 1920's there was no place for a woman like Susan. But she was determined to find one – even if it meant beating her wealthy parents at their own game . . .

STREET SONG – Emma Blair at her best . . . a passionate saga.

GENERAL FICTION   0 7221 1941 0   £3.50